Delayed By You

Chicago Steel
Book 6

Jessica Buss

Cover Design & Interior Formatting by Feed Your Dreams Designs

Ebook ISBN: 979-8-9879801-7-0

Paperback ISBN: 979-8-9879801-6-3

Dedication

To our best friends. The ones who laugh, cry, and love with us. We are stronger because of you. Thanks for believing in us, especially when we struggle to do this for ourselves. Love you, JL.

Chapter 1

Rocco

June 2006

"I'm so bored." I groan as I throw myself on the couch, letting my arm flop dramatically over my face. We're only a week into summer break and I've done everything there is to do. Kicking my feet against the gray cotton, my frustration simmers. Last week, I had a sleepover with my buddy Trenton before his family moved away. Then, I spent a day at the water park with my older sister and brothers, Rina, Ruben, and Raf. They're teenagers, and the last thing they want to do is spend time with me. They only agreed because Ma threatened their kneecaps if they didn't.

Ooh, I could play my Nintendo DS. Sitting up quickly, I lunge for it, knocking things off the coffee table. Ma clears her throat. Sheepishly, I look at her and see she has her arms crossed over her chest. Her face says "Don't even think about it." *That's right.*

Yesterday she told me I logged too many hours of *Mario Kart* on it already.

"You could read a book," Ma suggests before she returns to stirring a giant pot of what smells like tomato sauce. Being Italian, Ma is forever in the kitchen cooking. I'm not complaining; she and my nonna are the world's best cooks. Pushing off the couch, I go to see what she's doing.

"Ma, what are you making?" At seven years old, I'm already almost as tall as her petite five-foot frame. My father is just over six feet, and even at fourteen and seventeen, my brothers are taller than him. My thirteen-year-old sister is already 5'5" and still growing. *I wonder how tall I'll be.*

Ma ruffles my messy brown hair. "We have new neighbors moving in across the street, and I thought a nice lasagna would be a great welcome gift. What do you think?"

I nod, then say, "As long as there is enough for us too."

She laughs, making me smile. "Rocco, do you want to help?" I go wash my hands and bring my step stool to the counter. In no time, we assemble three trays of lasagna: two for our family and one to bring across the way to our new neighbors.

After we're finished, I run to the living room and look out the front window. Sure enough, there's a large moving truck being emptied of boxes and furniture. An SUV drives up, parking next to the curb behind an expensive-looking car. *Is this the new family?* Leaning forward over the back of the couch, I feel someone approach me from behind. "That the new neighbors?" Raf asks while taking a bite of an apple. I turn toward him as he wipes his mouth on his arm.

"I guess so." I shrug as I scoot farther away. *I don't want his apple saliva on me.* Turning back to the window, I see someone about my age getting out of the SUV, and it piques my interest even more. Studying the clothes, I see a ball cap. *Another boy my age has moved in across the street.* Just as I'm about to pump my fist in the air and run outside, the kid turns around. Blinking, recognition sets in and I freeze. Another boy my age hasn't moved across the street. "It's a girl," I sneer.

"So?" Raf questions.

Turning around in disgust, I flop back down on the couch. "Girls are annoying, bossy, and gross," I state petulantly.

He laughs at me. "You won't think that in a couple of years." Then he takes another bite of his apple and walks away, leaving me to stew in my frustration. *I thought this new neighbor was going to be the answer to all my summer woes.* Better come up with a Plan B.

Still pouting on the couch an hour later, Raf walks past me, asking, "Still bored?" I nod and he tosses something at me.

"What's this?" I say as I catch it.

"I got that a few years ago and never assembled it."

Looking down, I see it's the Lego set of Jabba's Palace.

"Really, Raf? You're serious?" I ask excitedly.

"Have at it, Rocco," he says with a laugh before he heads off to work.

"Thanks," I shout out as he closes the front door. Sinking to the floor, I make space on the coffee table before I rip open the box. Setting all the pieces into a pile, I flip open the instruction manual and start assembling. After a quick lunch break, I'm back at it again. The hall clock chimes five times, letting me know it's almost dinnertime and, as if on cue, my stomach rumbles. So close to having the entire set assembled, I'm hesitant to let it sit, but the amazing smell of roasted tomato, mozzarella cheese, garlic, and Italian seasonings dance around me. A timer goes off in the kitchen and I hear my ma pull something from the oven. I rise to my feet and head in her direction.

"Need any help, Ma?" I ask, knowing she'll have me set the table.

"Rocco, could you please set the table? I need to get this lasagna ready to run across the street." Once I've placed the plates, cups, and utensils in each spot, I turn to see the bubbly, cheesy goodness that is our dinner.

"Yum," I say on a groan.

"You want to help me take this across the way?" Ma asks. I know from her expression that she wants me to go. Squashing down my feelings about my new girl neighbor, I remind myself to be nice. *Maybe she isn't too bad?* I nod and follow Ma out the front door, dutifully carrying the lasagna.

The moving van is gone. It left sometime this afternoon while I was assembling the Lego set. Stepping up to the front door, Ma rings the doorbell. A short while later, a woman about my ma's age answers the door. "Hello," she greets us with a warm smile. Quick introductions are made and her daughter appears. All I can think is she's prettier than any girl I've seen before. Maybe she isn't bossy or annoying either. I notice her mom tug her forward. Mine does the same to me. Apparently, they want us to meet. *Let's get this over with.* Stepping forward, I look down at my flip-flops before muttering, "My name is Rocco." Ma tucks me back to her side. Still staring down, I see naked feet with pink toenails come into view.

"I'm Jasmine. It's nice to meet you, Rocco." Her voice is angelic and sweet. It creates a pleasant hum in my chest. Looking up, I'm desperate to see her up close. She's taller than I am, like most girls our age. She has long brown hair and piercing green eyes that remind me of Green Lantern. Peering closer, I notice freckles across her cheeks. Or I'm assuming they're freckles and not mud puddle spray. This girl doesn't look like she spends much time outside near mud puddles or tree forts. Even though that disappoints me, I still feel drawn to her. I want to get to know her, see if she's as bad as the girls at school. After all, she's the only other kid my age in our neighborhood, so she may be my only option to survive summer break. As we stare at each other, our moms talk about all the things parents find interesting. You know; the neighborhood, the schools, and the parks.

"How old are you?" I ask.

She smiles confidently. "I'm eight. How old are you?"

I'm younger. Lowering my gaze, I shuffle my feet. *Why do I care if she's older than me? It's only a year.*

Warmth covers my arm, and I look over to see her hand there. "Are you younger, Rocco?"

In answer, I nod my head. "I'm seven." Lifting my eyes, I see she's smiling at me again. *Maybe this isn't too bad. She seems nice.*

"Do you ride bikes?" I ask, wondering if she rides politely or if she's a bit of a daredevil like me. If I had to guess, she's never splashed through a puddle or raced down a hill.

Her sweet smile morphs into a smirk, and she steps away from our moms. "Mom, I'm going to show Rocco my bike. If that is okay?" Her mom nods, and Jasmine leads me over to the garage that is full of boxes. "Dad, are you in there?" she hollers.

"I'm over here, peanut. Far left corner," a deep voice answers. We weave around large and small cardboard boxes that are stacked higher than us until we find him. A large man stands up. His eyes widen in surprise when he sees me.

Even despite his size, he doesn't scare me. Since

I'm the youngest and the smallest in my family, I've had to learn over the years to capture people's attention. I do this by either being friendly or funny. In a large, busy family like mine, it's called survival. "I'm Rocco. I live across the street. My ma and I brought over a tray of our family's famous lasagna that we made this morning."

He steps toward me with his hand out, and I shake it. His hand dwarfs mine. "It's good to meet you, Rocco. And thank you for the lasagna. That's one of my favorite foods. What are you two up to?"

Jasmine stands on her tippy-toes, looking for something. "Dad, do you know where my bike is? I wanted to show Rocco."

Her dad motions for us to follow him. He slides a few boxes out of the way. "It's over here," he says before he pulls out a new BMX bike and sets it in front of Jasmine.

"Wow. That's a great bike," I say as my eyes trace over the shiny chrome frame. Leaning down, I run my fingers over the spokes, making an amusing sound that makes me smile. I love biking. Other than hockey, it's one of my favorite things to do. Starting both when I was five, my constant need to move hasn't let up one bit.

Chapter 2

Jasmine

Watching Rocco's eyes light up when he sees my bike is everything. He admires it. I can tell already that we like the same things. We're going to get along great. When I first saw him, I wasn't sure. He's a boy, after all, and I don't have too many friends who are boys. But he looked nice. His brown wavy hair is messy and his clothes are mismatched, which doesn't matter since it's summer. In only moments, I discover my favorite thing about him is that he has a great smile. It's warm and wide, and it instantly makes me happy. I can tell he's nice, cool, and funny. My type of friend, for sure.

Thinking back, I was so excited when my parents said we were moving. And this, right here, is why. I will finally have a friend who loves the same things as me. Even though we only moved from just a few towns away, it feels like this is a whole new world. Our last neighborhood was absolutely horrible. The girls were incredibly mean, calling me a tomboy. And the boys didn't pay me any attention because I was a girl. I had no real friends. They bussed in one girl that I got along with at school from another town, so things like sleepovers or playdates were a rare occurrence. But with Rocco being right across the street, we can explore together without venturing too far from home. It's a win-win.

After Rocco and his mom introduced themselves and dropped off dinner, and I showed Rocco my bike, they went home. As my parents and I stuff ourselves full of the amazing lasagna, we talk about our new neighborhood, and it's the first time I've felt hopeful in months. *I have a new friend.*

Waking up early the next day, I pull on some jean shorts and a tank top before I race into the kitchen. Stopping quickly, I see Mom is already prepping dinner, even though it's like eight hours away. "Mom, can I please go see if Rocco can come out and play?" I excitedly dance back and forth on my feet, waiting for her reply.

"Darling, it's only eight in the morning. I bet he is still sleeping, and we don't want to be rude and wake his house up." I let out a deep moan and collapse into one of the kitchen table's chairs. "Why don't you have some breakfast and then maybe around nine, you can go over."

Swinging my feet back and forth, I wish time

would pass quickly as I eat my bowl of Honey Nut Cheerios. I glance at the clock on the microwave every so often, willing it to change faster. When I finish my cereal, I clean my dish and then drag myself into the living room to wait. But it's as if the clock is going backward and time refuses to pass. When I let out a pathetic groan, my mom laughs. "Ever heard the saying 'a watched pot never boils'?" I shake my head. *What is she talking about?*

"Jasmine, it means if you're waiting for something to happen, it will take twice as long. If you busy yourself with something else, time will pass quickly. It's as simple as that." She returns to washing dishes, and I get up from the couch to help dry. Before I know it, the clock strikes nine and I'm racing out of the kitchen.

"Where are you going?" Mom asks. I give no response because I'm halfway out the door. My focus is solely on Rocco's house. I approach the light-blue two-story house without concern. Yesterday, when they were over, Rocco pointed out his house and then pointed out that his bedroom was in the basement. His window aligned with his mom's tulips. As I get closer, I try to sneak a peek into his room, but the lights are off and I can't see anything. *I hope he's awake and that he can play.* My nerves set in as I step up on their cement stoop. *I hope they're awake. Maybe I should've waited longer.* I lift my hand to the door and knock gently, hoping I'm not disturbing anyone. Silence meets me. Just as I'm about to head home, a loud stampede sounds from the other side of the door. Startled, I step back. *Am I in trouble?* My palms sweat as I wait to see what will happen next. Suddenly, the door swings open, and as I chance a look up, I'm relieved to be looking into the smiling face of the scraggly, brown-haired boy I met yesterday.

"Hi, Jasmine," he says.

"H-hi, Rocco. C-can you play?" I stutter.

He smiles even wider. "Come in and let me go ask Ma."

Stepping into his house, my eyes don't know where to go first. "This way," he calls as he leads me down a hallway lined with unmatched picture frames. *How big is his family?* Blindly following Rocco, I step into their kitchen. An adorably wrinkly older woman with gray hair pushed up in a banana clip sits quietly at the dining room table. Upon closer inspection, it looks like she's organizing dried weeds and leaves with her frail hands.

"Ma, can I go play with Jasmine?" Rocco begs. Mrs. Romano—Maria—who's at the stovetop, turns around at the sound of his plea and notices me in the doorway.

"Good morning, Jasmine. How are you today?"

Before I can answer, Rocco jumps in. "She's great, Ma. See?" He gestures toward me, and I smile. The old woman turns and looks at me, nods, then goes back to what she was doing.

Mrs. Romano crosses her arms over her chest. "Rocco, don't be rude. Jasmine can answer for herself. Plus, you haven't introduced her to Nonna."

Rocco drops his arms by his side dramatically, and I hold in a snicker.

Finally answering, I say, "Good morning, Mrs. Romano."

"Fine." He snags my hand and leads me over to his Nonna. "Nonna, this is my new friend, Jasmine. She just moved in across the street." Then he looks at me. "Jasmine, this is my nonna."

"Nonna?" I question, the word unfamiliar to my tongue.

"That's what Italians call their grandmothers." I nod my understanding while Nonna watches. Her eyes twinkle and her smile makes me feel like she's holding in a secret. *What is that about?*

Rocco marches back over to his mom. "Ma, can we please go play now?"

Like a skilled interrogator, she extracts the fine details of Rocco's plan for us within minutes. She also gives us rules: check in every hour, don't leave our street, don't talk to strangers, don't go too far into the woods behind the house, and when the lunch bell is rung, we better come running.

Heading out front, I run over to my house to let my

mom know the plan and to grab my bike. Minutes turn into hours, and before we know it, we hear a bell ringing and Rocco shoots up hollering, "Lunchtime!" He breaks into a sprint, yelling over his shoulder, "Come on, Jaz, we have to beat my brothers." In a minute flat, we make it back to his house, winded, dirty, and starving. "Let's go wash up." I follow dutifully along, removing my shoes at the front door.

After we've cleaned up, we make our way to the kitchen and Rocco shows me where to sit—right next to Nonna. I try my best to remember my manners and be on my best behavior, just like my parents taught me. Mrs. Romano walks to the table with her hands full. Roasted garlic, tomato, and Italian seasonings waft through the air. My mouth waters. Last night, the lasagna she gifted us with was magical, and whatever she's holding now smells incredible. Jealousy swarms in my gut. *Rocco gets to eat like this all the time.* My mom's cooking is bland; boring at best. It's edible but nothing you want to invite friends over for. Nothing like this. She sets a plate of spaghetti down in front of me. "This looks delicious. Thank you, Mrs. Romano," I say.

She just smiles at me as two older boys and a girl shove their way into the kitchen and snag whichever chair is unoccupied. "Children, we have a guest," Mrs. Romano admonishes them. They stop fighting and stare at me. I freeze mid-bite, with noodles hanging out between my lips. Covering my mouth with my hand, I quickly slurp them up. Rocco laughs at that.

"Hey, this is Jasmine. She just moved in across the street," he tells them, then looks over to see if I'm done. I nod. "Jaz, these are my siblings, Rina, Ruben, and Raf."

Chancing a quick wave, I whisper, "Hi."

Lunch remains fairly quiet as we eat. Once Rocco's siblings have finished their meals, they disappear with a "thank you" to their mom and a kiss to their nonna's cheek.

Rocco and I head back outside for the rest of the afternoon to busy ourselves with biking, climbing, and running. When it's dinnertime, we each head to our own house with a plan of meeting the next morning for another full day of exploring and adventure.

The summer passes quickly as we spend hours in the sprinkler, building a fort, and heading to special events at The Field Museum with Rocco's mom and nonna. It's the best summer I've ever had, thanks to my best friend, Rocco.

Before we know it, August has arrived and we're visiting our school to meet our teachers for the upcoming year. Pineville Elementary is familiar to Rocco, but it's new to me, and I'm nervous about it. *What if my teacher doesn't like me or the girls in my class are mean?* Even though we aren't in the same grade, we have recess at the same time. *Will he still want to play with me, or will he forget about me now that he's back with his guy friends?* He assures me that everything will be fine. But I'm not sure. *What if I was only a summer friend?* Sensing my concern, he hugs me and tells me he'll always be there if I need him. He is the best friend I've ever had.

Chapter 3

Rocco

Elementary school is a breeze, especially after Jasmine moved in across the street. I always have someone to sit with at lunch or play with at recess. But riding the bus is the best. I get undisturbed time with her. We sink into our seats and chatter on the way to and from school every day. In the afternoons, if we don't have homework, we play outside or hang out in our fort.

Hockey season started just as the temperatures drop, so as soon as I step off the bus, my ma ushers me to the family's car to take me to practice. On those days, I miss hanging out with Jasmine, but it can't be helped. Hockey is my passion, and I love playing it.

On the weekends, she often comes to the rink with my ma, dad, and nonna to watch my games. She's my biggest cheerleader, jumping up and down whenever I score. One weekend, she showed up at my house with a brightly colored homemade sign covered in glitter. My brothers teased me, but I thought it was cool, and after the game, I proudly displayed it in my room.

Because Jaz is a grade higher than me, when she moves to junior high a few years later, my sixth-grade year sucks. I can't wait to be in the same school as her again. We aren't as close as we had been. It seems like when she went to junior high, things changed between us. She spends more time with an obnoxious group of girls and less with me. *I'm not jealous. Okay, maybe I am.* But when we do spend time together, she doesn't want to do the same things we always had. Instead, we go to the movies, and most of the time it's to see some stupid romantic comedy. I don't care too much, because I get to spend time with my best friend. But it's becoming apparent to me that at some point, our friendship changed. *She* changed. She isn't the same Jaz I knew.

The biggest change is to her appearance. Instead of dressing in jeans and a t-shirt, she now wears girlie clothes like skirts and fitted tops. And then there's the makeup. Years earlier, I'd seen Rina go through similar changes, and they became more drastic when she entered high school. Now all she's concerned with is her clothes, hair, and social life. Schoolwork be damned.

My folks are constantly talking about grades and college acceptance, and that makes sense. It's a perfect fallback plan for me, or that's what I thought. At thirteen, I'm already determined to get drafted by the NHL. As the best player in our league and one of the best in the state, I'm on my way. I don't need to worry about a fallback plan.

Finally, my freshman year arrives, and I couldn't be more excited. I know I'll be the only starting freshman on the school's high school hockey team. In junior high, I'd built a good friend group, and I'm finally in the same school as Jaz again. Because we're in different grades, we have lockers on opposite sides of the building and no classes together.

Jaz is super smart, and even though she seems to ignore schoolwork, she gets all A's. I'm happy to maintain a solid B average. School isn't hard. I just have my mind focused on something else: hockey. My parents, coaches, and I have talked about the possibility of me going to play Juniors, but we're giving it another few years. I want to see what all the fuss is about high school. My brothers declared it was "the best time of their lives." And I'm all in, ready for whatever it throws my way.

For my first homecoming, I hitch a ride with friends. Decked out in our school colors, we're loud and obnoxious as Johnny's dad drives us to the game. The energy in the car is unreal. We're pumped and excited to finally take part in such an incredible milestone. When we arrive at the stadium for the game, I realize the upperclassmen are a million times more intense than my friends and me. Some guys are shirtless and have painted the school's letters on their chests. As a freshman, their size is intimidating to me. I'm tall—over six feet—but I don't have all the muscles they do. My legs are powerhouses from all the years of skating, but my abs and arms aren't anything special. It's at this game where I first get a taste of what girls will do for an in-shape athlete, and that becomes a new goal for me.

Knowing Jaz will be at the game, I scan the crowd, eager to see her. I find her among all the other popular girls, making goo-goo eyes at the half-naked upperclassmen. As I sit here, I see her focus and desire on display, and it unleashes something within me. I want that. I crave to be the object of her attention. *Where did that come from?* I'd never thought of Jaz as anything other than my best friend—my very platonic best friend.

Until today, I hadn't studied the curve of her hips like my life depended on it. I hadn't noticed the lift of her breasts as she jumped and cheered or the curve of her absolutely perfect ass when she bent over to grab a pom-pom. Then I practically swallow my tongue when she turns, notices me, and gives me a sultry smile. Surprised, my mouth falls open. Schooling my reaction, I turn quickly, noting who she could be looking at. No one registers as familiar. *So, was she really looking at me? Did that smile mean anything?* Recognizing my odds aren't great, I shove my interest down deep, never to be considered again. She will always be my best friend, nothing more.

But something about that day changes things for me. It's like a switch has been flipped, and Jaz had been the catalyst. Now, everywhere I look, I notice women and how amazing they are. *Holy shit. My eyes are open.* For the first time, I appreciate the female form like never before, and as I do, my pants grow increasingly tighter. I'm not unfamiliar with sporting wood. That's been happening for years. Every time I wake up, I know I'll have to deal with it before I can pee, or Ma would have me scrubbing bathrooms daily. But the ability to summon a boner with just a fantasy is something new.

Sure, when I see a pretty girl, I often feel my dick twitch, but I've yet to have it go full salute as I drool over the breasts in the row before me. Having two older brothers and being a competitive hockey player who lives in locker rooms, I've heard my share about sex, hard-ons, and masturbation. But at fourteen, I'm still pretty green to it. However, now that my hormones are rushing through my body like a car at the Grand Prix, I know I'll need to take them out for a test run to see what I'm really in for. I don't want to embarrass myself unnecessarily.

Following the game, as my friends and I wait for our ride, Jaz approaches me. She throws her arms around me, hugging me. She feels like heaven pressed up against me, and my body responds. I pull away quickly so she won't notice.

"Going to the dance later?" she asks, unaware of her effect on me.

Relieved, I shake my head. "I didn't ask anyone. Maybe next year."

She nods. "You know you don't have to have a date. I would have danced with you." Images of her in a tight dress pressed up against me almost cause my brain to misfire. My heart beats rapidly and my palms sweat. Being that close to Jaz would be a mistake because my attraction to her would be obvious. It would ruin what friendship we have left, and there is no way I'm going to let that happen.

"Jasmine, our ride is here," her friend Courtney calls. Jaz waves at her before she turns back to me. She frowns, then says, "It was so good to see you, Rocco. I've missed you." She looks like she wants to say more, but over Jaz's shoulder, I see Courtney looking impatient. Because I don't want to cause problems for them, I answer quickly. "I've missed you too. Have fun tonight." She forces a smile and then she's gone.

That evening, I stay vigilant. I'm watching her house from our front room, trying to get a glance at her all dressed up. At nine sharp, an unfamiliar car pulls up. Exiting the car, the guy turns and looks around the neighborhood. Instantly, I recognize who it is. Adam Turner is a junior starter on the varsity football team. *That's her date?* My heart drops. I've heard plenty of rumors about Adam and his flavor-of-the-month dating mentality. I can't believe Jaz would have agreed to go anywhere with him.

Ten minutes later, they depart the house with smiles on their faces. She looks absolutely amazing. Dressed in a tight white and gold dress, she is the epitome of a Grecian goddess. Her long brown hair is down in soft waves I want to run my fingers through. She has a thick gold belt that not only accentuates her waist but her full breasts. From the open window, I hear the jingle of her gold bracelets and the click of her strappy gold sandals that weave up her perfect legs. I am so transfixed on her, I don't hear Ma approach from behind.

"Stunning," she whispers before catching Jaz's eye. They wave as I try desperately to sink down out of sight. I don't want her or Adam to know I was staring like a lovesick puppy. "She looks beautiful. Doesn't she, Rocco?" Ma questions.

"She does," is all I say before slinking off to my room with the image of Jaz burned into my brain forever.

Chapter 4

Jasmine

Last year, as a freshman, I wasn't very involved. High school felt overwhelming, so I kept to myself. The pressure to fit in was intense. It seemed like you had to be part of the right crowd to make sure you had a good time. During the middle of the year, I caught the eye of a couple of the varsity football team players, Keith and Chad. They were in my Algebra II class. Traditionally a sophomore-level class, I was in it as a freshman, as math came easily to me. At the beginning of the year, our teacher had placed me in charge of a study group that both guys joined. Throughout the semester, they flirted with me, even inviting me to a few parties. Every time, I turned them down, but we became friends over the course of the school year. And over the summer, they invited me on some outings with them. We had a great time at the movies, a few hikes, and a day trip to Six Flags.

By the time we return to school in the fall, they've claimed I'm part of their group. I don't know what that means, but they've introduced me to a whole new crowd of people, and before I know it, I'm popular. I've even reconnected with some girls I hung out with in junior high, now that we find ourselves in the same social group.

Chad invites me out to lunch one day, and I jump at the chance to leave campus with a friend. While we sit at Subway, eating our lunch and talking, I feel someone approach.

"Chad-o," a deep voice calls out from behind me. My insides squeeze. *Man, he sounds sexy.*

Chad smiles and I crane my head to see who it is. A recognizable but unfamiliar guy approaches and fist bumps Chad before sliding into the booth next to me. Our legs brush, and I feel a zing shoot up my leg.

"Hey, Chad. You going to introduce me to your lunch date?" His melodic voice registers deep within me, making me blush. I take in his appearance and am instantly smitten. He looks like he walked off a Calvin Klein billboard.

Chad, who is like a big brother to me, introduces me to Adam, a junior, and I swear my heart skips a beat.

"Adam, this is Jasmine. She helps Keith and me with math. Jasmine, this is Adam, a junior running back on the starting line of the football team." Adam and I look at each other, and I freeze. He is the most attractive man I've ever seen. He's got high cheekbones, sparkling blue eyes, perfectly coifed blond hair, and the most amazing set of dimples. Basically, he's a fine work of art.

He leans closer, dropping his already deep voice, and says, "Hi, Jasmine. You're gorgeous."

He thinks I'm gorgeous?

"H-hi," I nervously stutter out.

Ever smooth, he adds, "The boys have mentioned you. It's nice to finally meet you."

I smile because at this point, my brain is mush and all I can get myself to say is, "It's so nice to meet you too." I keep staring at him with heart eyes while he and Chad talk about the upcoming homecoming game. Completely oblivious to their conversation, I miss it when Adam asks me a question. Instead, I just nod like a bobblehead. Next to me, he lets out a loud *whoop,* knocking me effectively out of my lust-inspired stupor. Quickly, I turn to Chad and mouth, *"What is that about?"*

Chad leans in and asks, "You're joking, right?"

Confused, I shake my head and shrug my shoulders.

"He just asked you to homecoming, and you said yes," Chad whispers. Looking over toward Adam, he's doing some sort of celebration dance that is so ridiculous it's charming.

Smiling, I look back at Chad and ask, "I did?"

He just nods.

Keep it cool. Okay, so I guess I'm going to homecoming with Adam. *Go me.*

Chad balls up his sandwich wrapper. "We need to head back to school." I look at Adam, then back at Chad. "Hey, Jabbawockeez wannabe, it's time to get back to school. Don't show Jasmine all your moves before the dance."

Adam laughs and then heads back over to the table. "Jasmine, can I have your number so we can coordinate our date?" He hands me his phone.

After I put my number in, I send myself a message. "Now I have yours too." His return smile is enough to make my knees go weak.

The rest of the week passes quickly, and other than a text or two, I don't hear from Adam. Assuming we're still going to the dance, I go shopping with my mom over the weekend. We find the most amazing dress and matching sandals.

ME

Hey, Adam. I didn't know if you
planned to match for homecoming,
but I got my dress today. It is white
and gold.

ADAM

Cool. Thanks.

ME

I'm planning to go to the game that
afternoon. What time do I need to be
ready for the dance? My mom wants
to grab pictures. Lame, I know.

A half an hour passes before he replies. *Maybe he's having second thoughts?* My stomach rolls at the thought of that. It would be so embarrassing. I've told everyone we're supposed to be going together.

ADAM

Sorry. I was at practice. I'll come grab
you at nine. Hey, don't knock the
pictures. When you look good, you
have to capture it, and I know you'll
look smokin' on my arm. What time
do you have to be home?

ME

My parents say I have to be home at
midnight.

ADAM

Okay, Cinderella. Midnight it is. I
know of a few parties we could hit
after the dance if you're up for it.

Parties? I've never been to a high school party. I've heard what goes on at them, and it doesn't interest me. But I'm not sure I can say no. Maybe I'll go and we can leave if I feel uncomfortable. Adam will keep me safe. *Right?*

ME

Okay. No drinking and driving,
though.

ADAM

Of course, babe. I won't put you in
any danger. You're safe with me.

As I read his text, I breathe a sigh of relief. *This will be great.* Or at least that's what I'm trying to tell myself as nerves spin recklessly in my mind.

Two weeks pass by and I head to the homecoming game with my girls, Courtney and Jennifer. We cheer the guys on to victory, and by the end of the game we're more than ready to get all dolled up and ready for the dance. I run into Rocco at the game, and it's great to see him. Even though we live right across the street from each other, our paths seem to be headed in opposite directions, rarely intersecting. At the times when I have a free moment, he's usually busy with hockey. When he's free, I'm studying or hanging out with friends.

It's sad to learn he isn't going to the dance. I would love to dance with him. I know we'd have fun together, just like we did as kids. Back then, we never cared what anyone thought, we just did what we wanted.

At nine o'clock sharp, my doorbell rings and Adam stands there wearing all black. He's so handsome, and he's right, we'll look amazing together. Once I've introduced him to my mom and dad, we quickly take a dozen pictures before we escape to the dance, fashionably late. Once we get there, we don't waste any time before heading to the dance floor. The hours pass quickly as we shake and grind. It feels amazing having Adam hold me so close during the slow songs. Until tonight, I'd never experienced being this close to a guy. I can tell he's enjoying it too. As we sway back and forth with my head against his chest, there isn't anywhere I'd rather be.

Lost in the moment, I feel Adam nudge my chin up. Looking into his blue eyes, I notice they've turned dark navy, almost black, and a shiver runs down my spine. *What is happening?* His hand that was at my waist dips lower, settling on the curve of my butt. *Is it wrong that I want him to go lower?* His gaze fixes on my lips, and my heart races. Excitement rushes through my veins. I want to shout out loud. *Is he going to kiss me?* It'll be my first kiss. My heart drops and my mind spins with anxiety. *I want to kiss him, but I don't know how.*

Slowly, Adam lowers his head and places his soft lips against mine. Scared, I wait to see what he does next. I plan to follow his lead. After a few seconds, he breaks the kiss and smiles at me. I tuck my head back into his chest and hug him close. *My first kiss was magical.* We dance a little longer and then Adam pulls me in close.

"A few of my friends are heading out to an after-party. Do you want to go?"

My worry sets in. *Will there be drinking?* I don't

want to get in trouble. But the hopeful look on his face is tough to say no to.

"If it's crazy, can we leave?" I nervously ask.

He tenderly kisses my lips again. "We can, but know I'll protect you." *Protect me? From what?*

I nod and we leave the dance and head to a friend of a friend's house. The music is already thumping and there are people everywhere. Immediately, I'm uncomfortable. Looking around the front yard, all I see is an ocean of unknown faces. I don't recognize anybody. My stomach tightens, and my palms sweat.

Everywhere I look, I'm surprised at what I see. As we enter the large house, I notice a group of people who have taken over the couches. Some are kissing and groping each other, while others look like they're having sex. Covering my mouth, I try to hide the gasp I just released. The farther we walk into the house, the louder it gets. There is complete chaos, and I question why Adam brought me here. I grip his hand as he leads me toward the back of the house. *How many people are here?* People with red Solo cups are everywhere, twerking and grinding against each other.

"Chad. Keith," Adam bellows as we move into the kitchen and he snags a cup off the counter. Not caring what it is, he tosses it back like it's a shot. Peeking around him, I see two familiar faces and breathe a sigh of relief. *This can't be too bad.* Then a girl wearing the tiniest string bikini goes running through the room, attracting everyone's attention, including my date's, and my mind changes. I tug on Adam's hand. He closes his mouth, blinks his eyes, and turns to me. "Isn't this party great, Jasmine? Let's get a drink."

"Okay, a soda sounds good," I answer.

"Yeah, I bet they have one of those around here," he answers over his shoulder as he leads me deeper into the chaos. *How big is this kitchen?* When we finally make it to the island, my eyes go wide. Half-empty bottles of liquor line the countertops. Looking to the left, I see two large stainless-steel containers on the edge of the dining table. A ridiculously long line of people is waiting to fill up their cups from it.

Beer, body odor, heavily applied perfume, and Axe body spray combine in the heated air, creating a nauseating odor that makes my stomach roll. Reaching up with my free hand, I cover my mouth. *I think I'm going to be sick. I need air, now.* Spotting a door leading to an outside deck, I tug my hand loose from Adam, bolting in that direction. The cool fall air whips me in the face as soon as I step outside. It clears my mind, and my heart sinks. *Adam knew exactly what he was bringing me to.* After a few cleansing breaths, my mind clears. I'd hoped for something different for the night, especially after that kiss. Because it was my first, it had been special to me. It meant something, and I wanted to spend more time with Adam, getting to know him, talking, kissing, being together. *But that isn't what he wants.* Disappointment sets in when I realize we had different assumptions about how our evening would go.

After another few deep breaths, I turn back toward the house, and before I even step inside, I'm shocked to see a girl in a tight pink dress all over Adam. Before I know it, they're making out. My breath catches. Adam breaks the kiss a few minutes later, and I wonder if he's remembered he's here with me. I stand frozen and whisper, "Adam."

He whispers something in her ear, and she smiles wide and then leads him away and out of sight. Sad and embarrassed, I look around to see if anyone saw it too. My heart shudders. I assumed he cared about me, but from what I just witnessed, that isn't true. Instead of us having an unforgettable night together, to my date, I'd been forgettable.

My eyes water and my nose stings as I try to keep my wounded feelings at bay. Glancing around, I realize I don't know anybody. How am I going to get home? I tug my lip between my teeth as my hurt morphs into worry. Stunned, I just stand here. *Why did I say yes to him?* I heard he was a player, but I was so excited to be asked by an upperclassman that I didn't listen to all the alarm bells going off. *I am so stupid. And now I'm stuck here.*

"Jasmine," I hear someone say. Turning, I see it's Chad. Dressed casually in slacks and a t-shirt, he's leaning against the wall, staring at me. Following the dance, he ditched the shirt and tie he'd been wearing. Tracing my gaze up to his face, I see his blue eyes are tough to make out under the ball cap he's pulled tight over his buzz cut. But I don't miss the pitying look on his face. It makes me want to scream and cry and laugh at the same time. He saw everything, and he knows I did too. Mortified, my shoulders collapse.

"He's an asshole, Jasmine. Don't let him ruin your night," he murmurs as he draws closer.

I scoff. "Ruin my night? Nope, he guaranteed he'd ruin my entire year. I have to be home at midnight, and now that doesn't look like it's happening. I don't even know where we are, and I'm not calling my parents from a party I didn't even want to come to."

Chad steps closer. "It's okay. I can take you home."

"Are you sure? Won't that ruin your night? Didn't you come with anyone?"

He hangs his head. "No. The girl I wanted to ask already had a date."

"I'm sorry. Hey, maybe you can ask her to the next dance?"

He smiles at me. "Maybe so. Let's get you home so you aren't in trouble."

Following him through the house, I ask, "Do you think I need to tell Adam I'm leaving?"

Chad laughs. "He's probably railing Malibu Barbie right now. Hate to say it, but the asshole's not thinking of you. Remember, he's the one who left you. You don't owe him anything."

The drive to my house is pretty quiet. Chad has been there before since I've been tutoring him and Keith for months. "Thank you for bringing me home tonight, Chad. I really appreciate it. I don't know what I would have done without you."

He smiles. "It's no problem, Jasmine. Happy to help a friend."

I lean over and give him a hug and a kiss on the cheek. Even though it's dark, I see the pink in his cheeks when I pull back. As I step out of the car, he says, "You looked really pretty tonight."

"Thank you. See you Monday." I wave to him as he backs out of my driveway.

A light coming through Rocco's blinds catches my eye, and I'm drawn to it. To *him*. Rocco has always been there for me. Over the last couple of years, I've kept my distance, because I didn't think he'd care about what I was going through. But at this moment, I realize how much I've missed him and that I need to tell him. I look down at my phone. It's half-past eleven. I have time before curfew. Hurrying across the street, I kneel at his window and knock. Rocco raises the blinds, and when his eyes land on me, he smiles.

"Jaz," he says as he opens the window. "What are you doing here? Aren't you supposed to be at the dance with Adam?" His voice sounds funny. It's filled with a tinge of... anger, maybe?

I tense up, hearing his tone. All I wanted to do was see a familiar face that always makes me feel better. *Why does he sound so upset?*

"I'm not, okay? I just wanted to say hi. But didn't know I'd be talking to a grump. Maybe I'll just head home. Night, Rocco." *What just happened? Maybe I was right, and he doesn't care about me and what I'm going through.* It feels like everything between us has changed, and I hate that. My stomach twists with uncertainty as I turn back toward home.

He groans. "No. Wait, Jaz. I'm sorry. I didn't mean to upset you. Did you have a fun time?" His voice isn't as angry, but it's still strained.

Instead of answering his question, I ask one of my own. "Feel like meeting at our tree house at midnight?" His brown eyes light up, and he smiles and nods.

When I was eight and he was seven, we worked on the perfect tree house. It took us years to reach that feat, and just when we did, I was entering junior high and tree forts weren't considered cool anymore. In fact, I haven't been in it in years. But tonight, I need to reconnect to my younger, less-popularity-focused self.

"Great. Let me get changed, say goodnight to my parents, and I'll meet you there." I stand back up.

Rocco clears his throat, then says, "You look really nice, Jaz."

"Thanks, Rocco," I whisper before heading back to my house.

Chapter 5

Rocco

hrowing on my hockey sweatshirt and grabbing a blanket to keep us warm, I replay the quick interaction I had with Jaz. I didn't miss that she avoided my question about the dance, and that meant only one thing. Something isn't right. She looked beautiful all dressed up, but instead of a smile on her face, she frowned and her eyes were red-rimmed. *Had she been crying?* It didn't look like she'd had a good time. Because of that, I bring a secret weapon with me when I sneak out of the house.

My nonna convinced me at a very young age that what I hold in my hands as I weave through my backyard is pure magic. It can cure any ailment. Before leaving the warmth of my house, I crept into the kitchen and grabbed a large slice of the tiramisu Nonna made for dessert. By the time I make it to the tree fort we built at the edge of my backyard, I've jostled the decadent dessert into an unrecognizable mess in the Tupperware container.

The treehouse is empty. Knowing she ran home, I set down the blanket and container. A minute later, Jasmine appears, dressed in sweats and a ragged t-shirt. "What's that supposed to be?" she asks in a snarky voice as she leans over the container and pokes it.

Rolling my shoulders, I try to dial back my annoyance with her. "It's tiramisu."

She gasps, then gushes, "Nonna's tiramisu? The magical one? Really? Is it for me?"

Handing it to her, I admit, "Sounded like you need some."

She gives me a hug. *That feels so good.* "Thanks, Rocco. I need something to make tonight better, and this is it. You and this," she proclaims as she opens the badly jostled dessert.

Handing her a fork, I laugh. "It may look scary, but I know it's amazing."

We talk and laugh just like in the old days. I don't mention the dance, even though I'm dying to know what happened. *If she wants to tell you, she will.* The way high school works, if anything scandalous happened, I'll hear about it from the rumor mill on Monday. I just hope she's okay, and that Adam didn't hurt her.

Sitting there on the floor of this poorly constructed wood fort, I feel like I'm getting Jaz back. Leaning into one another, sharing body heat with my blanket tucked around us, my eyes are getting heavy. I peek over at the best friend I've ever had and see she's fast asleep. Knowing we're safe here, I relax and fall asleep too, thinking this was the best night ever.

Over the next few years, the treehouse becomes our place. The one where we can escape life. Where we can catch up and reconnect. It's here where we share our secrets, like that she lost her virginity to Chad during her sophomore year. It was tough to hear, but I'd learned Chad wasn't a bad guy. She finally told me about homecoming night with Adam and how Chad had brought her home. They began dating shortly after that and stayed together until he graduated in May. He was heading to a Division-1 school to play football, and at the end of summer, they decide it's best to break up.

During our treehouse visits, we mostly talk about hockey, classes, and our families. While she confesses her relationship exploits, I keep mine to myself. Sex is off-limits. Every time I try to tell her about losing my virginity to Misty during my sophomore year, she flinches. It's confusing. Almost like she already knew something. I mean, I know they're in the same friend group, but Jaz avoids any conversations about her. Over the six months that Misty and I hook up, I just don't mention her. It isn't like it was serious or anything. I'm too focused on hockey to be derailed by girls.

At the beginning of what would be my junior year, I confess I'm leaving to play Tier 1 junior hockey. I'll still be in Illinois, just a few hours away, playing with the Springfield Rattlers. Because I'll be so busy with hockey and school, trips home will be few and far between. We vow to stay close, and saying goodbye to her is one of the hardest things I've ever had to do. My parents remind me that even though it's tough, if I want a chance to play in the NHL, this is what needs to happen.

Jaz graduates from Pineville High and is accepted into the University of Illinois in Chicago, where she plans to study business administration and management. I'm so proud of her. I make it back in time to see her walk at graduation. As if I'm wearing a special Jaz-focused magnet, once she crosses the stage, her eyes are drawn to me. Instead of heading back to her seat like the other graduates, she makes a beeline straight to me where I'm seated with her parents. She mauls me with the best hug I've ever received, and it leaves me shaken.

Throughout everything life has thrown at us, our saving grace is Facebook. It allows us to stay connected.

The next year, we reunite when I return to Chicago because I'm drafted to the Steel.

She means everything to me, and because of that, I know friendship is all we can ever have. Losing her is not an option.

S ettling into my second year in the NHL is more difficult than I expected. It's all a bit of an adjustment. There are so many practices and workouts. Strictly managing your eating and sleeping schedule are critical too. It's often tough to fit in anything else, like hanging out with your best friend. Jaz, on the other hand, is sailing into her junior year of college, kicking butt and taking names. She's swimming along, while I'm occasionally sinking.

Tonight, the stars must've aligned, or I paid it forward enough that karma's on my side, because I have a night off. And I plan to do nothing.

Relaxing in my apartment, I kick my heels up on the coffee table while sitting on my couch in just a pair of gray sweats. I flick on the television to the sports network. My phone dings, alerting me to a text. Do I look at it or ignore it? *It could be something important.* Feeling obligated, I flip it over, and when I see who it is, an instant smile appears on my face. *Jaz.*

JAZ

Do you have time to talk?

ME

Are we talking quick catch-up or
DEFCON 1?

JAZ

DEFCON? What is that supposed to
mean?

ME

It's how the military weighs levels of
threat. Never mind. I'm free for the
next hour. That work?

Seconds later, my phone rings.

I smile as I answer. "Jaz, it's good to hear from you. What a lovely surprise."

"Shut up, Rocco. I need to talk to someone, and you're it."

"Wow. Don't I feel lucky?" I tease. She scoffs. *Apparently, she's not up for sarcasm. I'll try levity.* "What's up, buttercup?"

Letting out a groan, she chirps, "What is it with you today? Buttercup? DEFCON? Seriously. I don't speak code."

She sounds on edge. *Danger.* With concern, I say, "Okay, Jaz. For real. What's up?" Silence fills the line.

She's not saying anything, but I know her mind is spinning. It's almost loud enough for me to hear. Finally, she folds. "I... I'm dating Anthony, you know, and last night he asked me an important question." The line goes silent again, and my stomach drops. *Way to leave a guy hanging.* Fear claws at my chest. *What did he ask? It better not be the big question. She isn't ready. They just started dating.*

Dialing back my concerns, I huff a laugh. "Yeah? I'm lost here, Jaz. I don't know what he said, so could you help a guy out?"

She whimpers. "I really like this guy, Rocco, and I don't know what to think."

I pinch my lips together in frustration—with her, him, the situation. "Jaz, just tell me. We'll figure it out."

"Well... um... he asked me to be exclusive."

I thought they already were.

Okay, that's not bad and definitely not the question I'd been fearing. If he had proposed, I'd have lost my shit. Coming back to the conversation, I focus on what Jaz says. "But I already thought we were exclusive. I mean, I haven't been seeing or sleeping with anyone else." Her gasp startles me. "Rocco, do you think *he* was? Do I need to go get tested?"

I shrug, even though she can't see me.

Jaz word vomits everything going through her mind. Unfortunately, I can't give her peace of mind. I'm the last person to ask. I am the king of hookups. I don't do relationships. And I'm not giving my best friend advice about another guy. Annoyed, I push my fingers through my hair and grumble, "You need to talk to him. Every time I've seen him, he seemed like a decent guy. Ask him those questions. Voice your concerns. Have him explain it to you." I pause. Panic sets in, washing all over my body. My fists clench. *I can't believe I'm encouraging their relationship. Where is Nicole? I thought best girlfriends were supposed to have these conversations.*

I don't want to be responsible for this.

"And when he answers everything, then you have to decide if that's what you want."

She lets out a deep breath. "Okay, that makes sense. Thanks, Rocco." A short while later, after we've caught up on other things going on in our lives, she tells me she needs to call Anthony so they can talk.

I wasn't lying when I said he seems decent, but is that good enough for her? I don't think so, but I can't make those decisions for her. I don't want to look like an asshole if I say anything. Plus, it's Jaz's first adult relationship. It's not likely it'll lead to forever. *Right?*

Chapter 6

Jasmine

May 2020

It seems like the older I get, the faster time flies. Next week I'm graduating with my bachelor's degree in business administration and management. I've already been to several job interviews for positions in my field. The one I'm most excited about is a management trainee position at a financial institution. My boyfriend of almost two years, Anthony Russo, who graduated two years ago, has been working for that same company. He raves about the organization and the opportunities offered to employees.

Tonight, my parents are taking me and Anthony out for a celebration dinner commemorating graduation. When I told Anthony about it last week, he said he had something special planned for me too. It's tough not to get too excited or up in my head about what that might be.

Anthony is driven, kind, thoughtful, and drop-dead gorgeous. When we first started dating, I was swept off my feet immediately. It took longer for him. A few months into our relationship, he asked me to be exclusive. The conversation caught me off guard, as I assumed we already were. But apparently not. While we were getting to know each other, he continued to casually date other women. Excited about being in my first real relationship, I'd rushed to assume things we never discussed or decided on, so he wasn't really in the wrong. After I told him his actions hurt my feelings, he explained his rationale to me. He was just exploring his options. When he committed to someone, he wanted to be one hundred percent sure of his decision. After he asked me to be exclusive, we were. And he has been completely committed to me ever since. This last year especially has been amazing, and it feels like he's been hinting at taking the next step. Butterflies take flight in my stomach every time I think about it. *Am I ready for that?*

Getting dressed for date night, I put on the final coat of lipstick and remind myself of what Nicole, my roommate since freshman year, has told me several times over the last few days. *"You and Anthony haven't even had a conversation about marriage."* She's right, we haven't. Having been around for our entire relationship, she knows everything. Both being in our early twenties, neither Anthony or I have mentioned anything more than a future desire to marry and have kids. We haven't outlined a specific timeline. I do love Anthony, but my focus right now is on the career I'll be starting. I could see us eventually taking that next step. But when? Maybe Anthony has other thoughts. All I know for sure is that we are perfect for each other.

The doorbell rings.

"Jasmine," Nicole hollers up the stairs of our duplex.

The air feels electric as I brush my hands down the simple, yet elegant, black wrap dress I've chosen. The skirt swishes as I take my time down the steps in my sky-high heels. A buzz of excitement surrounds me, making it feel like something is about to change. Catching Anthony's eye, I look for any tells he has.

Dressed in a black Ralph Lauren suit, he looks incredibly handsome. He has a bright blue tie on that makes his eyes pop. A smile that has made me drop my panties several times, spreads across his clean-shaven face, and he's holding a beautiful bouquet of lavender roses. He steps up to the first step, reaches out for me, and in his deep voice says, "Jasmine, you look fantastic." When I step down, he kisses my lips gently. The taste of him is so familiar. It's like coming home.

Blushing, I pull back. "Thank you." He hands the roses to me and I gush, "They're beautiful."

He smiles again before leading me toward the door.

"Nicole," I call out. My bestie pops out from the kitchen with a wide smile and her strawberry-blond hair tied up with a bohemian-print scarf.

"You look gorgeous, Jaz," she says.

"Thank you. Can you put these in water for me? Not sure if I'll be home tonight." I give her a wink, and she smirks.

"Right, Anthony?" I ask, while looking back at him.

"Yeah, sure, babe," he answers and then adds, "We need to get to the restaurant soon." I turn back and look at Nicole, confused by his halfhearted answer. *"Nervous?"* she mouths with a shrug. I frown back.

Dinner with my parents goes well. We meet at Nine, a high-class steakhouse that prides itself on having the best Wagyu beef available. Their sides are all served family style, and it is hands down the best meal I've ever eaten. Following dinner, Anthony whisks me off to Fork & Knife. It's another posh restaurant, but it's known especially for its decadent desserts. We both order a nightcap to enjoy while we devour chocolate cake that looks too incredible to eat. The first bite is filled with chocolate, coffee mousse, and candied hazelnuts. Thank goodness for the perfect pairing with vanilla ice cream.

"Mmm, this is so good," I say on a moan. Anthony smiles and lays his fork down. My stomach flips and my heart pounds in my chest. *Is this the moment? Is he going to ask me to marry him?*

He shifts in his chair and it looks like he's reaching for something. I try to control my breathing. I don't need to pass out while he's proposing. Across the table, he looks nervous, and he blows out a breath. I reach over and touch his arm. "Anthony, are you okay?"

He shakes his head, but I'm sure I see perspiration dotting his brow. "Yes. I just brought you here tonight because I wanted to make it special." I nod my head, encouraging him to go on. "We've been dating for almost two years, and I'm ready to take the next step with you, Jasmine."

I smile widely. *Here we go.*

"I wanted to ask you if you'll..."

"Yes, yes, yes, I'll marry you," I answer at the same time he's saying, "Move to New York with me."

His words finally register. "Wait, what?" Flustered, I look around, making sure we aren't drawing unwanted attention. My mouth goes dry as my heart pounds erratically in my chest. "You asked me to move to New York?" I pant, like I'm struggling to breathe. My cheeks are hot and I touch my face as I wait for the response I've already decided I don't want to hear. Feeling both embarrassed and sad, I look at him for understanding.

And he just nods his head. My mind spins wildly. I blink rapidly, holding back unshed tears. Then I notice the wide-eyed look of panic on his face. He heard me say yes to what I thought was a marriage proposal, and now he looks terrified. *Well, shit. That's not good.*

I push back my chair. My anxiety is building. It's a thousand degrees in here, and I'm suffocating. "I-I need air," I sputter while reaching for my clutch. "I need to go."

Anthony doesn't move. On shaky legs, I make it to the elevator. Stepping inside, it takes all my strength to remain upright. I push the button for the first floor. When the doors close, I pull up the Uber app and reserve a car that's only two minutes away. Numb, I walk outside into the dark, windy night just as a blue Toyota pulls up. The wind blows my hair, but I don't register the normal chill of it. Walking up to the car, I verify it's my ride and then climb inside, alone. Looking back up at the building as we drive away, I finally feel something. All my emotions crash down on me at once. Sadness, embarrassment, frustration, and confusion course through my veins, making me a weepy mess.

My phone rings. It's Anthony. I silence it and then pull up our text thread. Rereading the last few texts we exchanged, my heart feels like it's going to pound out of my chest. He'd been dropping hints about New York and I hadn't caught on. His question tonight shouldn't have been too much of a surprise, but that's just it. It was. We hadn't talked about moving. Chicago is home. He knows this is where my family is and that I plan to always live here. Everything I love is here. *What does that mean for us now?* I don't know. And right now, I'm too much of a mess emotionally to figure it out.

ME

I'm so sorry. I think we're in different places. I don't want to move to New York. I don't know what that means for us.

ANTHONY

I'm sorry too. I should have been clearer. I was wrong to spring that on you. I have to move to New York. That was my other surprise for you. I've already accepted a position with a prestigious trading house on Wall Street. Let's take a day or two and then talk, okay? I love you.

ME

I love you too.

Closing my eyes and resting my head against the back seat for the rest of the ride, I swear I feel my heart fracture when I realize that Anthony and I are going in different directions. This is where we end. If I weren't in the back of some stranger's car, I'd be curled in the fetal position. But that'll have to wait until I get home. The drive seems to take forever as I try to keep the floodgates closed.

When we finally arrive at my house, I thank my driver, give him five stars because he was nice enough to offer me a tissue, and head up to my door. Fumbling for my keys, I drop them before I find the right one. Just as I'm about to try again, the knob twists open and I'm looking into the surprised green eyes of my best friend. Dressed in a leopard print onesie that accentuates her curvy, petite figure, she's all smiles. With her long hair braided to the side and a mostly hardened mud mask on her face, she looks at me, confused. "What are you doing home? Where's Anthony?" she asks as I shuffle past her.

From the corner of my eye, I see her step outside to look for him. "He isn't there," I mumble. Her face cracks as she frowns at me.

"I see that." Heading back inside, she shuts the door, locks it, and engages the deadbolt. *You can never be too careful.*

She follows me into our living room, and we move to the couch. I collapse on it and do my best to curl up in the black wrap dress I selected especially for the evening. Flopping back and forth and grunting, I realize I'm confined in a full-body corset. The Spanx I wore below my dress barely allows me to take a breath.

"Stop moving and let me help you," Nicole patiently says, knowing exactly what I want to do. It's the heartbreak pose, and every woman knows it. And I need to be in it now. Otherwise, the pain radiating through my chest will never go away.

Rolling over, I present myself to her. With a flick of the wrist, she's got me untied, then unwrapped. Not worrying about modesty, I scramble out of the horrible undergarments. Nicole tosses a blanket on me so I'm not cold. Overwhelmed by her kindness, a knot forms in my throat. "Thanks," I mutter once I'm buried in the soft material.

"Do you want to talk about it?" she asks.

Not answering, I bury myself deeper in the blanket so I don't have to make eye contact. Because if I do, I know I will lose the flimsy grasp I have on my chaotic emotions.

"He didn't propose," I whimper. Just saying the words is all it takes to open the floodgates. I start to shake as sadness spreads throughout my body. My heavy tears soak the blanket, and my labored breathing makes my cocoon unbearably hot. Feeling dizzy, I throw it off and suck in a deep breath.

Once I've calmed down some, Nicole places her warm hand on my shoulder. "What happened, Jaz?"

"Everything was perfect. We went out to a nice dinner with my parents and then he took me to Fork & Knife, and it was so romantic. He talked about us and wanting more together, and he was giving major proposal vibes. And then he asked me to... move to New York with him. Can you believe it?"

Nicole gives me a sympathetic look, and I fold. "I didn't even tell you the worst part. When he was asking me, he hesitated for a few seconds, and I sort of jumped the gun."

"What does that mean?" she asks, confusion covering her face.

Hanging my head, I admit, "I sort of said yes to the proposal he wasn't offering. It was so embarrassing." Looking up at her, I swipe away a tear and add, "And to make it even worse, he looked terrified. He doesn't want to marry me."

Nicole leans over and wraps her arms around me. "I'm so sorry, Jaz. Just because he didn't propose tonight doesn't mean he doesn't want to marry you. He obviously sees living together as the next step. Did you talk about it?"

I shake my head against her shoulder and mumble, "I was mortified, and I had to get out of there. So, I left."

She gasps. "You left him there? What did you do?"

"Nothing. I texted him an apology while I was riding home. We're in different places, and we need some time to consider what we want and where that leaves us."

Nicole hugs me tight. "Oh, sweetie. What did he say?"

"He agreed and then told me he was going to New York regardless of my decision. He's already accepted a job. I guess I have to decide if I want to move, agree to long-distance dating him, or if it's best for us to break up." My chest aches and my stomach rolls. This decision is impossible. Every option will cause me heartache and grief.

I take a few days to carefully weigh all my options, and the only one that seems to make sense is staying in Chicago. It's my home. What I've always known. And because of that, I have another tough decision to make. Do I ask Anthony to try a long-distance relationship, or do we just break up? For me, the entire purpose behind dating is that you intend to end up together, eventually married. And how would that be possible if we live in two different cities?

For work, Anthony needs to be in New York. Even though I've always wanted to visit New York, I know I don't want to live in such a big and unfamiliar city. To me, moving means leaving behind my family, my friends, and everything I'm familiar with. It feels like moving is only about Anthony, his job, and the future *he* wants. I love him and want to continue dating, but it seems impossible. Trying to fit into a city I don't love or know makes little sense to me. The more I think about Anthony's request to move, the sicker I feel. Knowing that my saying no is going to let him down tears me apart. And because my decision has been made, it makes little sense to keep dating if our location wouldn't ever be the same.

Wednesday after work, Anthony and I meet up for drinks at some hole-in-the-wall bar. When I walk in, I see he's already nursing a beer. His tie is pulled loose and his suit coat is draped over the bar stool to his right. His body is bent over in defeat. He turns to me, and I see the bags under his eyes and his worried expression. My heart shudders. He's obviously had a rough couple of days too.

As I approach him, he stands up, sweeps up his coat, and offers me the stool. Instead of immediately sitting down, I step up and wrap my arms around him.

It doesn't take long for him to return the embrace. "Hi, Jasmine," he says into my hair.

"Hi," I whisper back before giving him a last squeeze and then dropping my arms. Once seated, I order a Diet Coke from the bartender. He delivers it and, sensing the discomfort, leaves us alone.

"So, what did you decide?" Anthony asks, his voice shaky.

"Anthony, please know this wasn't an easy decision for me. I weighed all the pros and cons before I came to my answer. I love you, but I'm staying in Chicago. This is my home. Where my friends and family are. Where I see myself putting down roots."

He nods.

"And you don't?" I ask.

He whispers, "No. I need to be in New York for my new job and for what I want to do." He hesitates for a moment, then asks, "So where does that leave us?"

I dip my head, not sure if I'll be able to get through this. Anthony's large hand pats my arm. I look at him with tears in my eyes. "I don't know how to say this, but I think it means that this is the end for us." His hand continues to pat me, like he's trying to reassure both of us. And then he pulls me into his arms and hugs me tightly. *Am I making a mistake?*

A few minutes pass as we cling to each other. It feels like our souls are saying goodbye. Finally, he sets me back on my stool and leans over, kissing me tenderly. Then he whispers, "Goodbye, Jasmine," against my lips before he places money on the bar and leaves. Watching him walk away crushes me. *What if I never find anyone better? Did I just make a huge mistake?*

I'm on autopilot the entire ride home. Normally, I enjoy watching all the different people on the train, but today is different. My body is numb and nothing registers. Not until I see Nicole standing in our kitchen, holding out a pint of my favorite ice cream and a spoon. She already has our favorite movie, *Leap Year*, cued up and the blanket fort assembled. She is the best friend I could ever ask for. Between her and Rocco, I'm so very lucky.

I purposefully kept what was happening between Anthony and me from Rocco. He always seems on edge when I talk about Anthony. They were virtual strangers. In fact, neither one had a definitive reason for disliking the other. It's just a feeling I always had. I'll tell him about the breakup maybe when the sting isn't so sharp.

When I finally get up the nerve to tell him a few weeks later, I send him a text message, like a coward. I don't think I'd be able to hide my reaction from him if he were anything but sympathetic. Thankfully, all he says is he's sorry.

Chapter 7

Rocco

It's playoff season, baby. The energy of each game is unmatched by anything else I've ever experienced. Since being with the Steel, I've been to the playoffs a few times, but we've never made it past the first round. It always seems like we're missing the "secret sauce" or something to earn us a victory.

Our team owner, Timothy McConnell, passed away the year before last, and his son, Trey, has taken over. He has a unique vision for the organization, and that started with acquiring an incredible player from New York: Lucas Bouchard. For the first time in my professional career, it feels like we may go all the way, and that feels incredible. Our team isn't a team, but more like a brotherhood. We're connected in a way I've never experienced before. Our play is at another level, and each time I step on the ice, I feel charged up.

We are home in Chicago for a few days since we just beat the LA Raptors in the third round of the Stanley Cup finals. Next week we head out again to face the Montreal Mammoths in our bid for the Cup. But seeing that I'm home, I plan to squeeze as much of the things I love into the days I have. First up is a call to Ma to invite myself over for some home cooking. Flopping on my couch, I pull up her contact.

"Romano residence," Ma answers. There's nothing like her soothing voice. It's always comforting for me.

"Ma."

"Rocco, my baby. Is that you?" she fusses.

"It's me." I chuckle into the phone.

"You are back in town, no? You must come over for dinner tonight. I insist." Even at barely five feet tall, she packs a punch, and my submission is hers for the taking. "Bring Jasmine too. I haven't seen her in ages."

Laying my head back, I stare at the ceiling. I hope she isn't busy. I haven't seen my best friend in weeks, and we've been playing phone tag recently. "Ma, I just got back in town, and I haven't talked to Jasmine yet. I'll call her and extend the invitation. I'm sure if she isn't busy, she'll come. You know she loves your and Nonna's cooking."

After finishing up the call with Ma, I dial up Jasmine.

After barely a ring, she answers. "Rocco?" she squeals with happiness. *That's good to hear.*

I nod my head and laugh. "Yeah, Jaz, it's me. I know you're at work. Do you have a minute?"

She lets out a dramatic sigh. "That's about all I have. We're swamped today. What's up?"

"I'm in town and Ma invited you to dinner tonight. Are you free?" I ask. *Please be free. Please be free.* My heart pumps at a feverish pace, anticipating her response. I need to see her. It's been too long.

I hear someone say her name hurriedly before she even has a second to answer. She groans. "I'll be there. You know I can't pass up a meal made by your ma and nonna. And bonus, I'll get to see you too."

"Dinner's at six. Want me to come get you?" I offer.

"I'll drive. I can't stay too late. I've got an early meeting in the morning. Speaking of, I have to go. See you tonight. Can't wait." She hangs up before I can say anything else.

Clapping my hands together, I let out a whoop. I cannot wait to see Jaz. To give her a hug and make her laugh. Just to have her near is a dream come true. Then I remember it will be a quick visit and my whole family will be there. *It's better than nothing.*

Sitting back, I wonder what I should do to distract myself for the next few hours.

Six o'clock cannot come fast enough. Because I'm bored, I head over to my parents' house early, which is a mistake. Nonna puts me to work making meatballs. Once I finish making the thousandth one, I wipe my damp brow against my arm. "What do you want me to do with these?" I ask, looking at the oddly shaped meatballs. I smirk. *Hey, if they wanted perfection, they should have done it themselves.*

"Cover them with sauce. We need to bake them for dinner," Nonna orders from her chair at the table. At seventy, she's really slowed down the past few years, and she does more quality control and advice-giving than cooking.

I quickly wash my hands and then bring the roasting pan over to Ma, who is stirring sauce on the stovetop. Once they're drenched with sauce, I cover the pan with tinfoil and put them in the oven to bake. Just as I'm finishing, my sister Rina walks in. While she distracts Ma and Nonna with the latest drama she's involved in, I sneak out of the kitchen. As if my feet have a mind of their own, they lead me outside, and I trek through our backyard and into the woods behind our home. Because it's early spring, everything looks dreary. The temperature has warmed considerably, but there aren't any leaves on the trees yet. The grass is still dry and yellow, and the woods are dull brown from winter. While growing up, I spent most of my free time exploring and playing in these woods with Jasmine. When we hit high school, our priorities changed, and we didn't hang out nearly as often. I still visited the woods periodically, though, even without Jaz. It became a safety net for me. Where I could breathe and think when everything—hockey, school, family, friends—got to be too much.

My long strides quickly bring me to the treehouse we constructed one summer. Looking inside, I see our makeshift furniture—a bookshelf, a lopsided table, and a couch we made from old plastic milk cartons that we flipped over and covered with a blanket. Memories flood my brain as I glance around the poorly assembled structure. We had such good times laughing and talking in our hideaway.

The snap of a breaking twig behind me startles me, and I whip around. There's Jaz, sauntering toward me, dressed to kill in a tight wrap dress, wearing her signature smile. *Damn, she is gorgeous.* Blinking my eyes, I can hardly reconcile what I'm seeing to all the thoughts flying through my head. Thoughts I shouldn't be having about my best friend. My *platonic* best friend.

Flexing my fingers, I want to touch her, but it's not to give her a friendly hug. No. I want to trace my fingers around her trim, sexy waist, run them up her abdomen, between her perfectly sized breasts, and up her sternum. When I reach her long neck, I'd trace them up to her chin and force her eyes on me. *What the hell am I thinking?* Panic sets in. I don't have thoughts like this about Jaz anymore. Needing to get my head right, I break eye contact, forcing myself to stare back into the treehouse.

"Your ma said you might be out here," she says as

she stands next to me. The heat from her body overwhelms me, throwing me back into the thoughts I'd just been trying to rid myself of. *She's too close.* I remain silent, and she leans into me, her perfume wrapping itself around me, invading my senses. Hints of cherry and sandalwood make my mouth water. *What is happening?* I *cannot* react to Jasmine like this. I thought I'd gotten ahold of those types of awkward feelings, suffocating them, burying them, forgetting about them. Lusting after Jasmine is not something I do anymore. With other women? Hell yeah. But not her. She is Jaz. Period. End of discussion.

Jasmine's right arm entwines with mine, and her other hand holds tight to my bicep. As we walk side by side, her hip bumps into me every so often. Her body heat, her scent, her presence envelope me until my palms sweat. My heart rate speeds up like I'm doing sprints on the ice. A bead of sweat runs down my back.

"Rocco, what's up? You haven't even said hi yet," she chides while still snuggled up against me.

"Hi, Jaz," I answer. However, instead of the deep and smooth sound I normally make, I sound more awkward and pitchy. Embarrassed, I clear my throat, hoping she says nothing.

We continue to stand in silence. Glancing at her, she looks serene, while I'm desperately trying to contain that I'm freaking out. *I don't understand what is happening.* But before I can figure that out, I hear my ma holler "Dinner."

Jaz laughs. "Looks like that's our cue. Better get in there before there's nothing left."

Laughing, I admit, "Well, you know how the Romanos eat. Let's go."

Over the next hour, we stuff ourselves with so much home-cooked food, and all of it's amazing.

"These meatballs are heaven." Jaz groans next to me. An enormous smile spreads across my face and I elbow her.

"I made them," I admit in a cocky tone.

"You did not," she shoots back. I give her my *are you kidding me look* and her mouth falls open. "Really?"

"Ma, who made the meatballs? Jaz doesn't believe it was me."

"I didn't say that. I was just surprised," she argues.

Nonna mutters something under her breath I can't quite hear. But Ma comes to my rescue. "You two haven't changed a bit. Yes, Jaz, Rocco made the meatballs tonight."

I elbow her again. "Told you." She sticks her tongue out at me, and we're back to being kids again. The tension of earlier melts away. *This, I can do.* Best friend Jaz. Not sexy Jaz.

When dinner, dessert, and dishes are done, Jaz reminds me she has to go because she has to be up early the next day. After hugs with my parents and Nonna, I walk her out to her car. Leaning against it, she lets go of a heavy breath.

"I'm sorry we couldn't catch up more tonight. I wish we had unlimited time for you to tell me all that's been going on," I say. She hangs her head and shakes it. "After the playoffs, we will," I promise her.

"Thanks for inviting me to dinner. It was so good to see everyone and to have a home-cooked meal." She looks across the street to the house she lived in while we were growing up. Her folks moved into another place a year after she went to college. "It's weird that my parents don't live there anymore, right?"

I scratch my head. "Yeah. They moved out a while ago, but I still look to see if their cars are there every time I drive down the street." Her soft smile warms me. This is my Jaz. *I've missed her.* "Hey, what are you doing next week?"

"Nothing really, why?" she asks, her green eyes bright and filled with curiosity.

Acting like it's nothing, I shrug. "Any chance you want to go to a playoff game? I have a few tickets."

She gives me a dazzling smile. "Really? Are you sure you don't want to give the ticket to your parents or siblings?"

I chuckle. "I'm more than sure. Don't worry, my folks and Nonna are covered. Management gave me four."

"Oh, good. I wouldn't want to take it from Nonna. Even at 4'3" that woman is scary. When she yells in Italian, I duck and cover," she confesses.

"What are you talking about? You have never been

in trouble with Nonna. She adores you. I, on the other hand, may have been swatted a time or two." Talking and laughing with Jaz is the best. I could do it all night long. In fact, we have many times.

An alarm on her phone goes off, and she groans. "I set it because I knew I wouldn't leave on time. After the Cup is over, can we please get together for more than an hour or two? I've missed you."

I pull her into a hug, feeling oddly content when the top of her head tucks under my chin. The soft skin of her cheek rests against my collarbone, and my heart beats faster. Unlike earlier, my body behaves. "Definitely. I'll leave the ticket for the game at will-call. If you want to go to more than one, let me know and I'll see what I can do."

With her arms wrapped tightly around me, Jaz hugs me with the strength of a boa constrictor. "Thanks, Rocco. Love you."

I kiss her on the forehead. "Love you too, Jaz," I say and then help her into her car.

<hr>

We've been neck and neck against the Mammoths during the entire series. In our last game in Montreal, we narrowly slip into the lead, and if we win this game tonight, the Cup is ours. Thankfully, we have a home-ice advantage. The energy inside the arena is mind-blowing. The air is electric and I swear it feels like the arena is buzzing. There's nothing like skating in front of thousands of fans rooting for you. And then you add in that it's not a normal game but one that could determine the winner of the Stanley Cup.

So far in this series against the Mammoths, I have one goal and four assists, and as I skate during warm-ups, my luck feels very much intact. This year's rookie, Ace Walker, has been on fire. He's got more intensity and drive than any other rookie I've played with. He is putting up numbers that are insane. The talk about him in the hockey community reminds me of when Lucas Bouchard was drafted by the New York Chargers. I was still in high school, but I remember well all the talk surrounding him and about the possibility of him winning the Calder Trophy.

Josh, our captain, goes around checking that everyone's head is in the game. I look to the section of the arena that my parents sit in, and there they are in their Steel gear. Nonna is tucked next to them with a blue and gold pom-pom in her waving hand. Seated next to her is Jaz, and my heart races at the sight of her. She's been to each of the home games versus the Mammoths, and it means so much to me.

We've been spending more time on the phone reconnecting lately. Often our conversations go late into the night, leaving us both exhausted the next day. But talking to her feels like coming home.

The horn blasts, letting me know it's time to head

back to the locker room before the start of the game. Skating off the ice, I try to clear my mind of any distractions. Right now, I need to focus solely on hockey.

Sitting on the bench, I check my gear and my stick while Coach Tristan talks about the importance of this game. His determination and drive make us want to do better, to *be* better. The advice he gives and the challenges he lobs aren't just empty words. The man has fought hard to be where he is, and he wants the best for us. We are an extension of him, and it's our job to show the hockey world what we're all about. This year, our team has had some growing pains, but it finally feels like we've hit our stride and we're all in for whatever comes next.

Each period of this game is different. The first is charged, fast-paced, and combative. Both teams want to win and we are battling it out on the ice. The second period is more strategic. Apparently, during intermission, both teams talked about what is necessary to win the game. The third period is where it's at. When it starts, the score is o-o. My first shift on the ice, one of their defensemen, Max Junger, comes after me as I skate into their turf with the puck at the end of my blade. Just as I'm about to shoot the perfect pass to Ace, Max slams into me, knocking my feet out from under me. The puck is shoved in the wrong direction, and as I fall to the ice in slow motion, I see Ace swivel, dig in with his skates, and race off.

Max's solid body lands on top of me, and I feel like I've been squished into a pancake. As he scrambles up, he uses his forearms to push me back down. Then he skates off, unconcerned. As quickly as I can, I push up onto my feet and head toward the action. All the while, running a mental scan of my body, checking for injury. Nothing registers, thankfully, because that was a brutal hit. The whistle blows and the referee seems to agree. Max gets a two-minute penalty for roughing. And that's all we need.

Our team maximizes the advantage, and Lucas scores during the power play. The next sixteen minutes are tense as we do everything we can to hold on to the lead. Both teams fill the period with penalty after penalty, and even with all the short-handed minutes, neither team scores.

When the buzzer sounds at the end of the game, they crown us Stanley Cup Champions. It's the first for our franchise. The arena goes wild, and for a few minutes, I can't hear anything as we all drop our gloves and sticks and rush toward our goalie. Piled on top of him, we cheer exuberantly. Simmons kept us above water, especially during that last period as he took shot after shot, in the end claiming a shutout. The entire team scrambles up to continue celebrating with hugs, fist bumps, and congratulatory words.

My eyes travel to the section of seats where my parents, Nonna, and Jaz are seated, and I'm rewarded with their bright smiles and euphoric cheering. Fans around the arena are so energized by the win, they are throwing things onto the ice. While they lay rugs across the ice to prepare for the Cup presentation, they hand us champions caps that we all discard our helmets for. An announcer talks, silencing the arena.

"Ladies and gentlemen. The moment we've all been waiting for... The Stanley Cup."

Two men dressed in suits with white gloves—one being the keeper of the Cup—carry the treasured hockey trophy to a stand in the middle of the rink. The crowd cheers as the commissioner speaks about our team. As tradition dictates, he invites Josh over and hands him the Cup. Our captain smiles wide and stands taller before he shouts and hoists it high above his head. After he's done that, we each take turns raising it to the chanting crowd.

When it's in my hands, I feel like I'm on top of the world. Looking around at the crowd, my eyes find my parents and Nonna again. Each wears a look of pride, and I know they are as thrilled as me. When I shift my focus to Jaz, I see she's crying. Smiling wide, she holds Nonna's hand, and my heart stutters. *This is a moment I will never forget.* When we were growing up, I'd told her that one day I was going to play for the NHL and my team would win the Stanley Cup. Now it's true. Our eyes meet and our silent conversation says everything. *"I'm so proud of you, Rocco,"* I see her mouth. Smiling widely, I hoist the trophy higher and yell.

After the on-ice celebrations, interviews, and locker room ruckus, I make my way out to the players' tunnel. And there stands my best friend. I checked my phone before I showered and she'd sent me a text telling me my parents and Nonna had gone home, but that she'd meet me.

"Rocco!" she shouts as she charges me. I open my arms, welcoming her in. She leaps into my embrace, and I swing her around. Laughing, she says, "Congratulations. You played incredible." Her words are breathy, and they register deep in my chest, making my heart beat harder.

Coming to a stop, I lower her to her feet, and everything between us feels different. I can't explain it. It's like I'm looking at her with fresh eyes. And what I see is how incredibly stunning she is. I've always known Jaz is pretty, but I've never been so intensely affected by it before. The thought of that steals my breath.

Nervous about all the thoughts and feelings flying warp speed through my body, I focus on the woman in front of me. *Jaz.* My hand twitches. I need to touch her. I reach forward and tuck a stray hair behind her ear. She dips her head. Tracing down to her chin with my finger, I lift her face, putting her eyes on me again. I smile and say, "Thanks, Jaz."

Her eyes sparkle, and I lock on them. Then I lean forward. She responds by lifting on her toes and meeting me halfway. Our lips brush, and instantly the contact unlocks my secret attraction to her. The one I've never mentioned to anyone or even admitted out loud. Dropping my bag, I pull her in close, taking things deeper. She gasps, and I push my greedy tongue into her mouth, seeking hers. When they finally touch, it's life altering. The shift in the universe causes my knees to almost buckle. I hold tighter to her, relishing the feeling of her in my arms. We've hugged so many times before, but this... This is different. I'll never be the same after this kiss. I'm forever changed. I lose all thought in the wanting of her. Needing air, I pull back, tugging on her bottom lip as I go. She groans, and I swear it sets my blood on fire.

Desperate for more, I'm just about to claim her lips again when a few guys come out of the locker room, chanting. She pulls away quickly and touches her swollen lips. Watching the look of panic on her face, I stutter, "S-sorry, I didn't m-mean to do that." Stepping back, I give her room while trying to make sense of what just happened. *Holy shit.* I kissed my best friend. And I liked it. A lot. Confused, I tug my hands through my still-damp hair.

"That was a mistake, Rocco. I got caught up in the moment," she whispers. I nod in agreement, but my mind whirls with questions. *Was it, though?* It felt right, like it was something I've always been missing.

Unsure about what to do next, I try to lighten the moment. "Want to get out of here? Go celebrate?"

Jaz frowns. "I... um... I already stayed later than I

thought I would. I have an important meeting in the morning with a new client. I really should just call it a night."

Disappointed, I motion to the exit. Walking her to her car, we exchange an uncomfortable hug, neither of us knowing what to say. Watching her taillights disappear into the night, I suddenly realize how exhausted I am. Between the playoff games and the last few minutes with Jaz, I'm drained. Both emotionally and physically. Once I get home, I'm going to sleep for an entire week.

Chapter 8

Jasmine

Work gets busy at the beginning of the summer and it doesn't slow down until late fall. It feels like one day I went to work and it was warm and sunny, and when I left, months had passed. During that time, work assigned me to a few large projects that monopolized my time and required an ungodly amount of overtime. I seriously considered whether I should just sleep in my cubicle. By the time I emerged from said projects, the sidewalks around town were littered with red, orange, yellow, and brown leaves. *Hello, fall.*

To many, these projects might have been a hassle, but to me, they were a godsend. They provided the perfect distraction at just the right time. Before then, every time I slowed down for even a moment, Rocco and the kiss we shared would flood my mind, overwhelming all of my senses. Even now, if I close my eyes, I can still recall every detail. From the weight of his soft lips on mine, to the musky wisps of his cologne in the air, to the way my knees went weak. I remember my heart galloping in my chest and my palms growing sweaty.

Needing some fun in my life, and knowing Nicole could use a break from her own crazy, busy life, I'm determined for us to enjoy a few fall favorites together. First, we stake out our favorite coffee joint to get the first PSL of the season. And a few weekends later, we're on our way to our next fall-themed adventure.

"Where are we headed again?" Nicole asks from the passenger seat of my Audi Q3.

Stepping on the gas as I merge onto the highway, I say, "To Peter's Pumpkin Patch."

"Peter's Pumpkin Patch?" Nicole giggles. "Sounds like that tongue twister. Is there anything else to do at Peter's Pumpkin Patch but pick a pumpkin?"

I laugh at her. "Yes. They have a corn maze too."

"Really? I've always wanted to go in one. I wonder if they have seasonal baked items for sale too." She takes another swig of her PSL.

Giving her a smirk, I tease, "You think you need more pumpkin spice items in your life?"

"Always."

We fill the remaining hour-long drive by discussing what we want to carve on our pumpkins. Neither one of us knows definitively what we want, but it's fun to banter back and forth.

Nicole bounces in her seat when she spots the sign to the pumpkin patch. "Jaz, it says hayrides too."

"I think that's how we get out to the pumpkin patch," I tell her as I park.

In no time, we're standing in line with a handful of people waiting for a hayride pick up. A heavenly pumpkin spice scent wafts past my nose, and I turn toward it, expecting it to be Nicole sipping on her coffee, but it isn't. Next to me stands an elderly gentleman wearing worn coveralls. I eye him just as he lifts a sparkly, round, brown item to his lips. After a hardy bite, he moans and then takes a drink of coffee. "Excuse me, sir. What are you eating? It smells delicious."

He clears his voice, turns toward me, and smiles. "These? They're fresh-made pumpkin spice mini donuts. And yes, they are heavenly."

"Can I ask where you got them?" I ask, hopeful he didn't bring them from home.

He grins and points. "They're selling them over there."

Without missing a beat, I hear Nicole's shoes turn on gravel as she announces, "I'm on my way. Don't let the hayride leave without me." She returns a few minutes later with a bottle of water and a bag of hot mini donuts for each of us.

"Thank you," I say before shoving the first donut into my mouth. I moan as the cinnamon and sugar dance on my tongue.

Nicole grabs my arm. "This is the best thing I've ever had in my life. Do you think they'd give me the recipe? I don't think it's feasible to drive out here every day. Plus, I'm assuming they don't offer them 365, and I need these in my life daily. Or at least weekly."

I can't tell if she's serious or not. So I just laugh as we board the tractor-pulled hayride. The pumpkin patch is huge. They have the traditional orange carving pumpkins, but they also have white ones, green ones, bumpy ones, and enormous ones. Picking a pumpkin is harder than you think. I must have gone through the whole patch before I finally selected "the one."

After loading our pumpkins into my car, we get lost in the corn maze for an hour. On the drive home, Nicole says, "Thanks, Jaz. That was the most fun I've had in a while. I haven't laughed that hard in ages."

"Hey, you were laughing at me, and it wasn't that funny," I declare with a smirk on my face. Tom the turkey at Peter's Pumpkin Patch was apparently fond of me. He followed us all around the patch, gobbling and strutting in front of me. When he tried to come into the corn maze, he was shooed away by some workers who informed me he was doing his mating dance for me. "Damn chicken legs," I mutter under my breath. The boys in our neighborhood had nicknamed me *chicken legs*. I hated it almost as much as my long, skinny legs. But I've filled out since then. Right? What was Tom's problem? Nicole, instead of protecting me from the intended courtship rituals of said turkey, just took pictures and video and laughed hysterically as I squawked and jumped around. My response had probably encouraged Tom even more. Thank goodness by the time we exited the corn maze, he'd moved on to another victim. One of his own kind.

That evening, we carve pumpkins and eat homemade chili, just like when I was a kid. Although, Nicole and I veer off course a bit by adding Hallmark movies. The night brings back fond memories. Even though my mom isn't a skilled cook, she makes amazing chili, and in October we would carve pumpkins together. Rocco was always invited to join us, until I entered junior high and declared, in all my teenage wisdom, that it was beneath me.

Rocco is present in practically every thought I have. Even as I narrowed down my pumpkin selection earlier, thoughts of all the pumpkins he and I carved together came to mind. And it made me miss him.

We've talked a little over the past few months, but nothing more than surface topics. With my work commitments and then his season starting, we never find a good time to get together. I want to see him. To see if things are different. To see if that kiss affected him as much as it did me. I can't even tell you how many times since that night I've mindlessly traced my finger over my lips, remembering the feel of his pressed to mine.

After the pumpkin patch adventure, Nicole and I decide on something a little different, and attend a few

Steel hockey games. I'm only a hockey fan because of Rocco. He's so fun to watch. As a winger, he's a definite playmaker on the ice. He and Ace are like a well-oiled machine. Their chemistry is insane. It's only the first of November and the team is already sporting an impressive record of 7-1. They don't disappoint tonight either, easily winning.

It was great to see him out on the ice, although I'm ready for some face time. *Lip time too.* That sounds amazing, but I don't know where we stand. My declaration that our kiss was a mistake wasn't true. I was just trying to give him an out. But I'm not sure he took it. Honestly, if I give it too much thought, I just end up more confused than when I started. We need to have a conversation. But I don't know how to start it, so I say nothing. Secretly, I'm hoping he'll bring it up.

Lost in thought as I step out of the arena, I don't notice the drop in the temperature right away. "Brr." An icy wind rushes past me, chilling me to the bone. I shiver as I pull my peacoat tighter. "It might be time for a hat and gloves," I say to Nicole. She nods her agreement. Being from Alaska, she can handle the cold better than anyone I know, but she always says Chicago has an extra bite to its cold. The change in our weather is often so quick it could give you whiplash. One day it's balmy, and the next it's frigid. The weatherman tonight even claimed snow is on its way. We haven't seen more than a dusting yet, so I'm doubtful about his prediction.

"Or a heavier coat," Nicole adds as she hugs herself in her light fleece zip-up. Our noses pinken as we wait for our Uber. Rocco's coming over to hang out after he's done with the press. It's been a while since we've spent any meaningful time together, and I'm beyond excited to get some real time with him.

When Nicole and I arrive home, we pop popcorn and turn on the TV. We love to torture Rocco with romcoms during the fall and Christmas seasons, and there is a multitude to choose from.

The doorbell rings just as we select our movie. Tossing aside the blanket I'm wrapped in, I hop off the couch to answer it, knowing who it'll be. Excitedly, I pull the door open and a bite of wind sneaks through. "Get in here, Rocco. It's freezing out there," I say while tugging him inside.

"Whoa, Jaz. Nice to see you," he says while crashing into my much smaller frame. His muscular body envelops mine in a warm hug that turns me boneless. "I've missed you." The husky timbre of his words tickles my ear, and shivers race down my spine, making me squirm.

"I missed you too." I laugh as he squeezes tighter.

"Ready for a movie and popcorn?" Nicole hollers from the couch.

Rocco sniffs at the air. "You had me at popcorn." He lets go of his tight hold on me. I hold out my arms as I wobble, trying to get my balance. After a second, when he sees I'm steady, he turns toward the living room, asking over his shoulder. "You coming?"

My eyes trace his body as I follow behind. Distracted by the way his jeans hug his ass, I freeze. *When did I ever stare at Rocco's ass?* Never. My eyes widen at my surprising revelation. I can admit that I've always known Rocco is attractive, but when I look at him now... Things are different. My knees go weak, I start to sweat, my heart races, and my mouth goes dry. *What is happening?*

"Jaz." Rocco says my name. I blink my eyes and focus on his face. His stupidly handsome face that is causing me mental chaos. Swallowing past a boulder in my throat, I nod. But then a thought strikes me. *Why did it feel so good in his arms?*

Settling next to him on the couch, our thighs touch, and the air crackles. The contact between us is like molten lava, heating my entire body, and making the idea of a blanket seem ridiculous. Earlier, when Nicole and I had set everything up, I'd been cold, but now I'm roasting and considering removing all my extra layers.

About twenty minutes into the movie, when I'm distracted by the storyline, my body finally relaxes and regulates. I shift, breaking our connection, and pull in a deep breath. Rocco places his hand on my thigh, and instantly, my heart races. "You, okay?" he asks. *I was until you touched me.*

Unable to form words, I force a smile. He returns it and continues to watch the movie. I stare at his profile.

Just being in the same space with him since our kiss last May has kept my body buzzing and my brain spinning. We still haven't talked about it, other than when I said it was a mistake. But it hadn't felt that way at all. It had been magical, and I'm not sure what that means or how to tell him that. My fear of the unknown plagues me, making me mute on the subject. I have so many unanswered questions. *Do I want more? Does he? If he doesn't, what will that mean for us? Could I handle just being friends?* Instead of asking any of that, I just sit here silently, unsure what to say.

Then Nicole heads to bed, leaving Rocco and me alone. My nerves fray. *What should I say?* The air feels heavy with unspoken words, and I force myself to take shallow breaths. My chest feels constricted, like I'm being squeezed too tight. But I'm not sure if it's from that or the discomfort in my heart.

The silence surrounding us is deafening. *When has it ever been this uncomfortable or awkward between us?* Nervously, I finger the edge of my braid while I consider why. As if a lightbulb goes off above my head, it occurs to me that this is the first time we've been face-to-face for more than a few minutes since our kiss. *It changed everything.* My heart sinks when I realize we don't know how to be around each other anymore. That kiss. It's slowly unraveling our friendship. The longer we sit in silence, the more painful it becomes. Even though I know I'm not alone, I feel very much like I am.

To keep myself from going stir-crazy, I grab the popcorn bowl and clean it up. When I step into the kitchen, the cold floor surprises me and forces me to suck in a deep breath. The tightness that was present only moments ago weakens as I stand still and focus on my breathing. Closing my eyes, I meditate on what I can control. *Myself.* Returning to the couch, I see Rocco's body is slumped and worry covers his face. *Maybe he doesn't know what to say either.* Carefully, I lower myself next to him and I nudge his knee. "Are you okay?"

He nods, avoiding eye contact, and forces a smile that doesn't reach his beautiful brown eyes. *Okay.* Knowing we both need a distraction, I ask, "Wanna watch the Food Network? Maybe they have a new baking show on."

"Yeah, that sounds good," he answers, still avoiding looking at me. Sadness sweeps over me as I turn the television back on. Even though Rocco is right here, he feels a million miles away.

"Jasmine," I hear someone whisper. Am I dreaming? My room is black, but I can't see anything. Behind me, I feel a solid mass of muscle keeping me warm and toasty. *Who's that?* Scooting to sit up, I'm immediately stopped by an arm banded around my waist. Confused, my palm tracks down his exposed skin to his large hand, which is curled around my naked hip. My eyes go wide and I strain to make sure I'm clothed from the waist down. *What the hell happened here last night?* Retracing the previous evening, my panic recedes. *It's Rocco.* Relieved, I let out a breath. I haven't had a sleepover guest since Anthony and I broke up over a year ago.

"Jasmine," the voice says again. I blink my eyes again and move them toward the sliver of light peeking through my door. Standing there, only a foot away, bundled in warm clothes, is Nicole.

"Morning, Nic. What's up?" I ask while stretching my arms above my head.

She smiles and waggles her eyebrows. Apparently, she's figured out Rocco stayed the night, as he's currently snoring in my bed. We didn't do anything. We were up late talking and hanging out, and when he decided to head home, we saw that snow had been falling hard for a while, leaving a lot accumulated. Instead of dealing with the roads, he just slept over in my bed, because the couch was much too small for him.

Nicole leans toward me and whispers, "We got snow last night, and I figure we can tag team shoveling so we both have a chance of getting to work on time."

"Ugh." I groan, making her laugh. Although I'm not a fan of shoveling, her idea of tag teaming it is solid. "Let me get some warmer clothes on and I'll meet you out front." Just as Nic's closing the door, I hear Rocco's deep baritone voice next to me. Thick with sleep, he asks, "Is it time to get up already?"

"No, Rocco," I answer. "Go back to sleep. Nic said

we got a foot of snow and we need to shovel before leaving for work."

I'm pulling up my sweats when I see Rocco throw back the covers. "You don't have to help. We've got this."

He scratches his head and then scoffs at me. "Jasmine, what kind of man would I be if I slept while you two shovel your driveway?"

Putting my hands on my hips, I reply, "The kind who doesn't live here and who's not responsible for it." He rolls his eyes and stands up. As he's pushing me through my bedroom door, he pulls on his Steel sweatshirt and a beanie he stored in the pocket. *That's handy.*

I try to shimmy past him and grab my coat and boots while he's bent over slipping his own boots on, but his huge frame blocks me out, and he growls at me. Nicole slips out, leaving me with my grouchy bear of a best friend. He grunts again before he leaves.

"Hey, Nic, is this the other shovel?" Rocco hollers as the door is closing. Meanwhile, I'm still trying to get my snow gear on.

Finally, not even five minutes later, I step out, pulling on my hat and gloves, and see Rocco has already almost cleared one side of the driveway. Slowly, I climb down the icy stairs. When I reach the bottom, Rocco just smiles at me over his shoulder before he goes back to shoveling. "Rocco," I warn. Nic ducks her head and tries to ignore us. She's told me a time or two we sound like an old married couple. He's now ignoring me. *What the hell?* I try again. "Rocco." Even I flinch at the harshness in my voice. Standing there staring at him, I tap my boot impatiently on the well-packed snow.

When he finishes his side, he looks at me and laughs. "Is that supposed to be intimidating? You are adorable." Then he laughs again. *What a jerk!*

"Hey, Nic. Need some help?" he offers while stepping closer.

"Sounds like you're in enough trouble," she answers. He just gives her a shit-eating grin. Her eyes go wide and she shakes her head.

"Nah. We're good," he side-whispers loudly to her, making sure I hear him. I roll my eyes.

"Okay, if you say so." They finish the driveway quickly and then we all scoot back inside. I'm still annoyed.

Rocco approaches slowly and then wraps me in a big bear hug, murmuring, "Jaz."

"I'm mad at you," I say against his muscular chest.

"I know," he croons before he laughs. Ever since I can remember, he's always been there to help me, no matter what I need. He's my honest-to-goodness knight in shining armor.

I head to my room so I can get ready for work, and Rocco follows. While I hop into the shower, he climbs back into my incredibly comfortable bed. I wish I didn't have to go in today. I'd much rather stay home, snuggled up in my bed. After showering, I reach for my towel to dry off. "Shit," I mutter to myself. In the chaos that was my morning, I forgot to bring clothes into the bathroom. Scrunching up my face, I tell myself to be quick. Wrapping my towel around myself, I tiptoe to the door and silently pull it open. *Maybe he fell back asleep.* Stepping out, I shuffle to my closet as best as I can while staying decent.

"Jaz." His husky tone startles me, and I pivot quickly, almost releasing the strangle hold I have on my barely long enough towel. Turning slowly, I catch his gaze as it traces over me. His eyes are wide and wild. I smile, trying to make the moment less awkward. He licks his lips slowly before smiling back. *What's that supposed to mean?*

"I-I forgot clothes," I stutter out.

He throws back the covers, and my eyes are drawn to his impressively tented gray sweats like a heat-seeking missile aimed at its target. "Do you need any help? Your hands look full," he offers.

"I've got it," I rasp out as I grab the closest dress I see. I hustle back to the bathroom before I flash him. In my quick grab, I forgot the most important things. Undergarments. Thankfully, the dress has a built-in bra, but I guess I'll be going commando for now, because there's no way I'm running out there in a towel again. With my luck, I'd probably trip on something, roll my ankle, and flash him with such pizzazz, he'd never be the same.

When I'm finally dressed, I slip from the bathroom and move over to my vanity to do my hair and makeup. Glancing over, I see Rocco's laid out in my bed with his eyes open. "Is it okay if I shower?" he asks.

Not even looking at him, I say, "Sure." Within minutes, he's done, dressed, and headed toward the door.

"I'm going to put on coffee," he says before slipping out of my room.

Finishing up, I add some jewelry. "Perfect," I tell myself as I glance in the mirror. I pull some heels out of my closet and put them on so I don't forget them. I'll change into my boots before I leave the house.

I click down the stairs. *That is the best sound.* When I enter the kitchen, I see Nic and Rocco talking. The little I hear of their conversation is about coffee. I roll my eyes when I hear him say, "No creamer for me. I drink mine black. People say it grows hair on the chest. And it does. Want to see?"

Nicole doesn't need to see him naked. Only I get to. *Wait, that's not right.* Feeling jealous, I try to hide it with a backhanded comment. "Not every woman is dying to see you naked, Rocco. Right, Nic?" *At least I don't think she does.* He just smirks at me, his brown eyes dancing. I wish I could read his thoughts, because I'm sure they're indecent.

I look at Nic, and her cheeks turn pink. Nervous, she fumbles over her reply. "Umm. Sure. Err. Nope, I don't need to see anything. Thanks." Then she practically runs to the door. *That was weird.*

After fixing my to-go coffee, Rocco and I head for the door. I'm going to work and he's going to the arena for an early practice. When he pulls me into a tight hug before we leave my warm house, my body melts into his. "Thanks for letting me come over and... stay the night. That was hands down the best sleep I've had in years." Hugging him back, I inhale the faint scent of my vanilla body wash on his skin. *Damn, that's sexy.* I picture him in my shower, naked and covered in water. My nipples pebble, my center clenches, and I squeeze my legs together. I'm thankful I slipped on panties after he started the shower so they could soak up all the desire rushing through my body.

Taking a second to compose myself before I answer, I whisper, "Me too. Let's not go so long between seeing each other, okay?"

He walks me out to my car and helps me get in. *Always a gentleman.*

The drive to work is hell. Ditch divers are everywhere, and it takes twice as long as usual. Because of the snow, we don't see as many customers at the bank, so the day passes slowly. At five o'clock, I'm chomping at the bit to leave. Since this morning, I've felt scattered and all I want to do is go home and pull on warm, fuzzy sweats.

When I pull up into the driveway, I see Nic beat me home.

"What smells so good?" I ask as I enter the kitchen.

"I made dinner and... figured we could talk," she explains while waving a wine bottle from side to side.

I laugh. "Are you trying to bribe me into talking by giving me wine?"

She shrugs her shoulders and her eyebrows raise while she says "No." I don't believe her, but I'm clueless as to what she wants to talk about.

"Fine. Hand over whatever smells so delicious and the wine, then you may begin your interrogation," I negotiate.

"Interrogation?" she questions dramatically while trying to look innocent. I scowl at her. "Okay, okay, okay." She takes a sip of wine before blurting out, "What's going on with you and Rocco?"

What?

Confused, I ask, "What do you mean?"

She focuses her eyes on me, daring me to talk. Exasperated, I sigh and then say, "He's one of my best friends and he slept over last night. It got late, and when he went to leave, we saw it was already snowing hard, so I told him to stay. And he did."

"But... He. Slept. In. Your. Bed." She crisply enunciates every word.

I shrug my shoulders and say, "So?"

Not done with her questions, she lobs another at me. "Did you shower together after shoveling?"

Annoyed at her insinuation, I glare at her. "No, Nic, we didn't. He and I are not together. I showered first and then he did while I was doing my makeup and hair. It's no big deal. It's not the first time we've done that. It's not like we saw each other naked."

Nic hangs her head. "Sorry. I know Rocco is one of your best friends, but he's a playboy, and I don't want you to get hurt."

I frown, feeling like I have to defend him or us. Yes, he's been a playboy. I know that. But I'm not like those other women. I'm special. He would never use me and leave me. Resolute, I answer, "I won't. I promise." *Or at least, I hope I won't.* If only these feelings would go away, then I'd have nothing to worry about. That damn kiss ruined everything. It made me feel things I'd never considered before. And that's been incredibly uncomfortable.

Pouring another glass of wine, I lift it to toast. "May we always have each other's back, and may we always be honest with each other, even when the conversations are uncomfortable or inconvenient."

Clinking her glass to mine, she says, "I agree."

Chapter 9

Rocco

It hardly feels like almost a year has passed since we won the Stanley Cup. Holding a picture Ma took on the day I had with the Cup, it brings back how emotional that time was for me. I laugh at the memory.

Unlike some people, I don't do anything crazy like eat or drink out of the Cup... because, yuck. No, I bring it home so that my nonna, parents, siblings, and friends can see it up close. Ma plays photographer, snapping a photo of each of my family members hugging the trophy. But my favorite moment she captures is one of Jaz and me, standing in front of our treehouse.

It's a Tuesday, and the only time Jaz can get away from work is her lunch hour. She rushes from the city, arriving at my parents' house ten minutes before she has to leave. We haven't talked or seen each other since the night of my last game, and I'm nervous about seeing her again. That night, things changed between us. To be honest, I'm still not sure what I feel about it or her.

"Stand closer, like you like each other," Ma directs as we pose with the iconic trophy in front of our broken, aged, mismatched treehouse we built over a decade ago.

As Ma lines up the perfect shot, Jaz turns to me and says, "You know, I'm really proud of you. I never told you that night, but it's true. I remember all the times we sat in this treehouse and you promised me you were going to win the Stanley Cup someday." Her sweet, tender voice tugs at my heart, and I want to reach out and hold her hand. But then I remember we have an audience, and I don't want them to figure out the worst thing ever: I have feelings for my best friend. Not sure how to respond, I say thanks and then face back toward Ma, who is happily snapping away.

"You must have gotten at least one, right? Jaz has to head back to work," I say to Ma, then turn to Jaz.

"I do. Thanks for inviting me out, Rocco." She steps closer, giving me a side hug that feels beyond awkward. That isn't right.

"I'll call you later," I holler at her. Looking over her shoulder, she gives me a smile that looks forced. The knot that has been in my stomach since that kiss weeks ago tightens.

Winning the Cup and hoisting it above my head while the fans screamed is something I will never forget. It's something I dreamed of since I was a kid. But even that doesn't compare to the kiss I shared with

Jaz. That evening was chock full of memorable things. And I hope for repeats of it all. Everything, including the highly improbable moment between Jasmine and me. Afterward, neither of us mentioned what transpired, choosing to pretend it never occurred. That night, it crushed me when she pulled away, declaring immediately that what happened was a mistake. Standing there, face-to-face, still panting for breath, I couldn't identify my feelings. But at no point did it feel like it had been a mistake. The kiss felt right but also forbidden. If I had to pick one word to describe it, I would say it had been unbelievable.

I hadn't been sure what to say or do with Jaz's response. Hearing her words caused me to pull back, as if something had stung me. The burn ached. Her words hadn't felt right, although I couldn't explain why. Instead, for her sake, I just pretended to agree. At the time, it seemed like the best course of action.

Now, almost a year later, I'm convinced it wasn't. For me, that kiss has become the proverbial elephant in the room. I've been too scared to bring it up. She wanted to forget about it, and I don't want to ruin the friendship we have by causing unnecessary drama. Jasmine means too much to me. At no point do I want to stir up something that could cause her discomfort. And because of that, every time I see her, I push down my still unresolved feelings. Instead, focusing on keeping everything platonic between us. And that plan works until it doesn't.

The last time we spent any real time together, it almost killed me. It was the night I stayed over in November after a hometown series. Waking up next to her warm body had been a complete mindfuck. Everything I had been repressing for months was again front and center in my mind, demanding answers. But I still didn't have any.

Since then, I've been distancing myself from her because I'm uncertain how to behave. When she got really busy during the summer, I breathed a sigh of relief because I didn't have to intentionally avoid her. Avoiding her feels physically horrible and so very wrong. Every time I think about her, my stomach cramps with guilt. My nerves are shot and my focus is shaky. My heart races, and I feel light-headed whenever there's a possibility we'll see each other. I know it's something I need to get a handle on if I ever plan to see my best friend again. Especially because I heard she's dating someone, and acting like a jealous, possessive jerk will only drive us further apart. I have to accept that we aren't ever going to be an "us" and move the fuck on. Being distracted by hockey would help with that.

T he playoffs come and go, and the Steel skate away with the trophy again. Winning the Cup again is amazing, but it's not as meaningful as the first time. Jaz wasn't there, and that hurts more than I'd like to admit.

Her new boyfriend, Mark, isn't a big fan of mine or hockey, so she stayed away. I'm not his biggest fan either. In fact, the only time I met him, I'd run into them at the grocery store. Everything about Mark makes me see red. I know nothing about him, but just from looking at him for five seconds, I could tell he isn't good enough for Jaz. When she introduced us, he puffed out his chest and tried to give me an overly hard handshake. Neither of the overcompensating behaviors impressed or threatened me. Throughout the brief conversation we had, his grimy hands on her distracted me. *What, was he claiming her? Why not pee on her, buddy?* What an asshole. And she allowed it. Almost like she picked that douche over our friendship. Anger boiled in my veins and my fists clenched. Assuming the next thing out of his mouth would trigger me, I chose to walk away. Unable to handle him any longer, I excused myself. From Jaz's expression, she knew right away what I was doing. I hoped their relationship wouldn't last too long. Or I might not see my best friend for a while.

In the middle of June, a group text from Lucas goes out to the entire team and Christian Fox. By now, he was the agent for over half the Steel players. In our eyes, he's as good as a teammate.

LUCAS

Fourth of July BBQ at our house.
Come ready to party!

ACE

I'm in.

MIKA

I'll be there.

JOSH

Count me in.

CHRISTIAN

On the books.

I haven't seen Jaz in months and wonder if she'd want to come. She'd gone the year before and we had a blast. I don't know if she's still dating the douche, but if she is, it'll require me to be on my best behavior. All my wayward thoughts about that kiss would have to remain buried. Then the thought of her in a bikini slams into me, sucking all the air from my lungs. *Holy shit. How am I going to control my response to that?* All her soft skin on display. It would to be the death of me. For sure.

ME

Can I bring a plus one or two?

LUCAS

Who are we talking about?

ACE

Are they hot?

ME

Just Jaz and Nicole.

LUCAS

Samantha says absolutely. She's
inviting Monica too.

ME

Thanks, man.

CHRISTIAN

Monica's coming?

LUCAS

Yes. Why, are you two fighting again?
If so, you'll have to play nice. I don't
need my fiancée pissed.

CHRISTIAN

Nah, we're cool.

Later that day I text Jasmine.

ME

Hey.

JAZ

Hey.

ME

What are you up to?

JAZ

Mark and I were about to go to grab
dinner. What's up?

ME

Oh. You're still dating him?

JAZ

Yes. Is that a problem?

ME

No. I was just going to invite you and Nicole to Lucas and Samantha's Fourth of July party. But you probably don't want to come.

JAZ

Are you serious? Last year was amazing.

ME

It was, and yes, I was serious. I don't want to stir up trouble with your boyfriend, though.

Why does the word "boyfriend" leave a sour feeling in my gut?

JAZ

Mark won't care. He knows I'm a social butterfly. He's more content staying at home. It'll be fun. Thanks for the invite. I can't wait to tell Nicole. She's going to freak.

ME

Okay, sounds great. I'll text you the address and time. It'll be good to see you. It's been too long.

How is this going to go? My stomach tightens at the thought that things still might be strained between us. But things would never get better unless we push through the discomfort, right?

Chapter 10

Jasmine

Rocco's timing is perfect. This summer has been too hot and I'm in desperate need of a pool. When he texted a few weeks ago and invited Nicole and me to the Steel's Fourth of July party, I could hardly believe it. I even had enough time to order all the makings for a prank I'd seen on social media.

During the lackluster months of my relationship with Mark, I learned he wasn't as good-humored as Rocco. He was far too serious, and I knew if I tried the prank on him, he'd get furious. Lucky for me, I had no intention of finding out. We aren't well-matched, and I planned to break up with Mark before the party. He was sent out of town for a work training, so I decided to wait until he got back to talk to him. I didn't tell anyone my plan because that felt wrong.

Sitting on my bed with the Amazon package in my

hand, I justify my prank is payback for all the pranks Rocco played on everyone growing up. I rip open the box and stare at the item I ordered to make pool time a bit more exciting. I toss it into my tote bag with my sunblock, towel, and sunglasses just before hopping down the stairs.

"All ready?" Nicole asks as she adjusts her cover-up over her hot-pink bikini. She's going to drive all the single guys crazy. The woman has a body I'd kill for. I'm the yin to her yang—tall and uninteresting, where she is petite and curvy.

"Yep," I answer as I tug my tote higher up my shoulder.

A few hours into the party, when we're playing in the pool, Mika calls us over to the side to introduce us the new owner of the team. "Damn, he's fine," Nicole whispers to me. When Trey reaches us, my best friend's cheeks go rosy and her smile brightens. In all the years I've known her, she's never reacted like that to anyone.

"Time to eat," Lucas calls out as he delivers food to the table Samantha set up. When we climb out of the pool, I watch as Trey moves closer to Nicole. Seeing their mutual interest makes me happy. Nicole hasn't had a boyfriend since high school, and I'm not even sure I'd call him that. He was an epic asshole who basically stole her virginity and then dumped her. Seeing her light up around Trey is incredible to watch.

Sensing they want some privacy to get to know

each other better, I wrap my towel around my waist and move next to Rocco. Ace sidles up to my other side, sandwiching me in between the over six-foot-tall walls of muscle. Gathered around a rectangular patio table, we laugh and eat the amazing food that Samantha prepared.

"Want to go back in the pool?" Ace asks with a mouth full of cookies.

Rocco swipes at him. "Stop spraying me with cookie crumbs and I'll consider it."

Ace finishes his cookie, washing it down with a big gulp of water before he tries again. "Rocco, do you want to go back into the pool?"

Rocco doesn't answer but shifts in his chair. "I hate wet swim trunks. They're the worst."

Laughing, I stand up and go to my bag. I pull dry swim trunks out of my tote and say, "I'm surprised you lasted this long in them. Here, these are dry."

He squints at me suspiciously. "Why do you have a pair of men's swim trunks in your bag?"

I roll my eyes and answer, "I put them in my bag in case I wanted shorts instead of my bikini bottom. Geez. Just trying to help you out."

Grunting, Rocco reaches for them and plucks them out of my hand without a word. Stalking off to the pool house, he emerges a few minutes later dressed in the tropical flamingo print.

"Thanks, Jaz," he says with a smile.

There's something about the way the afternoon sun

hits his exceptional body. The way his smooth, tan skin stretches over his tight muscles makes me thirsty. I lick my lips, searching for relief. My eyes trace over his eight-pack down to the slight dusting of hair that disappears into the bright pink flamingo shorts. Following it down, I silently beg to spot a bulge showing me exactly what equipment he's working with. I've gotten teases before, but I'm collecting data to support my hypothesis that he is incredibly equipped.

"You're welcome," I say, fighting a smirk.

Nicole whispers, "Those them?" Holding in a laugh, I nod as Rocco and Ace head back toward the pool. As they walk, they gesture to each other, and it's tough to follow what they're doing.

"Jace, come here," Ace shouts to another Steel player, who's relaxing on a lounge chair near the pool. Minutes tick by as the three are huddled together, discussing something.

"Come on," I mutter under my breath, desperate for Rocco to get in the water. Finally, they line up along the side of the pool. Channeling the precision of a synchronized swim team, the guys flip perfectly into the center of the pool. A massive wave crests and splashes out of every corner of the pool, soaking anyone unlucky enough to be in the unofficial splash zone.

Then the funniest sound I've ever heard pierces through the air. It's a high-pitched squeal. "Jasmine, what did you do to these shorts?" Rocco yells in a voice that is unbearably loud. Instead of the manly tone you'd expect, the sound he emits is high and pitchy, much like a teenage girl who sucked in too much helium.

I'm doubled over, laughing hysterically as Rocco angrily stomps over to me. In his large hand, he's clutching his rapidly dissolving swim trunks. It's the funniest thing I've ever seen. I can't contain the snort that comes out next. The sound causes Rocco to lose it; he drops the remaining pieces of the shorts, baring himself to everyone. Then he grabs me and throws me over his shoulder. Unashamed of his nakedness, he sprints back to the pool, launching us both in. I barely suck in a breath before we're completely submerged. I push away from him and swim to the surface of the water, greedy for air.

"Rocco," I pant.

"Yes?" he murmurs as he swims closer. I glare at him and he just smirks. And then I remember he's naked, and my pulse skyrockets. I fight the urge to look through the water and see what he's packing. I always suspected he was large from the way his clothes fit, but he's my best friend and I'm still technically in a relationship. It would be wrong for me to check him out. In fact, I probably need to get out of this pool before my mind gets muddled with thoughts and flashbacks of that kiss we shared over a year ago. At the time, it caught me off guard, and I assumed it meant nothing to Rocco, so I buried my feelings deep and told him it was a mistake. The truth is, I wanted more. I wanted him to confess it meant something more to him. But he'd remained quiet, agreeing that it had been a mistake, and I accepted he didn't have feelings beyond friendship for me. Accepting that had been difficult.

Every time I think of him, my heart flutters and butterflies take flight in my stomach. It took me almost a year to push my unrequited feelings aside and consider dating someone else. A month after that, when Mark was hired by the bank I work for, I thought maybe that was my chance at being happy. We had similar work and life goals. And he was attractive. I learned his dry humor isn't always enjoyable, though. But here and now, all those feelings for Rocco rush back, leaving me off balance.

Needing space, I swim over to the side of the pool, and without another word, I pull myself out of the water and look at Rocco.

"Jaz." All he says is my name, but his eyes tell me so much more than words could. The world goes silent as our eyes lock. The air around me shifts as I feel his focus change. Suddenly, the heat of his stare is intense as it travels up my long legs. I shift my weight when he reaches the apex of my thighs and his eyes widen in delight. My heart beats faster when he hits the curve of my hips. I wish it were his hands tracing my skin. My skin pebbles under his intense gaze. Wanting to draw his attention up, I lift my arms above my head. His hungry eyes eat up the distance from my stomach to my breasts, and I see him lick his lips. I long to feel those lips again. When his stare reaches my mouth, my body shivers. Finally, our eyes meet again and a thousand sentiments are exchanged. Unable to handle the intensity of it, and feeling guilty because I'm still technically dating Mark, I grab my towel off my chair and wrap it around myself. Then I go looking for Samantha. Maybe she needs help cleaning up.

Finding her in the kitchen, wrangling enormous platters, I laugh. "Need some help?"

Her wide eyes flip from the container she's carefully filling to me. "That would be amazing."

For the next hour, we busy ourselves with wrapping, organizing, and cleaning up all the food. "Hey, thank you for letting Nicole and me crash your party. If you're good here, I'm going to head out. We both have to work tomorrow, and I don't want to be dragging," I tell her.

"Good luck with that." She laughs.

"What? Why?" I ask. Is it later than I think it is? Looking around for a clock, I see it's nine thirty.

She grins at me and then looks out the patio door. "They look rather cozy." I follow her gaze and see Nicole and Trey seated closely together. They're laughing and smiling at each other like lovesick fools. It's adorable.

"Did they know each other before today?"

I shake my head no and say, "No, but they look like they've known each other forever."

Samantha looks at me. "It reminds me of you with Rocco."

Her words stun me, and I give her a nervous smile. My voice catches in my throat. "Thanks again to you and Lucas for hosting. I better go wrangle her away." I give a quick finger wave, ducking outside before she can say anything else that gives me irregular heart palpitations.

"Hey, Nic, you ready?" I ask as I approach. It's tough to miss the way Trey's delighted grin falls. Nic looks at her watch.

"Oh my. It's so late." She looks at Trey. "It was so nice chatting with you. Hope to see you again." They stand up and give each other an awkward hug. Then she tugs her cover-up over her bikini and we head out. As we pass the pool, I notice it's still full of the guys horsing around, and Rocco is right in the middle of it. He's busy splashing and hollering until he notices me. Needing to leave, I wave to the guys. When my eyes land on Rocco again, my heart drops. He's wearing a look of disappointment, and I wonder why. Not having the time to get into it, I force a smile and wave at him. His shoulders drop and my heart squeezes.

Chapter 11

Rocco

After spending all afternoon together at the barbeque, I was starting to feel like Jaz and I were getting back on track to our old selves. I have to give her props. The dissolving shorts prank was top-notch. By the time I'd figured it out, only scraps remained.

When I climbed out of the pool, I tried to remain covered as I stalked over to her. All decency flew out the window when she'd laughed, and I retaliated by throwing her over my shoulder, letting the remainder of the shorts flutter to the ground. The warmth of her body against mine and the squeal from her throat heated my blood, pushing it south. I needed to cool off before I gave everyone an eye-opening peep show. That would have been awkward.

Quickly, I tightened my hold on Jaz and launched us into the pool. The entire way, I was praying I wouldn't sprain my hard-as-steel dick when I broke through the water. Seconds later, I was cool, calm, and collected. Standing up, I waited for her to resurface. A high-pitched squawk filled the surrounding space when she popped up. I settled against the side of the pool, waiting for her full reaction. I was prepared for anything. I knew it could easily go any number of ways.

When I was young, I was the king of pranks. And normally I could tell how everyone would respond. But Jaz has always been a wild card. Her mood determined her response. So, the fact she was pissed enough to storm off had me confused. Usually, pissed means she'll slug me in the arm and call me a jerk. She's never stormed away before. Had I pushed things too far? Had she felt my hard dick rub up against her? I sure had, and the heat that traveled between us was intense. Is that what pissed her off? What did that mean for us? Before I could get any actual answers, she was gone, leaving me clueless. Not long after Jaz tucked tail and ran out of the barbeque, Jace asked me to go to Vegas with him and some of the guys. The offer couldn't have come at a more perfect time, considering all the unfamiliar and uncomfortable emotions warring for attention inside me.

Still confused about Jaz's reaction a few days later, the boys—Mika, Ace, and Jace—and I all head to Las Vegas. We're traveling in style. The private plane is big enough so we can all spread out and enjoy the flight.

We're only staying a few days, but there will be plenty of clubs, pool time, and gambling. We may even catch a show. Jace is in charge of the itinerary, so anything is possible. I'm just looking forward to a distraction and a few days of uninhibited fun.

Sitting back, I swirl the glass of bourbon the flight attendant just served me. Her accompanying bedroom eyes have me intrigued, but not in the way one might assume. Although beautiful, her offer doesn't tempt me one bit. It's strange. Flashes of Jasmine dance in my mind, and I grit my teeth. *Stop. You can't have her. She's not interested. She has a boyfriend. What do I do?* I don't fucking know. No matter how hard I've tried, I've never been able to reconcile my feelings for Jaz. Something changed after that kiss, but I'm stuck at a crossroads. I don't want to do anything that will mess up our friendship. But the question of *what if?* permeates all my thoughts. I fear losing her. To another guy. To my fears. So, this weekend is perfect. It's a test of sorts. To see if my obsession with Jaz is fleeting or if it's here to stay. And if it is... what then?

"Hey, Rocco," Jace says as he sits next to me.

Shifting my focus from staring out at the clouds, I smile. "Hey, Jace. What's up?"

"Just trying to get an idea of what everyone wants to do in Vegas. I've never been here before, so I want to hit everything. Other than the flights and the rooms, I've booked nothing."

Thoughts of Jace doing *everything* flood my mind,

and worry sets in. Panicked, I ask, "You did book us each separate rooms, right?"

Laughing, he answers, "Yes. I booked everyone a room." He elbows me and gives me a wink. "So if you want to bring a hottie or two back for the night, you'll have privacy."

With the way my mind is, we'll see if that happens. I scratch my head. "Thanks, man."

He nods. "Is there anything you want to do? Shows, pool, clubs?"

I shake my head. "I'm game for almost anything. Except for getting arrested. I'm not about to have Coach chew me a new asshole for going off the rails in Sin City."

"You sound like Mika." He laughs again, then puts his hands up. "I promise... nothing crazy. I don't want to end up in the press or get in trouble with the team either."

Our few days in Vegas fly by. The guys and I hit the hotel's gym for a workout each day before lunch. Then we secure a cabana at the pool and spend most of the afternoon eating, drinking, and goofing off in the water. Ladies come out of the woodwork and do whatever they can to get close. Being professional athletes, we draw quite an audience. I've taken so many selfies with scantily clad women, it's ridiculous. I guess if I were actively looking for hookups like Ace and Jace, I'd be in hog heaven, but every time I look at a woman with interest, my stomach knots and guilt washes over me. *Why? Jasmine*, my brain reminds me. But she's not mine.

One night, after I have my quota of drinks at Onyx, a club on the strip, I briefly entertain the idea of trying to fuck Jasmine out of my head. But when the moment arrives, I'm not ready to pull the trigger. I can't go through with it. It feels disloyal. And even in my inebriated state, I'm still not willing to cross that line.

The morning after, as I lie in my bed, alone, I consider everything. *Why am I still so hung up on Jasmine?* Do I just need to get her out of my system? A one and done? Or is it more? I don't know. What I do know is, I want to grab her around her waist, throw her on my bed, and memorize every inch of her silky, smooth skin. *Yes.* That sounds perfect. Looking down at my body, it agrees. My cock is tenting the thin white sheet that covers me. I'm a naked sleeper, and without the restriction of boxer briefs, I'm at full mast and standing tall.

Sliding my right hand under the sheet, I wrap it around my throbbing cock and squeeze. *Damn, that feels good.* A shudder rocks my body as I slowly stroke myself. After the third pass, I swipe the head of my cock, gathering the pre-come from it. My eyes roll back as I fist myself tighter. Trembling, I continue to pump as I imagine the last time I saw Jasmine in a bikini. Mentally, I trace the lines of her suit with my tongue, slipping underneath it to lap at her soft, tanned skin. When I near a sensitive spot, she mewls, and my cock grows harder. I reach the apex of her legs and I push the tiny scrap of fabric away. I conjure up an image of her pussy. From conversations over the years, I know she gets waxed. How much, I don't know, but I imagine she's bare. She glistens with the evidence of her arousal, and I lick my lips, eager to finally taste her.

Gritting my teeth together, I mutter, "Fuck." Squeezing my cock into submission isn't easy. He has an eager mind of his own.

I return to my fantasy. As I lower my head to her center to give her my mouth, I feel the telltale signs of an orgasm racing through my body. Leisurely, I lick her from back to front. Flicking her clit with my tongue makes her back arch. I insert my finger and her tight walls hug me. Sliding in a second finger, I wonder how many she can take. Jasmine moans and I pump in and out of her.

"Rocco. So good," she pants in my mind as she thrusts out her hips.

"You think that feels good?" I ask. "What about this?" I pull out my fingers and replace them with my throbbing cock. Only one push buries me to the hilt, and she lifts up with a giddy squeal that sounds more erotic than happy. It doesn't take long for her to orgasm, and watching her fall apart is remarkable. Within seconds, I too am on the edge. Pumping harder, a wave of pleasure rips up my spine just as cum shoots from the tip of my cock.

"That was amazing." I groan before I open my

eyes. It's then I remember she's not really here. My heart falls, not just because I'm alone, but because I'll never look at Jaz the same way again. Now that I've masturbated to my fantasy of her, I can't go back. Her image is forever burned into my memory. Right now, the only question running through my mind is, how close is my imagination to reality? *Maybe one day I'll know.*

Chapter 12

Jasmine

It's been a few weeks since the barbeque, and I haven't seen Rocco. The main reason is that when I broke up with Mark, my feelings were in freefall, and being around Rocco made things more confusing. The longer we dated, the more apparent it became that we're better coworkers than anything else. We have little in common, and although he's attractive, my interest in him had waned. It didn't feel right to keep dating when he doesn't have the thing I'm looking for. Plus, I've been unable to shake the feelings Rocco has stirred up in me. Between the kiss and our pool encounter at the barbeque, it's all been too much. My emotions are a chaotic mess, sending me down a bumpy path of uncertainty.

Laid out in my bed with my arm thrown over my eyes, I'm exhausted from a hectic week of work. My phone rings from the mattress beside me. I answer it without looking to see who's calling.

"Hello," I wearily say.

"Jaz, are you okay?" Rocco replies, panic lacing his tone.

"Oh, y-yeah. I-I'm fine," I stutter while sitting up. Running my fingers through my hair, I check what I'm wearing, like I'm expecting him to arrive at any moment.

He lets out a deep breath. "Good." Then he stops talking. *This is awkward.*

"What's up?" I ask, wondering why he's calling.

Another deep breath. *Is he okay?* "I was calling to see if maybe you wanted to go to dinner and catch a movie."

"I'm pretty tired. Could we do DoorDash and Netflix instead? Or we could hang out another night." I want to see him, but I'm nervous. I've been experiencing crazy, intense feelings for this man I've known most of my life. We've always been platonic, but things aren't the same between us anymore, I don't know what to do, think, or feel about that.

"DoorDash and Netflix sound great. Think about what you want and we can order it when I get there. I'm going to stop and grab dessert. Do you need anything? Anything for Nicole?"

"Nothing for me, and Nicole isn't home. Her douche of a boss is making her work late tonight. So she won't be home until late," I answer.

Thirty minutes later, he arrives with a homemade treat. Tucked in a Rubbermaid container is Nonna's infamous cannoli.

Licking my lips, I can almost taste them. "Is that the chocolate chip filing?" I ask excitedly.

He smiles. "Only the best for my girl."

He's used terms of endearment before when referring to me, and they've never elicited a reaction. Tonight, though, it's different. Hearing him call me his girl makes my heart race, my stomach flip, and my breath catch. *Is that what I want?* I think I do, but without knowing what he wants, I'm afraid of ruining the friendship.

"What are we eating?" Rocco asks, pulling me from the constant quandary living in my head.

"You know what sounds amazing and I haven't had in forever?" My mouth waters thinking about it.

He peers at me for a moment, then finally asks, "What?"

"A wet Italian beef sandwich."

"That sounds fantastic."

An hour later, we're unashamedly stuffing our faces. "This is amazing," I say on a groan as I take another large bite.

"All I have to say is I'm glad I ordered two." He laughs as he takes the last bite of sandwich number one.

I shake my head at him. *With that amazing body, I don't know where he stores it.* Mental pictures of his decadent form flood my mind. My skin flushes and I feel the heat in my cheeks. *Is it hot in here?*

"Uh, Jaz," he says cautiously as he stares at me while unwrapping his other sandwich.

"Yeah?" I answer, my breath shaky as my eyes lock on his chest.

Tipping his head, he asks, "Are your peppers spicy? Your cheeks are pink."

Uncomfortable, I clear my throat. "Y-yeah, it's been a while since I've had one. It is a tad spicier than I remember." *The peppers aren't spicy, but I need him to think so because I can't admit I was picturing him half naked.*

Standing up, he gets water for us from the kitchen. Our hands brush and a charge zings up my arm when he hands me the ice-cold bottle. "Here you go. This should help." *Not likely. My entire body is on fire and craving his touch.*

Once dinner is finished, we sit next to each other on the couch. Rocco sets his arm behind me, and I find myself cuddled into his side. The smell of his musky cologne puts me on high alert. If I wasn't responsive already, getting close just took it up another notch. The warmth of his body next to mine is mind-numbing. It doesn't take long for me to overheat, so I remove my sweatshirt, leaving me in just a tight tank top. When I settle back, I swear I hear him groan. That noise makes my lady parts tingle.

As we pick out something to watch, our bodies

move together. I swear I see sparks from where our thighs touch. Originally, we wanted to watch *Uncharted* with Tom Holland, because hello, gorgeous. But it isn't out yet, so we end up watching *Big Timber*, a show about lumberjacks. I don't know if it's meant to be sexy, but there's something about the way those men move that gets my blood pumping. The way their muscles pull and flex in their dirty, torn shirts. Or maybe it's the sexy man seated next to me.

During the first episode, Rocco puts his arm behind me. I lean into it, relishing the feeling of his large muscles against my skin. Although innocent, it creates a plethora of erotic scenarios in my head. No longer am I focused on the rugged lumberjacks. I'm up in my head, imagining all the things I want to do with my best friend. Curled in the warmth of his protective arm, I close my eyes. I feel my breathing grow heavier as I explore the deep recesses of my overactive and overstimulated imagination.

"Jaz." My name whispered against my ear wakes me up. I'd been having such an amazing dream about Rocco and me.

My eyes fly open. "Oh no. Did I fall asleep?"

The vibrations from Rocco's deep laugh tickle my side as I rub the sleep from my eyes. Why is he so close and why am I sideways? Moving my head, I notice we're lying down on the couch and I'm on top of him. *How did that happen?* We were just watching a show. Right? I couldn't have dozed off for that long.

Scrambling up, I bump up against something large and hard. "Ow." Rocco moans as he folds in on himself, grabbing at his crotch. *Shit.* Did I just hit his cock? Was that what I felt? *No way.* My eyes go wide in disbelief as I try to covertly snag a look for confirmation. Yep, he's consoling his cock. *Shit.*

"Are you okay? Can I get you some ice or something?" I offer, despite being mortified.

Squeezing his eyes together tight, his grimace tells me he's in a lot of pain. "I'm good," he rasps. "It'll pass in a few." *Getting off him might help too.* Standing up, I pick up the trash from our dinner and make my way into the kitchen. I see Nicole's lunch bag on the counter. *When did she come home? Did she see me lying on Rocco like he was my air mattress?* Embarrassment floods through me and my cheeks grow hot. I open the freezer to cool off.

Seconds, minutes, or hours later, Rocco comes into the kitchen and asks, "What are you doing?"

Shrugging my shoulders, I close the freezer. "I thought it would be a good time to inventory the ice cubes."

He just laughs.

"Are your balls, okay? I'm really sorry I hit them." I wince as I look at him.

He smiles, stepping closer to me. He reaches down and grabs my hand, and shivers tear up my arm and down my back. "It's fine. I'm fine."

Looking at him through my lashes, I ask, "Really?"

He pulls me into a hug. "I promise." Standing here, caged in his arms, I decide this is one of the best feelings in the world.

Chapter 13

Jasmine

The past few months—okay, a year and a half—I've felt off-kilter. My feelings for Rocco have changed everything about me. Food doesn't taste the same. Things I used to love don't bring me joy anymore. I can't sleep without dreaming of my best friend and the way he tasted. The feel of his lips against mine is seared into my heart. And there is nothing I can do about the way I feel. *Why?* Because I don't want to lose him. If I tell him I've been thinking of only him for months, I won't be able to handle the rejection if he walks away.

I've tried to pretend everything is normal, stuffing down my unresolved feelings. But it doesn't work. I feel like a pressure cooker. Every time I'm around Rocco, I feel more like I'm being squeezed by a vise. I'm lying to myself and to him, and the stress of that is eating me up inside.

During the season, I can avoid Rocco. We hang out occasionally for short amounts of time, always with others, because I'm not sure I can handle being one-on-one with him. My feelings would be transparent and then I'll be screwed.

I pray that as time passes, my feelings will lessen and I'll realize it's only a little crush. It's been a while since I've been on a date. Maybe I just need to get back out there and find someone to keep my mind off Rocco. *You tried that. Remember Mark?* Right, that didn't work out so well.

S ummer arrives, and avoiding him becomes impossible. So, I lie to him, making up every excuse about why I can't get together. And let me tell you, my reasons are crap, but he always accepts them. I'm just so scared that I'll blurt out my feelings and ruin everything. Every time we talk, though, I can hear the frustration in his voice. I know I'm messing up and will probably lose his friendship, which devastates me, but I can't stop.

When summer turns into fall, I realize nothing has changed for me. I'm still pining for someone I can never have, and I can't do anything about It. My feelings for Rocco are so intense. And unfortunately, unreciprocated.

I need a break. Maybe it's time for a change. I don't

know what that looks like, but all the possibilities are exciting. I scour the bank's job posts to see if anything catches my eye. One position does, but it's in New York, and I'm not sure I'm up for that adventure. Hell, years ago, I turned down moving to New York with Anthony, whom I loved. All because Chicago is and always would be home. Plus, I still think New York is huge and intimidating. I'm not sure I can handle it.

So, instead of doing pointless mental calisthenics all day, I do the one thing any rational person would do: I start a pros and cons list, carefully weighing all the things I would need to consider. When I'm done, the lists are similar in length. *What am I to do?* If I stay and remain in the same rut I've been traversing for years, nothing will change. I'll go stagnant while everyone around me moves on. What if Rocco finds someone to move on with? Watching that would gut me. But if I'm in a new city, I wouldn't have to witness it, and I might find my own happily ever after. My decision is made.

Chapter 14

Rocco

"Y ou're what?" I growl into my phone.

Jaz and I have been like two ships passing in the night and haven't seen much of each other lately. Life got busy and I couldn't check in with her as much. I had to get back into my rigorous training schedule and then the season started.

And I'm pretty sure she's been avoiding me. Every time I try to get together with her, she gives me some lame-ass excuse for why she can't. I tried to be understanding at first, but when the season ended and I had unlimited time, I figured she'd be available. But I was wrong. She continues making excuses and canceling plans. Anger and frustration don't even describe what's coursing through my body. She's throwing our decades-long friendship away, and for what? I don't know because we can't even have a fucking conversation because she seems nervous to talk to me. *What the fuck is going on?*

Fall arrives. I ease back into the season. I channel my confusing thoughts and feelings about Jaz into practice and games, gaining impressive stats on the ice because of it.

And here she is, calling me on Christmas Day, of all days, to tell me she's accepted a job in New York and is moving before the New Year. *What the actual fuck?*

"I'm coming over," I bark out right before I hang up on her. *I needed to get a grip.* Rolling my shoulders, I grind my fingers into my tight neck muscles, hoping to relieve the tension plaguing me. After a few minutes of massage, I tug my shaking hands through my messy hair, snagging a knot. "Shit." I need a shower, but there isn't time. I need to see Jaz, but I also need to figure out why her moving has me acting like an angry beast.

My gut churns. It feels like I've had my feet ripped out from under me. I wasn't expecting this. I thought we told each other everything. *But you don't.* I tighten my fists, pissed. *She's moving away.* Why? Needing answers, I stalk to my Range Rover and waste no time exiting my neighborhood. Speeding onto the on ramp, I feel the up kick of my heart rate as I reconsider her words. *She's accepted a new job, and she's moving.* It makes little sense. She loves her job and living in Chicago with Nicole. *Doesn't she?*

I'm on autopilot during the drive to her house. I

barely put the SUV in park before I hop out. Grumbling, I stomp up the stairs, my anger still getting the better of me. Impatiently, I pound my fist on the door.

"Hey, Rocco," Nicole says as she pulls open the door. Her eyes are red-rimmed and dried tears stain her cheeks. *Apparently, Jaz didn't tell Nicole either.* Stepping inside, I pull her into my arms.

"It'll be okay," I whisper above her head. She nods against my chest and sniffles. Across the room, the sound of someone blowing their nose pulls my attention. It's Jaz, and she looks as miserable as Nicole. If I wasn't so angry, we'd be a sad-looking bunch.

"Jaz, why the fuck are you moving to New York?" I growl.

Nicole lets go and steps back, her eyes wide. I don't mean to scare her, but I'm here for answers, and if I have to be the bad guy, so be it. My tone must startle Jaz because a fresh wave of tears streams down her high cheekbones.

"I need a change," she whispers.

Moving closer, I lower myself onto the couch next to her. "A change?" I question. She nods. "And New York is where you think that'll happen?" Knowing she'll go regardless of what I feel or say makes me incredibly sad. I'm losing my best friend. We hardly connect now. It'll be even less once she moves. She's leaving behind her two best friends and going to an unfamiliar city that operates differently from what she's comfortable with.

She looks at Nicole, then me, and shrugs her shoulder. "I don't know, but I need something different right now." *What does that mean?* It's hard to gain any perspective or understanding from her vague response. Is she trying to escape someone or something? Would she tell me if she was? *Doesn't she know how I feel about her?* I frown. No, she doesn't, because I don't know how I feel and I'm too scared to admit to her I feel something more for her than friendship. It would devastate me if I ruin things between us.

Channeling my unmanaged feelings, I say the only thing running through my head. "So, you're going to move to New York for a new job, find new friends, and forget about us?"

Nicole lets out a surprised squeak across the room. *Has she not considered that?* Great, I'm the bearer of more bad news.

"W-what? No," Jaz spits. "I will not replace or forget about you two. I've just felt unsettled for the past year and I want to try something new. I'm hoping new scenery or experiences may pull me out of the funk I've been in."

My heart drops at the thought I'll never see her. How can she do this to us? The ache ripping through my chest steals my breath. Leaning over, I try to get a deeper lungful. I'm losing my best friend. Does she even care? I can't fucking believe this! "And then we'll never see you? Sounds like a brilliant plan," I bite back, my anger refueled.

Jaz's face turns red. "I barely see you now, and whose fault is that?" Her chest rises rapidly, mimicking her hitched breathing. She's preparing for a battle with words.

Not feeling up for it, I grit my teeth together. "Well, I guess that's it then. Have a nice move, Jasmine. I hope you find what you're looking for."

I hear Nicole's gasp as I stand up and move to the door. Just before it closes, I hear Jaz crying. I know what I said hurt her, and I probably should go back and apologize, but I'm too hurt. She's leaving me and acting like she doesn't even care.

At some point, I make it back to my house. I don't remember the drive at all. My mind shut down. Ever since I heard her say she was moving, it feels like my world is imploding. I don't want to think about her not being here. She's always been my rock.

Sharp pain tears through my chest, my heart feeling like it's in a vise. The squeezing pressure is unbearable as I pull into my garage. Turning off the engine, I shut the garage door. Leaning my head back, I sit in the darkness, silently pleading with whoever that she'll change her mind. The truth is, with her gone, I'm not sure I'll ever be happy again. At the thought of that, my eyes leak. I quickly swat the tears away, not wanting to acknowledge how deeply I'm affected.

My phone buzzes in my pocket. It's probably

someone in my family wishing me a Merry Christmas. Since I planned to head to my parents' house for dinner, I don't bother answering. However, when I flip it over, I see a group text from Nicole.

NICOLE

Hey, guys. Big news. Jasmine is moving to New York City before the New Year to start a new job. Come say congratulations and goodbye to her this Wednesday from five to seven at Mateo's. I know you're heading out on Thursday for your next away series and she'd love to see you before she leaves. Please RSVP so I can get a head count. Thank you.

How is she okay with this? I don't understand. My stomach knots and my head throbs.

My phone buzzes again.

ACE

Jasmine is moving?

A minute passes.

ACE

Dude.

Another minute goes by and I still don't respond.

ACE

Rocco...

Get the hint, Ace. I'm not answering.

ACE

Are you there?

ACE

Are you okay?

ACE

Need me to come over?

Fuck me. "Persistent little turd," I growl out.

ME

No, I don't want you to come over.
I'm fine.

I finally head inside and make it as far as my couch before I crash. The emotions of this morning have done a number on me and I'm exhausted. My eyes are heavy and my mind is sluggish. Kicking off my shoes, I reach for a throw blanket before lying down. As soon as my head hits the decorative pillow my sister, an interior designer, said I needed, I'm out. Hours later, I wake up to my phone's constant ringing. Looking at the call log, I see missed calls from Ace, all of my siblings, and Ma. They've each left messages. *Wait. Did they hear about Jaz moving?* My stomach cramps. I don't want to deal with their reaction to my best friend moving away and out of my life.

I press play on my mom's message. Her sweet voice fills the line. *"Rocco, it's me. Everyone has tried to get a hold of you since you didn't show up for Christmas dinner. We want to make sure you're okay. Please call me back, my sweet boy. I love you.*"

Burying my head in the blanket, I feel awful. I'd been thoughtless and made them worry. Dialing my ma, she answers on the first ring.

"Rocco," she says, worried.

"Hi, Ma. I'm sorry I missed Christmas, but I wasn't feeling good. I laid down to rest and passed out. I just woke up." That's the truth, kind of. She doesn't need to know all the details. I feel raw. A barrage of emotions has been coursing through my body, and I'm not ready to hash it out with anyone, least of all my ma.

"Oh no. Do I need to come by and bring you a plate of food?" Ma, God love her, is a caretaker through and through.

"Naw, I'm fine. My entire body aches and I'm nauseous. If I caught something, I don't want to give it to you." I know I'm not sick. I just don't want to see her. I love her to death, but one look at me and she'll know right away something happened. And I'm not ready for that interrogation. No, the reason I feel like absolute garbage is because of the bomb Jaz dropped on me this morning.

Ma hesitates for a moment. She doesn't know how not to care for us, especially when we're sick or hurt. "If you're sure." Her voice is tinged with worry, and my heart drops. Guilt eats at me. I don't lie to Ma. Ever.

"I'm fine, Ma. I promise. I'm just going to get as

much rest as possible before we leave for our next series in a few days."

The other end of the line is silent. I know she's grappling with wanting to do more, but I can't handle it right now. Finally, she speaks. "Okay. But please let me know if you need anything. Nonna offered to make you her special soup too." I rub the ache in my chest. *Too bad it only works on colds and not whatever the hell I'm dealing with.*

"Thanks, Ma. I just feel like sleeping. I'll call you tomorrow."

She scoffs. "You better, or Nonna and I will visit you. I love you, Rocco."

Smiling at her threat, I reply, "I love you too, Ma. Sorry again for missing dinner."

After hanging up, I pull myself off the couch and head for the stairs. Sleep is the only thing that will take away the constant pain. As a winger in the NHL, I've taken my share of hard hits from defensemen into the boards during a game, but nothing has packed as much punch as this has. Jasmine's decision has knocked me off kilter, draining me of all my strength, and I don't have the energy to try getting up.

When I get to my bedroom, I lower all the blinds, blanketing everything in darkness. I strip out of my clothes and climb into my bed naked, and huddle beneath the down comforter. A chill settles across my body, covering my skin with goose bumps. Snuggling deeper, I hope it'll pass. A shiver runs down my spine, and I question if I might have caught a cold. But then my mind focuses on what it had been ruminating on, and it all makes sense. This morning, when Jasmine said she needed a change, her words were like an icicle penetrating my heart. They were sharp, cold, and devastating. *Why had she seemed so cold and vacant? Have I pushed her away? Is this all my fault? Is she leaving because of something I did? Or have I just worn out my welcome?* Perhaps she's tired of me coming and going from her life so often. Thoughts of all that swirl in my head, making me dizzy. I close my eyes and try to focus on my breathing. In no time, I'm asleep again. Blissfully avoiding the fact my best friend is moving away, and when she told me, I yelled at her.

Chapter 15

Jasmine

I didn't expect everyone to be excited about my new job and upcoming move, but I never would have predicted Rocco's anger. I knew he'd be sad, just like me, but it shocked me when he yelled at me, then stormed away. I tried calling him so we could talk about it like adults, but he refused to answer my calls. I even thought about going by his house. Honestly, I didn't know what to do. Nicole hugged me a lot and told me he'd come around and that I needed to give him space, but his reaction hurt.

On Wednesday, after a full day of work, I meet Nicole at Mateo's. She'd reserved their back room, ordered some finger foods, and invited friends and family. My parents are here, happy as can be about the position I'm taking at the New York location of the bank I work for.

Grabbing Nicole's hand, I pull her close. "Thank

you so much for this. It's nice to have one primary location to say goodbye to everyone at once." My eyes scan the crowd, looking for only one person: Rocco. My heart sinks. He isn't here. *Has my decision to move cost us our friendship?*

Guilt weighs heavy on my chest. Here I am worried that confessing my feelings to him would be what ended things for us, not moving a few states away. Still, when I close my eyes, I can still picture how his body shook with anger and the darkness of his brown gaze as it bored into me.

Maybe he's running late, I rationalize, after half an hour has passed. Looking left and right, I catch the eye of Ace, who's still wearing a brace from his surgery, and mouth, *"Where's Rocco?"* Ace frowns, shrugs, and slowly crutches his way over to me.

"Hey, Jaz." His normal happy, playful tone is muted as he hugs me.

Pointing to his leg, I ask, "How are you feeling? How's your recovery going?"

He gives me a sweet smile. "It's going... slowly."

I laugh. "I bet. Thanks for coming. It's great to see you." He lets go and moves back. An uncomfortable tension washes over us. "Is he coming?" I whisper.

He blows out a breath as he adjusts his worn ball cap on his head. Refusing to make eye contact, he stares at the floor.

"Ace." I say his name like a plea.

When he looks up, his eyes are cloudy. When he

speaks, his deep voice wavers. "Jaz, I don't know. He's refused to call me back all week. I went by his house a few times, but he never answered. I'm sorry."

Blinking back tears, I touch his forearm. "It's okay. I appreciate you being here and saying goodbye."

Ace's eyes go wide. "But is this truly goodbye? Are you leaving Chicago for good?"

Not having that answer, I shrug my shoulders. "For now," I say.

Nicole walks up to us. "Okay, you two. Stop with the sad faces. We're celebrating that Jaz is going to kick ass at her new job. And then she'll come back and visit us."

Ace and I stand there silently. "Right?" she questions.

Her tone puts me on alert, making me feel like I'm in trouble. I mumble, "Yeah. Right. Of course."

The festivities wrap up after another hour, and I'm bombarded with the warmest hugs one could ever want before moving away. They're great, except the one I want most, I never get. Rocco never showed up, and it feels like my heart has been shattered. However, I'm not able to deal with that because Samantha and Lucas pull me aside. They hand me a list they've compiled, ranking their New York favorites. Their list covers things to do and see, as well as where to eat. I will definitely put it to good use. Hopefully, I'll make friends quickly and they'll want to show me around and help me discover everything about NYC.

That night when Nicole and I finally arrive home, the exhaustion finally catches up to me. As I trudge up the steps, I see a small gift bag on the stoop. Looking at Nicole, I ask, "Do you think it's from one of our neighbors for Christmas?" She shakes her head and laughs, her green eyes twinkling, matching her knitted scarf and hat perfectly. My name is on the tag. Intrigued, I remove the silver tissue paper to reveal a plain white jewelry box. Flipping the tag over, I clutch my heart and gasp. "Rocco."

Nicole steps closer. "That's from Rocco?" With tears in my eyes, I nod. His not coming to my going away party was devastating. All night, I forced myself to shove down my disappointment and hurt. I had a good time, but every time I remembered he wasn't there, my pain grew.

"Are you going to open it?" she asks, her worried eyes fixed on me.

I shrug my shoulders. "Should I? I mean, if he had something to say to me, he could have done it in person."

Nicole places her hand on my arm. "Jaz, this has got to be difficult for him. Maybe this is all he could do?"

I know she's right, but I still don't understand. Nicole isn't too happy I'm moving, but she still did something nice and thoughtful for me. All he did was yell at me and storm away. *What about what's in your hand?* Tears well up in my eyes. "I'll open it a little later," I answer, knowing I'm not ready for whatever this little box holds.

"Are you okay?" Nicole asks, concern thick in her voice.

Overwhelmed with emotion, my words are thick and slow to come. I nod, then force out, "I need to finish packing."

Looking around my bedroom, a yawn overtakes me as I tackle another dreaded pile of clothes. I finish packing another suitcase, and breathe a sigh of relief. I only have a few days left before I leave, and I still have so much to do.

Taking a break, I sit on my bed. The get-together tonight was a much-needed lift to my spirits. The only thing that would have made it better is if Rocco was there. Everything about this move has been challenging and emotional for me. Not having his support has been devastating. Too often during the last few days, I've found myself consumed with that, and all I want to do is curl into a ball and cry. Thankfully, I've held it together, only breaking down a few times. Tonight, though, the weight of those feelings slammed into me, leaving me shaken. His absence was noticeable. He's always been there for me. *But why not tonight?* What message was he trying to send me?

Emotional and physical exhaustion settle heavily in my bones, and I need to rest. Lying down, I open the photos on my phone and flip through the hundreds of pictures. My chest warms remembering all the good times. My smile dips when I realize Rocco is present in many of them. It's both a good and a bad feeling. I'm grateful he's been in my life for so long. But considering the last few days, I wonder if that will continue. And that thought wrecks me. Tight squeezing pain replaces the warm, happy feeling. "Ow," I say out loud as I rub at my sternum. Not having him around has been unbearable. *Is he suffering too?* It feels like he stomped on my heart and then walked away. He didn't give any reason for the way he behaved, he just reacted. And he's gone radio-silent, which hurts even worse than if he'd kept yelling at me.

My fingers dance over his profile. I'm itching to call him. But what would I say? Nothing has changed. I'm still planning to move, and he's still angry about that. I wish he'd tell me why. He has me so confused.

Not wanting to deal with it any longer, I set my phone in the charger, and that's when I see the gift Rocco left me. *Am I ready for this?* Unsure, I slowly reach over and retrieve the box. It's light, almost weightless. My curiosity gets the better of me and I slowly remove the lid. A stunning snowflake necklace rests in the nest of fluff inside. I'm not sure of its meaning, but it's precious. Pulling it from the box, I notice it's heavier than I imagined. I run my finger over the pendant's pattern. Smiling, I unclasp the necklace and put it on. I can't imagine what Rocco was intending in selecting a snowflake, but the gesture of the gift speaks volumes. I only wish he'd given it to me in person. The feel of the snowflake against my skin reminds me that Rocco is always with me. No matter where I go.

I get up and get ready for bed. *Maybe tomorrow will be better and Rocco will reach out.* I toss and turn all night, my mind filled with lists, worries, and scattered thoughts. At about two in the morning, sleep finally wins out, but it's far from restful.

When Nicole wakes up at six to get ready for work, I get up and shuffle down the stairs for a cup of coffee. I know it'll be the first of many for me.

Leaning against the counter with my eyes closed, I sniff the heavenly aroma of my freshly brewed coffee and let out a groan.

"Morning, Jaz. How'd you sleep?" Nicole murmurs. I peek open my eyes and see her staring at me.

"I tossed and turned all night. You?" I answer.

She smiles and then dreamily answers, "It was incredible. I quit my job because an incredibly sexy billionaire wanted me to be his assistant. He was controlling and demanding in all the provocative ways." Her cheeks flush, and I know she's reliving it. I quirk my head to the side, giving her a knowing smile. "No matter how much I protested, he wouldn't take no for an answer. He was a major bosshole, but I couldn't resist him. And the best part of the dream was, when I quit, I finally told Curt what an asshole he is."

"Sounds like the books you read, but it would be

amazing if it were to really happen," I say. Even in my exhausted state, her excitement is infectious. She's right, her boss, Curt, is an asshole. He's been that way since her first day, but because Nicole hasn't finished her degree, she doesn't want to quit and not be able to find something else. So she's stuck for now. *Maybe she doesn't have to be.*

"You know... you could quit and move to New York with me." I smile hopefully.

"Jaz, you know I can't. Without my degree, I'd struggle to find a job that would help with rent. Plus, I couldn't afford to take classes. I'm so close to finishing my degree. I just need to stick it out a little longer and then I'm saying goodbye to Curt."

Taking a large swig of my coffee, I force myself to wrap up my raw emotion before responding. "I know. I know. I'm just going to miss you, that's all. I figured there was no harm in asking."

Nicole laughs. "I know we'd have fun, but it's too big of a cost for me."

I step closer and wrap my arms around her. "Will you visit at least?"

She smiles big and nods. "I will definitely visit. But I'll wait a bit until you're more familiar with the city. That way, you can show me all your favorite places."

"Deal," I say before I let her go.

She glances at the clock and grimaces. "Time to go to work. Lucky me."

Watching her head out, my eyes mist. Swiping at

them, I acknowledge this is the end of another chapter of our lives. Pouring another cup of coffee, I head back upstairs for a full day of packing. At the top of the stairs, I hear my phone ring. *Is it Rocco?* Feeling hopeful, I hurry down the hall to my room. I set the coffee on my desk and lunge toward the still ringing phone. Not looking where I'm going, I slam my foot into the bag I finished packing last night. "Ow, ow, ow," I chant as I dance around the room on one foot while cradling the other. The phone rings again and I hobble over to it, but it goes silent just as I pick it up. "You've got to be kidding me." *Was it Rocco?* I hadn't been able to see, so I open the home screen and pull up my missed calls. My shoulders fall when my eyes land on the name across the screen. Amanda from my new job. I slowly sit on the edge of the bed and return her call.

"Thank you for calling Investor Bank. This is Amanda. How can I help you today?" Her perfectly pleasant voice fills the line. My shoulders go tense as I hold back a groan. I'm obviously in a shitty mood, and I need to keep it under wraps so I don't scare off my new coworker.

"Good morning, Amanda. It's Jasmine returning your call. Sorry I missed you. I was packing and got distracted."

She laughs. "It's no problem at all. I wanted to let you know that all the paperwork for your transfer was perfect, and the team looks forward to meeting you next week after the new year begins."

I kick my jittery legs like I'm practicing for a swim meet. Relieved, I drop my head back and say, "I'm so glad it arrived safe and sound. Is there anything else you need from me before Tuesday?"

"No. Everything's great. Hope everything goes well on your move."

Me too. "Thank you, and I look forward to seeing you again on Tuesday." *I'm not kidding. Amanda had been the nicest person I'd met when I'd gone to New York to interview a month ago.* The trip had been quick. In fact, other than my boss, no one knew I went. I'd been keeping it close because I was fearful, even then, of the fallout. Mostly about how Nicole and Rocco would respond.

I know Nicole is sad, but her support means everything. I still haven't heard from Rocco, and each hour that passes is like another slice to my weary heart. I need this change, and he refuses to see that. All he sees is that I'm leaving. But he's done that to me repeatedly with each hockey season, and I never threw a fit. Plus, he's got plenty of money. It's not like he can't visit whenever he's free.

Shaking my head, I refuse to let my hurt feelings win. "It's his choice not to try to keep our friendship alive," I tell myself as I stand up and gather the next suitcase.

A few hours later, I've finished packing everything besides my essentials to get me through the next day. I have a flight the day after tomorrow, which happens to be New Year's Eve, and I hope the airport isn't insane. *Yeah right.* My timing isn't ideal. Moving into New York City while the end-of-year festivities are being set up in Times Square is going to be crazy, but I don't really have a choice. My new job starts on January 2nd, and I want a day to get my bearings. Thankfully, my newly furnished apartment isn't too close to where the celebration is being held. I tell myself it'll be simple. I'll grab a taxi from the airport and have the driver take me straight to my apartment. After that, I'll find the nearest market, and stock up on food to last me a few days. Totally doable, right? *I hope so.*

Exhausted from my seesawing emotions and sleeping poorly the night before, I climb back into bed to take a nap before Nicole gets home from work. Snuggled deep under the covers, it doesn't take long for me to fall asleep.

Chapter 16

Rocco

"**W**hat the fuck?" I grumble to myself as I pace my condo for the millionth time since storming out on Jaz. That was a day ago... I think. I haven't eaten, slept, or showered. Hell, I'm a mess, and I don't even fucking care. All I care about is that Jaz is leaving me and she said nothing until the decision was already made. *WTF?* If she was unhappy, maybe I could have done something. If I'd known. But from what I can tell, no one knew. She'd kept it all a secret. And I fucking hate secrets, especially from her. What else is she not telling me? *What are you not telling her?* Stuffing that question down deep, I refuse to acknowledge I'm keeping anything from Jaz. We've always been honest with each other. *Mostly.* The only thing we never discuss are any of the women I've been with. From as far back as I can remember, I just kept that to myself. I don't remember why—probably because none of them ever mattered—but right now, with all things considered, I'm not questioning it. *So, see, I'm not really keeping a secret.* I don't have to tell her about all the feelings I'm having about her. I'm sure they will pass... eventually. "Gah." I grunt as I tug my hand through my messy, unwashed hair.

Ring, ring.

My cell phone goes off across the room, and I ignore it.

It rings again and again. "I don't want to talk to anyone," I growl.

Then there's a knock at my front door. *That's weird.*

"Open up, Rocco," a voice calls through the door before they knock out an oddly familiar beat. As I near the door, I roll my eyes. I know who's on the other side.

Pulling open the door before he can finish his snappy tune, I snap, "What do you want, Ace?"

His sunny smile is all I get before he attempts to shove his way inside. Being on crutches has slowed him down a bit.

"What is that smell?" He grimaces, looking like he sucked on a lemon. He dares moving in closer to me. "It's you!"

His accusation pisses me off and I say, "I don't fucking smell." *Do I?* Lifting my arm, I take a whiff of my pit. *Damn, he's right.* I shrug my shoulders. Who the fuck cares, anyway? I scowl at him. If I were alone right now, it wouldn't matter. "If my smell bothers you, you're welcome to leave," I tell him as I cross my arms over my chest. He just stands there, leaning on his crutches, which angers me even more. I haven't even asked how he's recovering. I feel my body tense further. *Why can't he leave me the fuck alone?*

Noticing my posture, Ace's eyes go wide. "What is wrong with you? I haven't heard from you in days and you didn't show up at Jasmine's goodbye party." His focused stare makes me uncomfortable. I want to crawl out of my skin and run far away. But I can't. He's waiting for an answer. So, like a mature adult, I do the only thing I can. I stomp away without saying a word.

I can practically hear him roll his eyes, and I look at him from the corner of my eye. Sure enough, he shakes his head and crutches back to the still-open front door. *Maybe he's leaving.* My hope dies in an instant when he slams the door shut. *I guess I'm not that lucky.* Knowing he'll follow, I escape into my living room and sit on my couch in the divot I've made over the past two days. Sitting there in silence for a few minutes, I wonder what will happen next. Ace and I have been teammates for years. We're incredibly close. Our friendship has always been relaxed and easy. We play, have fun together, and joke around. Nothing between us has ever been serious.

"Rocco," Ace says. Turning my head toward him, I see an unfamiliar look in his eyes. Usually light and happy, today they are dark, full of worry and concern for me. "What is going on with you?" The emotion in his voice makes him sound raspy, like a pack-a-day smoker. I just shrug in response. Ace sits back in the chair he's commandeered and fidgets with his crutches. The asshole; he's waiting me out. Trying to get me to break first. I can do this all day. But then a few minutes tick by. It feels like nothing, but it also feels like the room is shrinking in around us.

Needing relief, I ask, "Why are you here, Ace?"

He stops moving, looks over at me, and admits, "I'm worried about you... how you're dealing with Jasmine moving."

I scoff. "Nothing to be worried about. I'm fine," I answer, hoping I sound convincing, unlike how I truly feel, which is destroyed.

"But Jasmine," he protests. And I don't want to hear any more.

"She's off to new adventures and opportunities. I wish her well."

Again, he shakes his head. "That's bullshit." He glares at me. "If you supported her, you would have been at her going away party, not sulking in your house."

"I am not sulking. I'm doing fine," I grit out.

"Would Jasmine say the same?" he challenges.

I let out a breath. When I finally answer, my voice

sounds sad. "It doesn't matter. She's moving away. What she thinks is irrelevant. It changes nothing."

"Thought so." Ace smirks, his suspicion confirmed that my shitty mood has been due to Jaz leaving. His words are like pouring salt on my wounds. They sting and burn. My fists flex. I never wanted to knock out a friend before, but right now I'm seriously considering it. Who cares about the broken leg situation? Just getting that cocky smirk off his smug-ass face would make my day. Hell, probably my week, all things considered.

With anger pulsing through my veins, I say, "What the fuck is that supposed to mean?"

"In all the years I've known you, I've only seen one thing affect your mood. Jasmine. If she's happy, you're happy. If she's angry, you become a wild protector, wanting to right whatever wrong she's experienced. If she's dating someone, you withdraw and become sullen. And right now, you're just being an asshole. With her leaving, it doesn't bode well for you. I'm not sure how you're going to be, but if the last few days are any sign, it will not be pretty."

Ace's words hit hard. And I'm a big guy, so normally I can take it. But today, they're hitting too close to home and aren't rolling off my back. No, each one is like a barb, sinking deep and refusing to let go. I don't want to hear any more. Pushing up to my feet, I yell, "If I'm such an asshole, then why are you here? Draw the short end of the stick?" Standing up with his crutches he moves until we're toe-to-toe, our chests bumping. Mine's filled with rage, while his is filled with challenge. He isn't stepping down. Instead, we're like two bull moose during rutting season and it's a fight to the death.

With nostrils flared and shortened breaths, he answers, "No, I didn't draw the short stick. I'm here because, like it or not, you, you moody asshole, are my best friend. I know that Jasmine leaving is fucking with you, and even though you're trying to push me away, I'm still here, calling you out on your shit."

I grit my teeth and deliver the death blow. "I don't care what you say. Get out. I don't want you here."

Immediately, Ace's chest deflates and his shoulders hunch. "Fine. You win. Be a moody asshole by yourself. I won't feel sorry for you one bit. I hope Jasmine finds all that she's looking for in New York, because it'll be better than what she has here." Then he storms out of my house.

Exhausted, I drop back onto my couch. Burying my head in my hands, I groan. In the course of a few days, I've pushed away both of my best friends. "What the fuck is wrong with me?" *Jasmine.* Thoughts of her invade my mind and pain shoots through it as if I'm being squeezed. Lying back, I rub at the affected area. She can't be leaving. *What if things change between us? What if she finds someone to replace me?* If I don't fix things, she won't even think twice about replacing me. I was a complete asshole and I owe her an apology. I just wish I could understand why her leaving is so distressing to me. I must lie here for hours, trapped in my thoughts, because when I finally shake off the haze, I see it's grown dark outside. Just as I'm about to make myself get up off the couch to take a shower and go to bed, my front door swings open. It's Ace again. *Damn, he's persistent.*

"Ace," I mutter, scrubbing my hands over my face. As he marches up to me, I take in his appearance. Normally put together, he now wears workout clothes. His face is red and sweaty, like he just came from the gym. When he gets in front of me, he points his finger at me.

"Rocco, you are the dumbest guy I've ever known. You have perfection in front of you and you are completely oblivious."

"It's been a long and confusing day for me. What are you trying to say?" I ask.

"You love Jasmine," he announces.

"Wh-what?" I ask, stunned by his accusation. "Sh-she's my best friend. Of course I love her."

"Just as a friend?" he questions, his face full of skepticism.

"Yes. Just as a friend," I answer, as confidently as I can muster. "I mean, it's Jasmine. That's all she sees me as too." *Even though I've always questioned if we could have more. I mean, she's perfect.*

"Are you sure about that?"

Slumping onto the couch, I lay my head back and

groan. "I don't fucking know." Would I want more with her? Hell, yes. But I've done nothing about it. *Except for that kiss.* My heart pounds in my chest. Sitting up quickly, I know I need to deal with how I feel about that kiss. I've pushed it away for so long. I've been telling myself I made a mistake. But had I? Even back then, I knew I wanted something more with Jasmine. And she'd been receptive to the kiss. However, instead of talking about it, we swept it under the rug, refusing to deal with it. The only problem is, I haven't forgotten how it felt to have her lips on mine. I remember the way she tasted and the soft moan she made. *How could I be so stupid? She's been right here all along. And now she's leaving.* "Fuck!"

A voice to my right says in a cocky tone, "Sounds like you figured something out. Realize you have feelings for your best friend?" Looking over, a smug-faced Ace sits next to me. "If that's the case, you truly are fucked." He smiles.

"Thanks, asshole." Watching him out of the corner of my eye, I see him kick his feet out and make himself comfortable.

"What are you doing to do now?" he asks.

Giving him a half laugh, I reply, "I don't know." Frustrated, I pull my hands through my hair as idea after idea pops into my head. But nothing feels right. "What am I going to do?" I ask the surrounding air.

Silence fills the room as we both sit there and ponder my situation. Ace claps his hands together.

"I've got it. You go over there and demand she stay in Chicago."

I flash him an unamused look and scoff. "Have you met Jasmine? You can't demand she do anything. Not if you like your balls where they are. And I do, very much."

He laughs. "Okay, fair point. How about you go over and tell her how you feel?"

I drop my head back and focus on my ceiling. *How I feel.* "That sounds like a brilliant plan, if only I knew how I felt."

My admission shocks him. "Oh shit." I just nod my head. Truth is, on top of not knowing how I feel about her, I don't want to screw up our friendship—more than I may have already.

Turning to me, he blurts out, "But, Rocco, what if she meets someone in New York, never knowing you have feelings for her, and she gets involved with them?" At the thought of that, my stomach bottoms out and I break out into a nervous sweat.

I answer back in a shaky voice, "I don't know, man."

"Then you have to tell her. Before she leaves," he says confidently.

"This isn't a Hallmark movie. I will not go over there, spill my chaotic mess of feelings, demand she stay, then live happily ever after. No, Jasmine is an independent woman who is going to move to New

York, meet new people, tackle new hurdles, and live her best life."

"And you're not even going to try?"

I shrug, not having an answer.

Ace gets up, looks at me, shakes his head, and leaves. His disappointment is thick in the air, but I just don't know what to do.

Chapter 17

Jasmine

As I look around, all I see are skyscrapers reaching into the heavens... and people. So, so many people. I'm not sure what I was expecting, but this isn't it. I'd heard that New York City is a bustling place, but I never imagined it was this busy. It's been overwhelming, to say the least.

After a week of being here, when I'm sure I showed up to work looking frazzled, one of my new coworkers, Melinda, took me aside. During lunch that day, she was an enormous help in explaining the flow of the city. Most importantly, she gave me tips on how to best navigate the subway, which was a complete godsend because the first days were hairy. By the third time I ended up in a neighborhood that wasn't my own, I seriously questioned why I moved. And to the most populated city in the country. *You needed to get away.* By week two, I had a better working knowledge of the subway and could get to and from work and to get groceries. This weekend I'm planning to meet Melinda for brunch across town, and it will be my biggest adventure yet.

After riding the R train for ten minutes, I get off on Canal Street and find myself in a lively area of Chinatown. Being my first time here, I find myself mesmerized. It's utter chaos, but it's hard not to see the beauty in it. In the hustle and bustle, I notice mostly the street vendors peddling their wares.

As I walk, I see colorful bits of paper scattered everywhere. Curious, I stop and asked a young woman about it. She tells me it's the Lunar New Year and families bought confetti poppers to celebrate. While we're talking, I hear multiple pops near me, along with the squeals and cheering of children. My heart soars. It's beautiful to see a live celebration. Every inch of the space before me is bursting with rhythmic sounds, colorful sights, and exotic smells.

"Jasmine." I hear my name called from a nearby storefront. I turn and see Melinda. I wave at her before I maneuver my way through the crowd to where she waits.

"Hey there," I say when I finally reach her. "Is it

always this busy?" I ask as a group of tourists push past us.

"On the weekends, for sure." She laughs. "This way," she says as she leads me down the street and farther away from the sizeable crowd. After a few minutes of walking, she opens a door with "The Eatery" written on it in a white font, and we shuffle inside the cozy restaurant.

While we wait for a table, she tells me, "This is a newer restaurant to this area. I've only eaten here twice, but both times were amazing."

A server shows us to a rustic wood table, hands us our menus, and scoots away. A short time later, we're ordering. Avocado toast for her and French toast for me.

"Do you live near here?" I ask.

"My place is about twenty minutes away. I live with my boyfriend Henry, and one of his best friends from college," she says.

"A two bedroom. That sounds nice."

She grimaces. "It is until you have to pay the rent. There would be no way Henry and I could afford it if Paul didn't live there too. I'm not sure what we'll do when he decides to move in with his girlfriend."

"Is he planning to leave soon?" I ask.

She shakes her head. "Not that I know of. But I try to be realistic and plan for the inevitable."

"That sounds smart. I know I got lucky finding a tiny place with one bed and one bath. An even bigger win is that it's reasonably affordable. Because if I needed a roommate to supplement rent, I'd be in some major trouble. There isn't much room, and one of us would have to sleep in the shower." Melinda laughs at that.

We share small talk while enjoying our breakfast. "Do you want to look at the shops while we're here? I need to find a gift for my sister's birthday, and you can usually find some fun things in Chinatown."

"That sounds fun," I say while pulling my hat and mittens on to fend off the chill in the air. "At least until my feet are frozen." I laugh.

"Right? I didn't plan ahead either," she says, holding her foot out for my inspection of her footwear. No boots for her either.

Linking our arms together, we head out. Time passes quickly as we move from vendor to vendor, looking for the perfect thing.

"Jasmine, over here," Melinda shouts, clutching a bag close to her.

"Did you find what you were looking for?" I ask, hopeful that we can end our impromptu shopping excursion sooner rather than later. I've been wiggling my toes in my canvas shoes for the past fifteen minutes, trying to make sure I still have feeling.

Smiling widely, she nods. "I did. I found something perfect." Holding up a satchel she found, she tells me her sister is obsessed with bags and she will absolutely flip over this one.

"That's so great. I hate to cut this short, because I had a great morning with you, but my feet are freezing and I need to get home before I lose a toe."

Tipping her head back, she let out a big laugh and adds, "Same here." We hug goodbye before we head our separate ways.

The subway is crowded on the way back to my apartment, but I always enjoy the opportunity to people watch. I absolutely love what a melting pot New York City is. It's rich in diversity, and you never know what you'll encounter.

Thankfully, my apartment is near the subway stop because my toes are tingly. Riding the elevator up to my floor, I wiggle my frozen digits, muttering to myself, "We're almost home. I'll get you warmed up soon." Stepping off, I see my handsome next-door neighbor. "Hello, Mike," I say as I wave to him. I met him the first day I moved in, and learned we're about the same age and that he's an architect.

"Hey, Jasmine. How are you?" he replies in his deep baritone that always makes my knees go weak.

"I'm great, despite being half frozen." I laugh.

"Frozen? What have you been up to this morning?" he asks, stepping closer and rubbing my arms to warm me.

His touch makes my heart skip a beat. It's been a while since I've reacted like this to a man. Maybe moving away from Rocco and the constant draw I feel toward him was a good thing. I can officially move on from my unreciprocated crush on my best friend. Smiling, I tell him about brunch and shopping with Melinda in Chinatown.

"Ah, now I know why you're freezing. It's cold today, and if you were shopping in Chinatown, you got little opportunity to stay warm. And here I am, delaying you even more." He looks at his watch. "You get inside and warm up. I have to get to something. Maybe we could do dinner this week?"

"That sounds great. Here, let me have your number in case anything comes up." After we exchange numbers, Mike pulls me into a warm hug, and I can't help but melt into him. *That feels so good.* As we pull apart, the elevator opens at our floor and my eyes connect with those of someone I wasn't sure I'd see anytime soon.

"Rocco," I whisper, mindlessly touching the snowflake necklace he gave me. Mike turns to see who I'm staring at and his mouth pops open like a goldfish breathing. Rocco steps from the elevator. Wearing a long, black wool coat and a matching camel-colored wool cap and scarf that highlight the hazel flecks in his dreamy brown eyes, he's so handsome. In this moment, even though he looks exhausted, he's stolen my breath from me.

"Jasmine," he rasps out. His eyes widen as he focuses on my neck, and you'd think I'm standing here naked, what with the hungry look in his eyes.

"Y-you're R-Rocco Romano," Mike stutters out. Rocco nods without removing his laser focus from me. It's unnerving, but in the best way. A shiver runs down my spine. He's never looked at me like this before. And I realize I like it. His gaze traces over my body, leaving a path of heat behind. Suddenly, I'm not feeling frozen anymore. Rather, I'm wishing I could remove some of my layers. Still focused on Rocco, I barely notice Mike step away. Once he's out of sight, he's forgotten. I fix my attention on the man who's always been there. *Well, except for when you told him you were moving.* Pain seeps into my heart, and my shoulders fall.

"Why are you here, Rocco?" I question, tears gathering in my eyes. Before I left Chicago, he made me wonder if our friendship was over. The last time we saw each other, he yelled at me and stormed away. And then there had been the gifting of the necklace. Every day since then, I've missed him more. He's always been my best friend, the one I've loved unconditionally, and he shoved me away. My brain refused to accept it, though, hoping that he'd eventually show up and right his wrongs. Is that why he's here?

Rocco lowers his head, dropping the eye contact. "I'm here for you."

Stunned by his words, my hand flies to my chest. *What does that mean?* He lifts his head and worry fills his eyes.

"I don't understand."

"Can we go into your apartment? Maybe not have this conversation out in the hallway," Rocco asks. Turning, I unlock the door and push into my small space. He's my first official visitor. Looking up, I see his gigantic frame takes up much more room than mine. His being here makes the space feel tight, claustrophobic.

I point to the couch. "You want to sit down?" He nods, but before I can move, he steps closer and pulls me into a tight hug. Burying his head at my neck, I feel his warm breath against my skin, and my body temperature climbs to dangerous levels. *Pretty soon, I'm going to be stripping to my birthday suit to cool down.*

"I'm sorry, Jasmine." His voice is filled with emotion. I push back and look into his eyes. They're dark and stormy. Still needing air, I step away, pull him to the couch, and encourage him to sit beside me. Stroking his hand, I see his body let go, unwind, and he mutters again, "I'm so fucking sorry."

Wanting to comfort him, I squeeze his hand. "It's okay, Rocco. I know you're upset I moved, but you never told me why. Can you do that now?"

Leaning his head against the back of the couch, he blows out a deep breath. "Please?" I beg.

A few minutes pass in silence, and I wonder if he'll actually tell me. "I miss you, Jaz. Having you this far away is killing me. I need you to come home. Chicago is where you're supposed to be," he finally says, not really clearing anything up for me.

"I hear what you're saying, but for years I've been stuck. Moving here forced me outside of my bubble. It's good to try new things, and I needed a new environment with new people and fresh problems to work through. It's not like you can't see me. You play in New York several times a year, and you're wealthy. You can come see me anytime your schedule allows. Chicago and New York are pretty close."

He licks his lips and nods. "Yes, but what if things change between us?"

I scoff. "For the last seven years, you have spent most of that time traveling and being gone from Chicago, and although I missed you, there was nothing I could do about it." He goes to object, and I cut him off. "Plus, that is the nature of relationships... they change over time. It was bound to happen."

Rocco furrows his brow and crosses his arms over his chest, pouting. "It's not supposed to happen to us," he growls.

Then my phone rings. It's Nicole, and I'm in desperate need of a break from the conversation with Rocco, so I answer it.

"Hey, Jaz." Her happy greeting sucks up some of the heaviness in the room.

Happy to hear from her, I say, "Hey, Nic. What's going on?"

"Not too much. Still hate my job and that you're a million miles away."

She's ridiculous. I laugh. "I am less than 800 miles away. In fact, it's a short flight if you ever want to visit."

"I do, but you know funds are tight right now. It's why I'm bugging you." This ought to be good.

FaceTime Request Sent.

"I'm thinking about getting a side hustle," she confesses when I accept the video call.

I frown. "What type of side hustle?" I don't know many that aren't pyramid schemes, so I'm nervous for my friend.

Nicole sticks her tongue out at me. "I need something that isn't makeup, bags, or food. Something relaxing, especially after dealing with Curt all day. That, or I need a man in my life. Speaking of that, have you found any hotties in New York yet?"

I turn red just as a deep growl comes from next to me. Panicked, Nicole's eyes go wide. "Is there someone with you?" I shift my phone, showing her Rocco, who is channeling the Hulk. He's scowling and his fists are squeezed tight.

"Eep," she squeaks.

"Hey, Nic," he gruffly says as he gives her a little wave.

"Rocco, hey. Are you playing a series in New York?" she asks, sounding confused about why he's here.

Before he can answer her, I whip the phone back

and scowl. "No, he's here because he's trying to convince me to move back to Chicago."

"Jaz," he croons. Thankfully, he doesn't know what that sound does to my body. *Great, now I'm all hot and bothered again.*

"Really, I should go. Jaz, I just needed to ask you a quick question and then you can get back to whatever you two are doing," Nicole rushes to say.

I let out a dramatic sigh. "We aren't doing anything but fighting. Our M.O., right? What do you need?"

"So that bachelorette party in college for Molly. Do you remember the sales lady there? Do you remember the company she worked for?" she asks.

Thinking for a moment, I say, "I think it's called Intimate Moments. Why? Did you already find a man in the weeks I've been gone?"

Rocco clears his throat. "Why would that matter?"

Nicole laughs and I roll my eyes before I explain. "Because, Rocco, Intimate Moments is where someone can buy sex toys, lingerie, and other intimate stuff."

"Or can sell them," she adds. Surprised, my mouth drops open, and Rocco groans. *What is he thinking?*

"What do you mean, 'or sell them'? Are you going to become a sales rep for them?" I ask, confused.

"Yeah. You know, the side hustle I was considering so I could make the rent."

And suddenly I understand. Before I can offer any help or ask any more questions, she spits out a goodbye. Rocco says bye before she ends the call.

"Well, that was informative," he says with a smirk.

Rocco

Before I left Chicago, I promised myself that I'd tell Jasmine I'm in love with her. But I've been a complete chickenshit. After our brief conversation when I first showed up at her apartment—where nothing was resolved and I kept my mouth shut about my feelings—I spend the entire ten-minute walk to a neighborhood bistro hyping myself up to tell her how I feel. By the time we sit down and are handed menus, I'm on the edge of a breakdown. My heart pumps incredibly fast and I'm sweating. I rush out a raspy "thank you" to the young man who delivers our water and basket of bread. Bringing the cold glass to my lips, I take a healthy swig. It's refreshing, but I still need a second to control my anxious thoughts. Tipping the glass back again, I down the rest. When I lick my lips, I still feel parched. I rest my hands on the table, mentally calculating my next move. *Tell her during dinner.*

After ordering, we sit, staring at each other. All the things I want to say flood my brain, making it a chaotic place, and I struggle to get my words out. Frustrated with myself, I look down at the white tablecloth.

"Rocco, are you okay?" Jasmine asks. *Am I? I don't*

know. I want to confess to my best friend that I have feelings for her, but the fear of doing just that has me frozen in terror.

Forcing my gaze up, I see a concerned look stretched across her beautiful face. Her expressive mocha-colored eyes are swimming with worry. *You need to fix that.* I let out a deep breath and say, "I am *really* glad to be here visiting you." The smile that graces her bubblegum-pink lips steals my breath.

"Me too," she replies. A sense of relief washes over me at her answer. "And while you're here, what do you want to do?"

"Honestly?"

She gives me a shit-eating grin before she replies, "Of course. It's the best policy, or at least that's what they say."

"Who's 'they'?" I ask while laughing.

"I don't know. It's just a saying." Exasperated, she groans, then says, "We're getting off topic. What do you want to do while you're here?"

She's fucking adorable. I smirk; I love to watch her get riled up. "I just want to spend time with you. I don't want to do or see anything in particular."

Over our dinner of ratatouille, which is like my nonna's caponata, we catch up on our time apart.

"This is amazing. It reminds me of something your nonna makes," Jasmine says before she licks her lips. I nod my agreement as my gaze follows the movement of her tongue.

Shaking my head to clear the fantasy brewing, I distract myself with a few questions. "How was the move? Do you like the city?" I'm asking, secretly hoping she'll tell me it was terrible, and she's moving home immediately.

She grimaces while taking a bite of her dinner. "The move went well. Renting a furnished apartment helped a lot because I didn't have to figure out the logistics of furniture. Also, taking a cab from the airport with my two extra-large suitcases saved me. I know doing it differently would have caused severe frustration and a likely migraine. Just imagining trying to get on the subway with my bags gives me hives. All I know is it would have ended up with me in tears. And the city..." She pauses, thinking for a moment. "The city is overwhelming and magical at the same time. My first few days were truly terrifying as I tried to navigate the subway system, but after a coworker gave me helpful hints, I feel like I have a better grasp on it. At least I can get to work, the store, and home." She smiles at that.

"Well, it sounds like you're settling in nicely." I hate to admit that. She needs to come home. I miss her there. That is where she belongs.

"It's been a learning experience, for sure, but mostly, I'm enjoying it," she admits, and my heart sags. Hearing that, I question if it will be pointless to confess my feelings to her. Despite my heart wanting to claim her, I stop myself. It sounds like she's happy here, and she doesn't do long-distance relationships. Not wanting to mess things up between us again, I keep my mouth shut. If she ever decides she doesn't like New York, I can try to get her to move home and then tell her what I'm feeling.

Chapter 18

Rocco

My second morning in New York starts slowly. When we finally make it out of her apartment, it's lunchtime. I get the best idea as we're riding in the elevator. "How about Greek food for lunch?"

She side-eyes me. "Okay. Any reason why?"

Smiling, I answer, "it sounds good."

She laughs at me. "Okay, let me text Melinda and see if she knows of any good Greek restaurants."

A minute later, her friend recommends The Olive Branch. After an entertaining twenty-minute subway ride, we stand on the sidewalk in front of an older building. Staring at it, I notice the storefront's painted blue, an obvious nod to the flag of Greece. Stepping inside, I see it isn't too big, but it's bustling and loud. A smile spreads across my face when I realize that most of the noise is laughter and singing, and it's coming from what looks like the kitchen.

"I have a good feeling about this," I say as I nudge Jasmine. We take a seat at a small table that seats four.

"What are you going to get?" Jaz asks as she looks over her menu. Taking it all in, I see that although their menu isn't huge, it has everything I'd expect at a Greek restaurant. *And now to choose.*

"That's tough. It all sounds amazing." Glancing around at the plates of the other diners to see if anything grabs my attention, I mutter "wow" under my breath as I spot something I have to try.

I flag our server over.

"Are you two ready to order?" she asks with a smile.

Jasmine chimes in with "yes" at the same time I answer. "Almost. I just have a question first."

"What would you like to know?"

Pointing to a table near us, I ask, "What is that?" When Jasmine sees what I'm referring to, her eyes go wide and she nods her head.

"That is the Greek fries. It's our traditional fries with lemon salt, chunks of feta, chopped kalamata olives, red onion, and fresh Italian parsley."

I nod and smile. "Does it come with tzatziki sauce?"

The server laughs. "Of course."

My stomach growls.

"Okay, I'll take an order of that with a lamb gyro." My mouth waters in anticipation of what I've ordered.

Turning to Jasmine, the server gets her order of a Greek salad and a hummus plate. I'm glad we each got something different so we can share. As if she's reading my mind, Jaz laughs. "I'll share only if you do."

The food at The Olive Branch is amazing. There's not too much conversation between the two of us because we're busy gorging.

Being January, it's still cold, so we decide to head back to Jasmine's place to watch a movie after we eat. *Home Alone* is our pick, even though it's almost a month past Christmas. Over the course of the movie, we laugh about all the shenanigans that Kevin gets into while defending his home from two burglars.

Things get heated, and not in a good way, while we're eating dinner.

"This Mongolian beef is good, but not as good as Golden Dragon," Jasmine says while she fixes herself a plate of food from the various takeout containers covering her kitchen countertop.

"Well, you know you could move home and have all the Mongolian beef, fried rice, and dumplings you want from Golden Dragon." My smile is met with resistance when Jasmine rolls her eyes and frowns at me.

"We talked about this, Rocco. I'm not ready to come home yet. And you need to stop pushing me." Her tone is a clear warning that I've crossed the line.

Holding up my hands, I say, "I got it. Moving home isn't a safe topic right now." *Guess I'll never be telling her how I feel.*

The rest of the evening, I feel off. Even though my mission for the weekend was to tell Jaz how I feel, I also want to focus on bringing her home. Unfortunately, every time I push her, she pushes back. Like me, she's stubborn, so I don't know why I was expecting it to go any differently.

T his morning I have to fly back to Chicago, so I take her out to an early breakfast before I deliver her to work.

Over skillets, I try sharing my feelings again, even though I fear how she'll respond. Having her shrug it off as nothing, would destroy me. Trying my best to maintain eye contact, I admit the less scary feelings to her. "Jaz, until you moved, I didn't realize how much I'd miss you."

Her beautiful face grows soft. "I miss you too, but I needed to do this. Being here is all about me and discovering who I am and what I want. Maybe that's New York. Maybe it's not. Only being here just under a month, I don't think I've allowed myself to fully experience it all. I've met some great people, and although they aren't my best friends, it's a good reminder that there are good people everywhere. I'm not trying to say New York is home, because Chicago is and always will be. But it's a stop in my journey and although it's scary, it's exciting too."

When she finishes, I nod my understanding. Everything she's said is important to her, but I'm struggling to get past my own selfishness. I need her home. I need *her*. *If only.* Wanting her to be mine is a big ask, and I'm obviously not ready for that, but every time I think of my girl, single in the city, my gut tightens. My mind floats back to what I saw when I stepped off the elevator the night I arrived. Her arms had been wrapped around that oh-so-friendly next-door neighbor I'll call asshat. Just knowing he's here makes every possessive trait I didn't know I had swell with intensity. She's mine. *She doesn't know that.* But what can I do? It feels like I can't do anything, and just knowing that makes my heart spasm and ache.

Standing on the cement stairs of the bank she works at, I wrap her in my arms and hold her tight, not wanting to let go. She pulls back, refusing to make eye contact.

"Jaz, look at me," I say quietly as I tip her chin up. Her eyes are filled with unshed tears. And it shreds my heart. Swallowing hard, I rasp, "I'm only a plane ride away." She remains silent and just nods her head.

"Last night, I'd looked at my calendar and saw a two-day window where I can visit. Smiling at her, I confirm, "I'll be back next month."

Her eyes go big, and a hopeful smile tugs at her

soft, pink lips. "Really?" I badly want to seal my promise with a kiss. But instead, I press my lips to her forehead before I pull her into another hug. The feeling of her body against mine drives me wild, and I need to end it before my attraction to her becomes obvious. Our relationship is on fragile ground, and it would shift off balance if I rub my erection against her.

"Okay," she says before pulling away and turning toward the building. My eyes follow the delicate sway of her luscious hips, and my fingers flex as they itch to wrap around her. On instinct, I know my thumbs would anchor her hipbones as I pull her into me.

When she reaches the front door, she turns around and gives me a wave before blowing me a kiss.

"Bye, Jaz. I'll miss you. I love you." I whisper the last three words so only I can hear them.

I fight myself every step to the Uber I ordered. *Why didn't I tell her how I feel?* Then, the entire flight home, I berate myself for being a coward. I don't want things between us to change, but the *what ifs* give me hope what we have could be even better if we throw love in the mix. I just have to bite the bullet.

When I get back to Chicago, I hurry home to drop off my luggage before heading to the arena for practice. Out on the ice, Coach has us skating sprints. Feeling winded after twenty minutes, I question for a moment if playing hockey is what I want to do for another five years. But it's undeniable; I want to play hockey for as long as I can. There aren't many things I want for myself other than hockey, but the longer Jasmine is in New York, the more apparent it becomes that I want her permanently in my life. And not just as my best friend.

Lost in thought, I don't notice a teammate skate up to me until they bump into my side. "Watch out," is off my lips before I even process who it is. "Mika. Sorry. What are you doing?"

He laughs. "Coach ended practice a few minutes ago, and the Zamboni needs to get on the ice, but your old, lazy ass has been standing in the way for the past five minutes."

Looking around, I see the rink has been abandoned, and they've pushed the nets against the boards, ready for the ice to be resurfaced. "Sorry, Jim," I shout to the Zamboni driver as I finally skate off the ice.

"No worries," he calls back as he waves.

"So, how was the trip to New York to see Jasmine?" Ace asks as he walks into the busy locker room. He isn't practicing with us yet after breaking his leg, but he often does his physical therapy at the same time.

I go to my locker and begin stripping off my gear. "It was good. But I didn't manage to convince her to move back." I hang my head, knowing that the next month is going to suck. "I'm heading back next month to see her and make another plea for her to come home."

Ace sits next to me as I remove the tape from my

socks. He looks around, drops his voice, and asks, "Did you tell her how you feel?"

Sighing, I reply, "No. I couldn't get the words out. It was never the right time."

"The right time? Really? Rocco, when will it be the right time?" His questions grate on my nerves, making me defensive.

"I don't know," I growl.

He abruptly stands up, annoyed, and questions, "Will it be the right time when she's dating someone else and deciding to stay in New York permanently?" Then he walks away.

"Fuck." I breathe out. His words cut deep. I can't let that happen. The next and last guy Jasmine will date is me. I'm going to make sure of it. Dressed in just my hockey pants, I sit there on the bench in a mostly empty locker room, planning my next steps. He doesn't know it, but Ace's words are the call to action I needed.

Almost a month later, my plans are coming together. I'm only days away from traveling to New York to see Jasmine again. This month has been so hard. It's as if a piece of me is missing. Only my phone calls with her somewhat ease the near-constant discomfort I'm suffering. I have an ache in my chest directly over my heart that throbs all the fucking time. When it first appeared a few days after I got back from my initial trip to see her, I tried my best to ignore it. Still feeling it a few weeks later, I mention it to Matthew, one of our training staff, and within the hour I'm being hooked up to an EKG.

"While Christine is getting you ready, I need to ask you some other questions that may help us determine our next step. Okay?" Matthew says, and I nod my head, showing him I understand.

He holds his iPad ready to record my answers. "Besides the chest pain and discomfort, are you experiencing any of the following symptoms: fatigue, heartburn or indigestion, cold sweats, nausea, lightheadedness or dizziness, or shortness of breath?"

"No. Just the constant ache," I answer as they place the last lead.

Ten minutes later, he stands next to me, holding a long strip of paper with squiggles all over it. "Rocco, your EKG looks fantastic. I'm not sure what you're experiencing, but I want you to do a stress test just in case."

What is wrong with me? Worry washes over me. I break into a cold sweat. *Didn't he just ask about those?* "You aren't thinking it's a heart attack, right?" I ask, concern swimming wildly in my gut.

He holds up the EKG strip and looks again at the rhythm, then shakes his head. "Everything looks great. No evidence of a heart attack. It's all baffling, really. Let's have you do the stress test and see if that shows us anything."

Once the stress test is done, it shows my results are perfect. I'm in peak physical health. Matthew reaches out to a renowned cardiologist the team contracts with, and I go to practice. Hours later, after I've finished my ice time and weight room visit, he finds me in the locker room, hanging with my guys.

"Hey, Rocco. Do you have a minute?" he calls from the doorway.

"Sure," I say while tucking my shower stuff back into my cubby.

Jogging over to his office, I rap on the doorframe with my knuckles.

"Come in and close the door, please," he says while gathering up some papers from his desk.

I lower myself into a chair and look at him. "What's wrong with me, Matthew?"

"I talked to Dr. Bernard, and after sending him your test results, he also thinks that you aren't experiencing symptoms of a heart attack." I breathe out a sigh of relief. "But he asked something that I couldn't answer."

The relief of hearing it isn't my heart is short-lived as I wonder what he'll say next.

"Do you experience panic attacks or anxiety?"

His question confuses me. "No. Why?"

Matthew flips around a piece of paper he's printed out on panic attacks. "Some say that the symptoms of a panic attack are like a heart attack, and he wondered if maybe you had some anxiety and had panic attacks."

I take the piece of paper and slowly read over the information. Yes, the symptoms are similar, but some are different. Trembling and racing heart. I have both. I suck in a breath.

"Rocco, are you okay?" he asks, concerned.

I wrap my hand around the back of my neck and squeeze at the tension I feel before I admit, "This is exactly what I've been experiencing. But I've never had issues with anxiety before."

Scooting his chair back, he asks, "Anything you're worried or anxious about right now?"

Jasmine.

"Yeah," I mumble.

"Are you more worried or anxious than normal?"

I laugh to myself. *That can't be what's causing this.* "Yeah, it's more than normal." Admitting that relieves some of the ever-present pressure in my chest. *That's interesting.*

"Is there anyone you can talk to about it?"

I shake my head no. "It's just... I have to make some big decisions soon, and the pressure of it all is driving me crazy." Another band of pressure releases its hold on me, making it easier to breathe.

Matthew looks at me. "I'm not a therapist, but I think talking to someone you trust is worthwhile. Sometimes another person's perspective is all we need to help alleviate the stressor."

"Thanks. I hear what you're saying and I appreciate all your help."

"You're welcome. Take care of yourself. And I hope everything works out for you."

Taking a shower before I leave the arena, I plan to call Ace and see if he wants to grab a beer. I know he's sick of my Jasmine drama, but he'll still listen.

Calling Ace from my car, we make plans to go out to dinner on Thursday night.

Two days later, Ace and I are sitting at a table at Meat & Potatoes, nursing our beers while we wait for our food.

"Any plans for the weekend?" he asks.

"I'm going to see Jasmine tomorrow," I confess.

Tilting his head at me, he asks, "Are you going to tell her how you feel this time?"

I take a swig of my beer just as they deliver our food. We thank the server and then I take a bite of my loaded mashed potatoes without answering his question.

"Well?" he says with a snap.

Finishing my bite, I nod my head. "Yes, I plan to tell her." Then I whisper, "I just hope it doesn't fuck up our friendship."

Ace's scowl morphs into an expression of concern. "I don't think that will happen. I think you've both been fighting your attraction to each other for a long time. And I think one of you needs to bite the bullet and come clean."

"I hope so, man. I don't want to waste any more time."

"It'll be fine," he assures.

The rest of our dinner is pleasant, and we enjoy amazing Wagyu steaks that melt in your mouth like butter.

Taking in the ambiance of the restaurant, I ask, "Who told you about this place? It's amazing."

"Do you remember Janica from the library? She's a big reader and saw a review a few weeks ago in the paper. She told me she wanted to come, but her boyfriend, Captain Dickface, won't take her."

Laughing at the name, I add, "Well, he sounds like an asshole."

"He is," Ace agrees. "I wish she'd just break up with him. She deserves so much better."

His tone makes me curious. "Like you?"

"She's incredible, but she's too good for me too." His voice strains heavy with want. I can tell he cares about her a lot.

"Naw, man. There's no one better than you," I add.

Then his phone rings. Seeing that it's Lucas, he answers it. "Hey, man, I've got you on speakerphone. Rocco's here with me. What's up?"

"I just got off the phone with Samantha. She and the girls are at a bar celebrating her first drink since Chloe was born, and they ran into a friend of yours. Janica."

"Oh yeah? That's nice. So, is that why you're calling?" Ace asks.

"Well... I'm not sure how to tell you this, but she's really drunk. The girls have tried to get her to leave, but she refuses. She doesn't recognize them, seeing as she's only met Nicole once. Could you maybe stop by and help get her home?"

All the color has drained from Ace's face and he's pasty white. His eyes are full of worry. He doesn't answer Lucas, so I do.

"Hey, Lucas, it's Rocco. What bar are they at?"

"They're at Dragon's Lair. I'll let the ladies know you're on the way." Then he ends the call.

Ace is frozen. Reaching over, I grab his arm and shake it. He startles and looks at me. "Let's go get your girl," I tell him as I rise from my chair and throw a couple of hundreds on the table.

"Okay," he mumbles, looking scattered.

Dragon's Lair is a popular bar. Most of the interior of the establishment is black. Red lights are strategically placed, giving the space an eerie, demonic feel. It doesn't take long to locate the ladies. They're circled up around a petite woman who is crying. Her makeup is running down her patchy face, and her eyes are red and swollen. I'm not good with crying, but I know Ace is. Being the oldest of his siblings, he definitely learned to dry the tears and bandage the cuts of his younger siblings. Although he's been in a trance since before we left dinner, as soon as he sees Janica, he strides over to rescue her.

"Janica," he says in a low voice.

Whimpering, she wipes away tears and squints her eyes. "Ace, is that you?"

"It's me," he replies while opening his arms to her. She stands up and rushes to him. Wrapped tightly in his arms, she sobs. He shushes her, telling her it will be okay.

After a while, she quiets down and Ace pulls back. "Janica, what happened?"

Sniffling, she wipes her nose on her sleeve. "I just found out Trevor has been cheating on me for the past six months. I got home from the library today and found them in our bed."

My body goes tense. I don't even know Janica, but I know she's special to Ace, and I want to beat Trevor up on her behalf. Then I hear the low rumble of my best friend. "That asshole," he growls. I'd hate to be Trevor right now. He just became Ace's enemy number one. Tipping her chin up, he looks into her eyes. "And what is your plan now?"

"I don't have one. Tonight, I just wanted to forget it all. Tomorrow, I'll deal with the fallout and move on."

Janica's body slumps against Ace's. All the drinking has done her in. "Rocco, can you give us a ride to my house and then I'll put her in my room for the night? Tomorrow I can rent a van and help her move out."

"I got you, man. And I can help tomorrow too," I say.

"But you're supposed to go see Jasmine. That's important."

"Jasmine will understand. I promise. I'll make it up to her," I tell him.

Samantha and Shiloh step forward. "We just texted the guys and they can help tomorrow too."

"Thanks everyone," he says as he supports Janica's dead weight. The drive back to Ace's house is quiet as he holds Janica close to him. I've seen nothing like it before.

When I get back to my house after dropping them off, I pull up Jasmine's number, and my heart sinks. I know she'll understand helping a friend. But I'm so ready to confess my feelings to her. I'm afraid if I don't do it now, I'll always find an excuse. I have to do it in person, and who knows when that'll be? Our season is packed until after playoffs, so it will be a while until I'll finally be able to go see her. Pushing off the anxiety that's back and has my chest in a tight squeeze, I roll my shoulders, trying to relax as I FaceTime her.

Chapter 19

Jasmine

eep, beep.

Beep, beep.

A strange, unfamiliar noise rattles my nightstand, and I roll over to look at the clock. Two fifteen in the morning. *WTF?* Rubbing the sleep from my eyes, the sound finally registers. It's a FaceTime call. Knowing it can only be one of two people, I grab the device. Squinting my tired eyes, I key in my passcode on the first try and answer the call. "Hello," I say in a scratchy voice, my eyes blinking to identify who has woken me up.

"Jasmine, I am so sorry to wake you," Rocco croons, his deep, smooth voice sounding like caramel. He gives me a sweet smile, and all is forgiven.

Pushing up, I pull up my blanket to make sure I'm covered. Sometimes the girls slip out of my tank top when I sleep, and I'm not sure that would be the best greeting. "Why are you calling so late? Aren't you supposed to be sleeping so you're well rested when you come see me in a few hours?" I tease.

His brow furrows and warning bells go off in my head.

"About that," he hedges.

My heart drops. *He isn't coming, is he?*

"I need to stay in town this weekend and help Ace. His friend Janica came home tonight and found her boyfriend in their bed with another woman. It didn't go well, and she needs help to move out of her apartment. Ace is going to need help, so I told him I'd stay in Chicago this weekend." His voice is sad and his shoulders are slumped. *He isn't happy about not visiting.*

Disappointment rushes through my body and my eyes threaten to leak. "So, you're not coming at all?" My question wavers as it leaves my lips.

Rocco hangs his head and mumbles, "No."

"Okay, I understand. I'll miss having you visit, but it's important to help friends out when they're in trouble." My shaky words exposed how upset I am. This past month has been hard. I thought moving to New York would be an adventure full of excitement and fun. But all it's been so far is lonely and intimidating. The only friend I've made is Melinda. My handsome neighbor, Mike, has avoided me ever since that day with Rocco. And I've been scared more than twice by extremely large, beady-eyed sewer rats in the subway. I've been so excited about his visit, needing a taste of home to get me through another month. I'm trying to give this new opportunity a fair shot, but I'm hopelessly homesick.

He looks up, his eyes stormy. "I really am sorry, Jaz. I'll make it up to you."

Forcing a smile I don't feel but know he needs, I say, "I know you are. And I know you will. You have a big heart. It's one of those things I love most about you." His return smile warms me to my soul.

I cover a yawn with my hand. "I'm going to go back to bed if that's alright. We can talk sometime this weekend, right?"

"Looks like you and I have a date," he says, his panty-dropping smile in full effect. *Date? I wish.*

"Goodnight, Rocco. I love you."

Dropping his voice, he answers, "Night, Jaz. I love you too." A shiver travels down my spine. He never says *I love you too*, only love you too. Am I reading into it? Maybe it's because that's what I want him to say, and mean it more than just friends.

Setting my iPad on my nightstand, I snuggle back under my blankets. I'll have to get up for work sooner than I want. When I wake up a few hours later, I feel the groggy effects of my early-morning call. Thankfully, the day passes quickly and I'm home, kicking off my heels by six o'clock. I've just barely changed my clothes when my phone rings. Hoping it's

Nicole, I answer on my iPad and switch it to FaceTime.

"Heeeey, Nic," I call out.

She laughs, answering, "Bet you assumed it was me before you even answered."

"No, I hoped it was you."

"Sure. Anyway, how are you, bestie?" she asks.

Thinking for a second, I hum to myself. Should I tell her how I really feel about New York? How I don't want to live here anymore, and that I would give it up in a heartbeat? Over the past few months, I have struggled to remain positive about being away from home. Often, I try to cover it by telling her she should quit her job and move here. I even told her that the rent would be covered if she just lived with me. I'm pretty sure she thinks I'm kidding, but I'm completely genuine in my offer. But I know she'll say no.

Concerned about me, she asks, "Jasmine, what's going on?"

My feelings overwhelm me, and my voice shakes as I say, "Nothing much. I just wish either you or Rocco were planning a visit soon."

Watching her expression, I can tell she's focused on my emotions. If I'm honest, I'm struggling. My eyes flick to a motion she's making. She's rubbing her brow, and she says, "You know, you can come home anytime you're ready. It doesn't sound like New York is making you happy."

"Parts of it are making me happy. Like my job. Others, not so much. But it'll be okay. I'll figure it out."

Frustrated with me, she grits her teeth and hisses, "You know, coming home means nothing other than you're following your heart."

"I hear you. I do. But I'm not ready to throw in the towel just yet. Okay?" My voice is piercing as I defend myself.

Ding dong.

"Someone is at the door. Hold on," I say while setting my iPad on the counter. After I confirm who I am, the delivery driver hands me a giant bouquet of colorful flowers.

When I step back into view, Nicole gushes, "Oh, wow. Those are gorgeous." Then she gasps. "Wait. I thought you were single. Who's sending you flowers?"

I laugh. "I am very single." I pluck out the card and read it. My heart warms and I smile. "They're from Rocco. He was supposed to come to visit this weekend, but at the last minute, he had to stay in Chicago and help Ace with something."

"That's sweet of him. Why are you two not dating?" she asks.

"Because we live in different cities, Nic," I tell her. I know it's a lame excuse, but it's all I have.

Nicole clears her throat defiantly before she challenges, "That's a recent development. In fact, since you were kids, you've lived in the same city and practically in each other's houses."

"True," I answer.

"And nothing ever happened between you two. Why?"

I shrug my shoulders. "I don't know. It never seemed like the right time. And I've never been sure of his feelings for me."

She smiles at me. "Jasmine, I've always known there was something special between you. Why haven't you ever asked him how he feels or made a move?"

My emotions are raw, and I wipe a tear from my eye. "Because I'm afraid. If I'm wrong, what would happen to our friendship?"

"Can I ask you a question?" she whispers. I nod. "Do you love Rocco?"

Even though I try to remain strong, my face crumbles as heavy tears fall, giving her my answer without words.

"Why do I feel like there's more to it?" she asks, and I freeze. "Jasmine, what am I missing?"

"It's nothing, really," I rush out. Nicole furrows her brow, showing me she doesn't buy what I'm saying. *Thanks, FaceTime. If she couldn't see me, I could pretend she doesn't know I'm upset.*

"Try again, Jaz."

I can't lie to her.

"So you remember the Steel won their first Stanley Cup in 2021. Well, that night, I stayed after the trophy presentation to congratulate Rocco, and...

we sort of kissed," I admit, rushing through the last bit.

"What do you mean, *sort of*? Did you trip and your lips landed on each other? Did you need CPR and he performed it? How did it happen exactly?"

I go to explain, and she cuts me off. "And did you say 2021? That was three years ago and you're just telling me now? What the hell, Jasmine?"

I shrug. "When it happened, I was so confused. I didn't know if it meant anything or not, so I said nothing, hoping all the feelings it stirred up would go away. But they didn't. They were always in the periphery, waiting for the next move. However, it never came, so I told myself the kiss was a careless mistake. We were just lost in the moment's excitement."

"And you still haven't talked about it or how you feel?"

I just shake my head no.

"I wish I were there to give you a hug right now," she says, and the tears continue to fall down my cheeks.

After crying for some time, I wipe the tears away and say, "Okay, you didn't call to hear me cry. What are you going to do about your job and Curt?"

"I want to quit," she confesses.

"Then that's what you should do. You're making decent money as a rep for IM, right? Can't you work for a temp agency in the interim until you find something?"

Nicole smiles at me. "Yes, I'm actually making more money working for IM than I dreamed, and you're right, if I get desperate, I can temp while looking for something new."

"Sounds like you have a plan. Good luck with it. Can't wait to hear when you're done with that asshole. We'll have to celebrate."

"I'll call you as soon as it's done. Now, you better call Rocco and thank him for those beautiful flowers."

"Yes, Mom. Love you, Nic. Talk later."

Blowing me a kiss, she answers back, "Love you too."

After the call ends, I turn back to the card.

Jasmine–

I am so very sorry I'm not there with you now. You are the light to my day, the joy in my heart, the bounce in my step. Every day is better with you in it. I can't tell you how much you mean to me and how much I've missed you. Now, please come home.

I love you,
Rocco

Tears fall as I read his beautiful words. I love him so much more than a friend, and I wish I could tell him that. *Does he feel the same?* I wish we'd just talk about it, but it will destroy me if he ever walks away.

Hitting his contact, the line rings and rings, eventually sending me to voice mail.

I leave a message. "I know you're probably moving Janica right now, but I just got the most amazing bouquet, and it had the most special note with it. Thank you so much. I love you too. Talk soon."

The next day, as I'm cleaning my apartment, I'm surprised when there's a knock on my door. Looking through the peephole, I can hardly believe my eyes. I pull open the door and squeal, "Nicole, are you really here?"

Looking scattered, her strawberry-blond hair peeks out above the multicolored knitted headband she's wearing over her ears. Her hair in a messy bun. She's bundled up in a brightly colored pea coat. A matching scarf and mitten set sit on top of a small suitcase.

"I'm here," she pants, sounding exhausted from her travel. "This place is insane."

New York can definitely be overwhelming.

I just smile, ushering her into my tiny apartment. "But you're here. For how long?"

Peeling off her crossbody bag and coat, she nods. "Only until tomorrow night, because Curt the douche wouldn't allow me to take a day off."

"No problem. I'm so excited you're here!" I say as I tug her in for a hug.

"I've missed you so much, Jaz. It was so nice of Rocco to pay for a ticket, even if it's only for a day and a half."

What? In disbelief, I pull back. "You let Rocco pay for your ticket? Really?"

Nodding her head and laughing, she answers, "I did. He insisted, and after we talked, I knew I needed to see you."

"He insisted?" She just smiles and nods. *That was so incredibly sweet of him.*

Grinning back before I pull her into another hug, I squeal, "I'm so glad you're here."

"Me too. Now, you have twenty-four hours to show me what's so cool about this city."

My mind is already busy with ideas. "Challenge accepted."

After a quick call to Melinda, we have tickets to see a new Broadway show.

"Guess what we're doing tonight?" I say when she exits the bedroom.

Her eyes grow wide with excitement. "What?"

"We have tickets to see Hugh Jackman in *The Music Man.*"

Her mouth drops open. From her posture, I can't tell if she's happy or not.

"S-sorry. What did you just say?"

"I just got us tickets to see the Broadway production of *The Music Man* with Hugh Jackman. You know, the actor from *The Greatest Showman.*

Wolverine from the X-Men."

She waves her hand. "You had me at Hugh Jackman. He is extremely sexy."

"He really is. The man is a triple threat. Beyond being sexy, he can sing, dance, and handle a weapon."

Nicole does some sort of dance that reminds me of Elaine from *Seinfeld* and squeals, "I'm so excited."

Until the show, we keep ourselves busy by visiting neighborhood food carts. We dine on pretzels that are as big as your head. I'm sure Nicole's first ride on the subway will be entertaining, so we do that too.

"What's that smell?" she asks as we wait for the train.

I laugh. "You probably don't want to know."

"You're right. It's probably not healthy to inhale," she mutters.

As soon as our butts land on the uncomfortable plastic seats, Nicole's eyes grow even larger. She takes people-watching to a whole new level. I'm glad she doesn't talk to anyone because New Yorkers are private and they won't find her as endearing as I do.

After a quick ride, we climb the subway stairs up to the sidewalk above. A quaint bookstore called Booked is just a block over. Its brick front and large front windows displaying books about all things love draw you in. The bell above the door earns us a "welcome to the store" from the owner, Joan, who is behind the checkout counter. She's a spry sixty-year-old woman with curly gray hair.

"She is absolutely adorable. Does she have pink highlights in her hair?" Nicole asks, a giant smile on her face.

"Yep. Isn't that great? She is the sweetest lady I've ever met."

We spend the next hour wandering the store. By the time we leave, I have a few new romances to add to my collection and keep life stimulating.

Before we head back to my apartment to get ready for the show, we stop at another street cart, this one selling hot dogs. Considering it's February, I'm grateful it isn't too cold.

Sitting on a bench nearby, I open my tinfoil wrapping, and the escaping heat warms my face as I lower to inhale the heavenly scents. The onion sauce the vendor put on top of the steamed hot dog smells incredible, and my mouth waters, anticipating my first taste.

"Oh my gosh, this is amazing," Nicole mumbles, her mouth full.

There's an audible snap as I bite into my hot dog, the flavors exploding in my mouth. After my first bite, I'm in love. Never have I had a hot dog this delicious before. *Only in New York*. That's what the vendor's sign promised. And boy, does it deliver.

The Music Man is outstanding. Even though our seats aren't the greatest, the performance Hugh and the rest of the cast put on sweep us away. The entire show, from the singing and dancing to the acting, is noteworthy, and it's an experience I would highly recommend.

By the time we wake up the next morning, we only have a few hours together until Nicole has to head back to the airport for an early evening flight.

Still warm from sleep, I roll over to see my bestie curled up in the blankets next to me. Because of my tiny apartment and lack of sleeping space, we shared my bed last night. It's not the first time we've done that. Over the years that we've been friends and roommates, it's happened a handful of times.

Once I see her eyes open, I ask, "How do you feel about a bacon, egg, and cheese sandwich for breakfast?"

Smiling sleepily, she nods. "That sounds great. I can be ready in ten minutes."

"Are you hungry?"

Nicole sits up and her stomach growls.

"I guess so," I say while climbing out of bed. "I need a shower first. I'll be quick, though."

Twenty minutes later, we're bundled up and heading to the corner bodega, Figaroa's, to grab the breakfast of champions.

While I make my way through the two-row store, hunting for drinks, Nicole happily watches the cook prepare our breakfast sandwiches.

"How do they look?" I ask after I finally find the bottles of juice.

"So good. The cook asked if you wanted ketchup,

and I said yes. I remember you eating ketchup on eggs when we were in college. I didn't mess that up, did I?"

"Not at all. Thanks."

A minute later, we're handed our breakfast. We bring them back to my apartment because it's cooler today than yesterday.

Seated on my couch, Nicole unwraps her sandwich. "It smells amazing and looks delicious. I can't wait to try it." A moan comes from her after she takes her first bite. I can't help but laugh.

"That good?" I ask, and she just smiles and shakes her head. This isn't my first breakfast sandwich from Figaroa's, so I know it'll be outstanding. And I'm not disappointed. The eggs are fluffy, the bacon is both crispy and salty, and the cheese is gooey. But the bread... that's what ties it all together. A soft, buttery, and flakey bun that's like a croissant. Basically, it's perfection. It melts in your mouth.

With breakfast done, we head down to Chinatown so Nicole can shop for a few New York trinkets. Of course, we take a million selfies, even sending a crazy one to Rocco.

ME

Thank you for sending Nicole to NYC
to visit. We're having a blast.

ROCCO

You two are ridiculous. I'm glad
you're together again. Maybe she can
convince you to come home.

ME

Oh, she's tried. Thank you again.
You're the best.

We grab dumplings with chili sauce for lunch before heading back to my apartment. Before she leaves for the airport, I wrap her in the longest, tightest hug. "Thank you for coming to see me. I missed you so much."

"You know, you can always come home," she tells me one last time before getting into her Uber.

A quick wave and she's gone. My heart sinks. I'm alone again.

Chapter 20

Rocco

It's May, and we aren't in the running for the Cup anymore. After a slow start to the playoffs, we found ourselves in Colorado for a two-game series versus the Mountaineers. We'd already lost two games to them. If we won the games, we'd have another chance to see who would advance to the next stage of the playoffs. However, we lost the third game and then half our team came down with Norovirus before we could even play the fourth. Through rounds of puking, I'd heard we had to forfeit, earning us another loss. With the two previous losses against the Mountaineers, we were out of the playoffs.

Since my failed visit in February, I haven't been able to see Jasmine in months, and I'm going crazy. Phone calls and FaceTime can only do so much. I need to be in her bubble and physically touch her. So as soon as I knew we weren't in the playoffs and I'd fully recovered from the effects of Norovirus, I booked a one-way ticket to New York. My intention is to finally tell Jasmine how I feel and bring her home. I'm a desperate man, and I'll beg if I have to.

Arriving in the city hours before she gets off work, I find my hotel. The concierge is very helpful in locating a florist too. At half-past five, I grab the bouquet I ordered and head toward the subway. If I planned it right, I'll get to Jaz's apartment right after she does.

The subway ride is eventful as always. Most people keep to themselves, listening to something on their phone or reading. A few women comment on the flowers, though. Stop after stop, I double-check to make sure I get off at the correct one. Last time I was here I used cabs or Ubers to and from my hotel so all morning long, I fretted about it. But again, the concierge had been ever-helpful in providing fantastic directions. And now, as I stand in front of her building and look up, my nerves increase tenfold. Worry and fear race through my body, my palms and brow sweating. My stomach churns *What am I doing?*

"Rocco." I hear my name called out and I whip around. Approaching me is the most beautiful woman I've ever seen. Her long brown hair is curled and hangs around her shoulders, swaying as she moves closer. Her green eyes are wide and sparkling. Apparently, it's been sunny in New York because her emerald-green dress accentuates not only her incredible curves but also her sun-kissed skin. When my gaze lands on her lips, I want a taste of her, and I lick my lips. Ever since the kiss we shared years ago, I haven't been able to get it off my mind. I want more.

"Jasmine," I breathe out slowly, relieved to finally see her. She walks straight into my arms. Even though she's wearing heels, I still tower over her. "It's been too long," I tell her as I squeeze her, relishing the closeness of our bodies. Pulling back, I lock eyes with her. "It's so good to see you."

Pulling me in for another hug, she rests her head on my chest before she says, "I agree. Let's go upstairs so I can get changed out of my work clothes and into something more comfortable. Then you can share your agenda with me." After she unlocks the front door to the building, I hand her the red roses I purchased.

"These are for you." Her cheeks flush and she dips her head to smell them, humming her contentment.

After a few seconds, she lifts her head. "These are so beautiful, Rocco. Thank you."

I smile. "You are too," I admit. *That may not be my full confession, but hell, it's a start.* Her cheeks pinken at my words, and it makes her even more stunning.

"The elevators are closed for repairs today," she says as I follow her into the building. Looking at the stairs, she adds, "Thankfully, I only live on the third floor and the climb isn't bad."

Following Jaz up the stairs is agonizing. The heavenly curves of her perfect body are complete torture. I feel my cock thicken as I imagine running my fingers over her rounded ass and tight waist. My fingers itch to touch her, and I rub them against my jeans, trying to make the sensation subside. When we finally reach her door, I thank the gods. *Get it together, Rocco.*

Jasmine disappears into her bedroom to change and comes out in an outfit that's sure to kill me. All I can say is emerald green is her color. *Damn.* Wearing a halter top that highlights her trim waist and ripped jean cut-offs isn't enough. The naughty peekaboo holes of her shorts reveal all of her smooth skin that I'm desperate to touch and lick. Holding back a groan, my gaze traces hungrily over the rest of her.

Jasmine finally notices my eyes glued to her. "What? Do I look okay?"

Does she look okay? She looks good enough to eat. But I can't say that. She still doesn't know how I feel. I don't need to frighten her off with my amorous talk, so I shake my head, getting my mind back on track. "You look beautiful, Jaz." She smiles and blinks at me before she grabs her cross-body bag off the counter, loading her wallet, keys, and phone into it.

"I was thinking we could grab dinner from Athena, it's another Greek restaurant nearby. They have the most amazing kabobs and their Mediterranean platter has everything you could ever want," she raves.

"That sounds amazing," I reply as I grab her hand. I'm relieved when she doesn't pull it away and actually laces our fingers together. My heart rate increases and I can hear the blood rushing through my veins. *I hope my hands aren't sweaty.*

The walk to the restaurant is much too fast, because as soon as we step inside, our hands separate, and I'm not ready for it. It feels like a piece of me is being torn away.

We opt to share a bunch of appetizers, and they're delivered in record time. "Mmm, this is delicious," I say as I grab another kabob. Jaz was right, they're incredible. They're tender and the spices used are divine. The gyro meat from the platter is out of this world too, especially when I pair it with the still-warm pita bread, tomato, onions, and tzatziki sauce.

Jaz is all smiles, watching as I devour everything in front of us. "I see you like it." she giggles.

Smiling back, I say, "Yeah, Jaz. It's awesome."

We fill our dinner with small talk about the end of the season and her past few months in the city. She tries to put on a brave face, but it's hard to miss the sadness in her eyes and the weariness in her voice.

Back at her apartment later, while we're snuggled together on the couch, I finally broach the topic that brought me here. "Jaz, I need to say something, but I don't want you to get upset with me." *Does she hear the trepidation in my voice? I don't want to make her upset with me, especially before tomorrow.*

"What is it?" she whispers while she's cuddled into my side. *Damn, that feels good.*

"Tell me if I'm wrong, but it doesn't seem like you

like living here in New York. You always sound sad, and I hate that. I just don't understand why you don't move home." She stiffens next to me, and for half a second, I want to take it all back. That is, until she begins to answer.

Jaz shifts, turning her body toward me. "I'll be honest. I haven't had the easiest time since moving here, but I want to give it a fair shot. I've only ever lived in Chicago, and this was my first actual attempt at being on my own. Truthfully, it's been hard, and I wanted to come home more than once, but every time I considered it, I felt like a quitter."

Pulling her into a hug, I kiss her hair line. "I understand that, really. But if you're so unhappy, there's no shame in coming home. You've been here almost six months already. I'd say that's giving it a fair shot."

Her shoulders slump. "It's not like I can pack up and fly home on a whim. I have a job and a year-long lease to consider. I don't want my reputation or credit to be negatively affected. Maybe I just need to give it more time. Meet more people. Try new things."

"Those are all good points. But I don't want you stuck here, trying to make it work even though you're miserable. Plus, I want you home."

Jaz sighs, and I know she's staying. My heart sinks. I'm not lying. I want her home. With me.

While watching a movie, she lays her head on my lap and I stroke her hair. It's like second nature. I've been doing it since we were kids, when I mindlessly started playing with her hair during a movie that wasn't holding my interest. She told me later she really liked it, and I've been doing it ever since. I hadn't realized until tonight how comforting it is to me.

At some point, she falls asleep, and I just watch her, enjoying the delicate rise and fall of her chest, the way her lips part, the rhythmic dance behind her eyelids as she dreams. It's all remarkable and something I cherish. I've always thought Jasmine was beautiful, but being this vulnerable takes it to a whole new level. *I am head over heels for this woman.*

Thinking about tomorrow fills me with unease. What if she doesn't feel the same? Instantly panicked, my body goes stiff, and she flinches in her sleep. I need to get rid of these edgy feelings and move before I wake her up. Turning off the television, I carry her to her bed and place her in it. Pulling up the covers, I make sure her phone is on her charger and then kiss her head before I leave.

Ordering an Uber as I head down the flights of stairs, I see it isn't too late. I can fit in a good run and work off all this energy before I head to bed. An hour later, I've finished a hard five-mile run on a treadmill in the hotel's gym. Swiping my brow, I walk into my room to shower before I collapse into bed. *Tomorrow is a big day.*

Early the next morning, I head to Starbucks to grab Jasmine's favorite morning drink, a vanilla latte. Then I

Uber over to her apartment. Stepping off the elevator, I run into her neighbor again. "Hey, Rocco," he says.

"Hey, man," I answer, not remembering his name.

"Mike," he informs me.

"That's right. How are you?"

"I'm good. I've got to get somewhere. It's nice to see you again. I'm sure Jasmine is happy you're visiting." He waves and then he's gone.

Knocking on her door, I'm not sure what I'll find on the other side. I hold out the latte just in case she's just waking up and the only thing she wants to see is coffee.

"Rocco, you're an angel," she gushes as she takes the still-hot beverage from me. Turning away from me, I notice she's dressed in a soft cotton robe that hits her upper thigh. I try not to groan as my gaze traces her smooth, tan legs up to the bottom hem of the robe. It's almost short enough to be indecent, and I'm wishing it were so I could get a peek of her perfect ass. I lick my lips as all the blood in my body speeds to my groin. My cock thickens and pushes against the zipper of my tan shorts. *Glad I'm not wearing athletic shorts, or I'd certainly have some explaining to do.* She takes a large drink of her coffee and then whips around to face me. I hold my breath, hoping I'll get a flash of some cleavage, but I'm not that lucky. *What is up with me?* This is the first real time I've spent with Jaz since I admitted my attraction to her, and all I can think about is wanting to get her naked. *Not how you want to start things.*

"Can you give me fifteen to get ready?" I nod

because, right now, I'm wound so tight I don't know what my voice will sound like—a grown man or a prepubescent boy. She heads off to her bedroom as I move to the couch to have a one-on-one with my overzealous cock.

"Calm the fuck down. Get yourself under control," I whisper to us both, thankful her door is closed and she can't hear me losing my shit. For the rest of the time she's getting ready, I fill my mind with images that will move me from full salute to floppy.

A vanilla-scented cloud exits her bedroom before she does, and an instant semi appears in my shorts. *Fuck.* Dressed in a flowery romper, she looks ready to play. Her long brown hair is elegantly braided to the side, revealing the sexy skin on the other side of her neck. Glancing down, I see she's wearing a pair of aqua Chucks that match the little flowers on her outfit as well as the sweater she's holding. To say she is adorable is an understatement. She's perfect.

"Okay, I'm ready. What's the plan for the day?" she asks as she sits next to me on the couch.

Pulling a subway map out of my pocket, I tell her I want to visit Central Park. "First stop, of course, has to be the zoo." She nods her head. I have been a zoo junkie since I was a kid, and visiting the one made popular in the DreamWorks movie, *Madagascar*, is on my to-do list.

Jaz takes the map from me, setting it out of the way. "I may not have been to Central Park yet, but I've mapped the route at least a dozen times. We have to take the R train to our stop at 59th Street. Then it should be a short walk to Central Park," she explains.

"After the zoo, can we go to the Central Park Boathouse? We can grab a picnic lunch from them and rent a boat." It's on that boat that I plan to tell her the secret I've been hiding for years. Because of it, my nerves have been frayed the last few days. Every possible what if is on a constant circling loop in my mind.

An hour later, scanning my zoo map, I look to see when they offer feedings for the sea lions and penguins. Flicking my wrist to check my watch, I see we're early. The keepers feed the penguins at ten thirty and the sea lions get their turn at eleven thirty. While waiting for the show, we visit the polar bears, as they're one of Jasmine's favorites. The animals put on quite a show, especially the sea lions who bark and splash. We visit the rest of the zoo before heading over to the Boathouse.

Once we grab our picnic lunch, we claim our rowboat for the next hour. While I row us out into the middle of the lake, Jaz unwraps our lunch, which is really a deconstructed charcuterie board. Being a big guy, I get worried when I see the limited amount of food we have. We dine on fresh baguettes, salami, and cheese. Once we've eaten it all, my suspicions are correct. I know I'll need another meal soon or an early dinner.

Sitting in our boat, looking up at the sky, I remember the promise I made to myself. Glancing around, I see our nearest neighbor is a ways away. I clear my throat. "Jaz, there was something I needed to talk to you about. I've been putting it off for a while, but now I just need to tell you before you hear it from someone else."

Chapter 21

Jasmine

itting in the middle of Central Park Lake with a full belly and warm sun beating down, I can't imagine anything better. Everything seems right in the world. Is it perfect? No. But I'm enjoying the moment. And then Rocco says something that stops the world from rotating. Dread sinks heavy in my gut and, once settled, sours. *He needs to tell me something before I hear it from someone else? He's been putting it off for a while?* My mind spins and it's tough to breathe as my panic threatens to strangle me.

"Okay," I gasp out, my fragile heart threatening to crack. I can't look at him. My eyes feel heavy with tears. It's then I remember we're in the middle of the lake. The only way back to land is by rowing or swimming. Depending on his admission, I might have a wet afternoon in my future. Fear pierces my heart and a sharp pain rips through my chest. I place my hand over my heart, trying to will it to settle. *He's going to confess that he's secretly been dating someone. Then he'll tell me he's in love with her and is going to ask her to marry him.* I feel an anxiety attack coming on. My breathing is labored and my vision clouds. I start to sweat.

A hand lands on my knee. "Jasmine, are you okay? You're as pale as a ghost and your breathing is funny. Dammit, are you seasick? I didn't think a rowboat could make anyone sick. Is that what's happening?"

I shake my head no. "Please tell me whatever you have to say. Get it over with," I mumble.

"Are you sure? It can wait. My concern is that you're feeling all right."

I place my cold, sweaty hand on his and squeeze it. "I'm fine, promise. Just tell me what you need to say."

Rocco swallows hard before he licks his lips. I brace for impact, my feet going to the sides of the boat and my hands centering me on the edges.

"What I've been wanting to tell you for months is that I... I have feelings for you, Jasmine." I hear his words, but they don't register. It's almost like I tried to listen through noise-canceling headphones.

"Huh?" I ask, legitimately confused.

He puts his other hand on my other leg and scoots toward me. "I have feelings for you, Jaz. I want to be more than friends."

That time, the words register, but all I feel is shock.

"You do?" I squeak. His admission has me surprised, and my heart gallops in my chest.

He grins at me. "I do. Ever since that kiss three years ago, I haven't been able to get you off my mind."

"Really?" I smile widely, making me feel foolish. He just nods, waiting for my response. My tongue slips out to wet my parched lips, and I notice Rocco's focused on them, his eyes turning almost black. He licks his own lips, which triggers a shiver to run down my spine.

"But you've said nothing for three years," I say, still unsure about admitting my feelings. I mean, I'm relieved he feels something more, but what does that mean? I'm still confused. What does he want?

He dips his head. "Jaz, we've been best friends forever. We had no secrets until that kiss. I felt something, and I didn't want to tell you because I was afraid that it'd push you away. And that's the last thing I wanted to do. You are my person, my ride or die. I couldn't screw that up."

I reach over and take his hand. "I wish you would've said something sooner." His head pops up and his brown eyes have gone wide.

"Why?" he gasps.

I clear my throat and give him a smile. "Because I would have told you that the kiss changed things for me too." His mouth drops open, and I laugh. It's both adorable and funny.

"Really? How?"

Tell him.

"I really liked it. That day, I felt something I'd never felt with you before, and I wanted more. Wanted to explore it and see if it was anything. But neither of us talked about it, so I just assumed you felt nothing more than friendship. Believing that, I tried to move on."

"Mark," he grumbles, and I nod.

I frown, and he mirrors it. "But it didn't work. Every time we were around each other, I felt a pull toward you. Every time you touched me, even though it was platonic, my heart skipped a beat and my skin buzzed with excitement. It also hurt to be near you. Knowing you didn't want me too." I remove my hand and sit back, looking around. "I needed some space." My heart stalls in my chest and I hold my breath. *What is he going to say?*

Rocco scoots closer, and the boat rocks. My arms fly out reflexively, and I anchor them on the sides, praying we won't tip. That, for sure, would mess up this moment. And we are having a moment, right?

Then he rasps, "That's why you moved to New York." His voice is filled with such sadness. A moment passes before I nod.

"I couldn't handle the possibility of seeing you with someone else. I needed to get away and start over. Find something that would make me happy."

"Jasmine," he growls. "I only wanted you. There has been no one since that kiss."

Shock registers, and my eyes bug out. "Wait. What are you saying?"

"No woman even compares to you, so I just haven't bothered."

"No one?" I question. He shakes his head. "How is that possible? I mean, it's been three years, Rocco. During that time, you've traveled with the team a lot, gone to Vegas with the guys, and visited plenty of bars and clubs, and you've not hooked up once?"

He holds up his hand. "Scouts honor."

I slap it away. "You were never a Boy Scout. Are you being serious right now?"

"Yes, I am. My hand is the only action I've had for the last three years." *What? How is that possible?* His cheeks turn pink at his admission, and it's adorable. I know it's the truth because we tell each other everything. My mind and heart can hardly believe his confession. I'm both flattered and annoyed. *Why didn't he say anything sooner?*

"So, the question here now is... Where do we go from here?" I ask, wondering if he's going to make a move. The thought of that excites me, making it feel like I have a thousand butterflies taking flight in my stomach. But will he? I mean, it's been three years. That has to be the worst case of blue balls anyone has ever given themselves.

"Isn't it obvious?" he asks, and my heart rate picks up, waiting for a hint that something is about to happen. I nod, leaning forward. He moves closer, and my skin buzzes with the anticipation of his touch. Just when we're inches away, he says, "You move home." I expected the faint whisper of his lips against mine would light my body up, but his words are comparable to having a ten-gallon bucket of ice water dumped on you.

"What?" I question as I jerk back. The boat rocks, and Rocco tries to steady it as our eyes have a silent conversation.

"Jasmine, you aren't happy here. I'm in Chicago, and we can be there together, finally." His explanation makes sense. But what about my job, my lease, adulting on my own? If I return to Chicago now, I'll feel like I've given up too soon.

Rocco's eyes plead with me, and I look away. "The reasons I gave earlier still apply. I'm not ready to walk away."

He takes my hand in his, squeezes it, and asks, "But then what happens with us? Jasmine, it's been three years, and now that I know you want more, I want to be the man to give it to you. But how will I be able to do that if we're in different cities?"

"What about long-distance dating?" I ask half-heartedly. I want the commitment, but that's hard when you live in different cities.

"Is that my only option?"

I nod. "It's the only one I can come up with."

He pulls me closer. "Then I'll take it. Can I kiss you now?"

"Please," I whimper, just before our lips touch.

Chapter 22

Rocco

I've imagined this moment for so long. Feeling Jasmine's lips on mine is absolute heaven. My heart thumps out a chaotic beat as I try to catch up to all the thoughts flooding my brain. Pulling her closer, I slide one hand behind her neck. Tipping her head, I adjust the angle to accommodate our kissing. Our tongues wrestle, and she gives just as good as she takes. When she pulls back, I panic for a second until she sucks in my bottom lip, giving it a nibble. A deep growl releases from my chest and I feel her shiver in my arms. My internal dialogue is chaotic. *I'm finally kissing Jasmine. She tastes and feels so good. I want more.* I go to pull her onto my lap, and the boat rocks, reminding me of where we are.

"Shit. I don't want to get you wet that way." She giggles against my lips. Pulling back so I can see her eyes, I notice they're bright and wild, filled with lust. "Do you want to continue this at your place?"

She bites her lip. "Please." After a quick peck on the lips, I grab the oars and row us back to the dock at a record pace. After we've returned the boat, we make a beeline for the subway, eager to get somewhere private. The entire ride back to her place, my blood pressure inches dangerously high. Holding her hand and having her tucked into my side feels divine. My mind imagines all the things I want to do to her, and my cock thickens in my shorts. I'm not as subtle as I want to be when I adjust myself. Surprised, Jaz gasps and makes an O with her lips, giving me another idea.

Groaning, I lean close to her and whisper, "See what you do to me?" She licks her lips and nods her understanding. "What are you doing to me?" I question, causing her to laugh.

"One more stop," Jasmine pants. She's as excited as I am. *Holy shit! This is going to be amazing.* When we finally get to our stop, she takes me by the hands and pulls me from my seat and toward the doors. Taking two steps at a time, we do our best to avoid all the people coming from the sidewalk above. The crosswalk on the next street is our next cockblocker. It takes forever to change. I consider jaywalking, but I know if I were to be ticketed it would take longer, and the officer probably wouldn't let me out of it if I explained my reasoning for breaking the law. Plus, it's New York, and you have to be on your toes as a pedestrian. These drivers are crazy. Being dead or gravely injured would definitely put the kibosh on all the fun I'm hoping we're about to have.

The signal finally changes, and we power walk to her apartment building. Even though the elevator is working today, I still follow Jaz to the stairs. "This will be faster," she says. Dutifully, and with a raging boner, I do my best to climb the steps. But I can attest it's nearly impossible with the steel rod in my pants. When I finally make it to the third floor, Jaz is already there with the door open.

"What took you so long? Aren't you the professional athlete?"

I don't even answer her. I stalk up to her, push my groin against her, and say, "You try climbing stairs quickly with this." She laughs and we make our way into her apartment. As soon as she's got the door closed, I push her up against it and attack her lips.

"Rocco," she whimpers into my mouth. I thrust my groin forward into her heated center, and she rubs against me.

"That feels so fucking good." I moan before releasing a growl. Desperate to feel her closer, I tug at her legs and lift her. She wraps them around my waist, and when our bodies make contact, she rotates her hips. *Holy shit.* I push us harder against the door, giving me better leverage to grind against her.

"Ahhh," she moans into my mouth, and I do it again and again at a syncopated rhythm until she rips her lips from mine, throws back her head, and screams, "Right there, Rocco! R-right there!" I feel her spasm against me, and I can't hide the smile that appears on my face. *I did that.* But I'm just getting started. Sweeping back the stray hairs that have gotten loose from her messy bun, I lock eyes with her.

"You good, babe?" Jasmine nods, then gives me a sultry smile. When she bites on her bottom lip, I almost lose it. "You are so fucking gorgeous."

Walking back to her bedroom, I lower her onto the down comforter. She scoots back, just watching and waiting. I tug my t-shirt over my head, and her eyes go wide. She reaches for me and delicately traces her fingertips across my muscled chest, leaving a trail of heat in her wake. "That feels so good." Tipping back my head, I try to calm my body down, but it's no use. My cock throbs in my shorts. I palm myself, reminding him I'm in charge. Returning my gaze to hers, I see she's staring straight ahead at my very obvious erection. I run my finger down her cheek to her chin and tip her head up to me. She licks her lips, and when her eyes find mine, she smiles widely. "You want this?" I ask, making sure she knows the decision to go any further is hers. I told her I want more, and I'm ready to take it, if she gives me permission.

"Yes," she sighs, and I remove my shorts, leaving me only in a pair of black boxers.

"Jaz, you're wearing too many clothes." She blinks rapidly before she pulls off her romper. And then, sitting before me in a matching aqua blue satin bra and panty set, is the woman of my dreams. She looks exquisite. My breathing picks up, my heart rate skyrockets, and my mouth begins to water. Scooting farther up the bed, she lies back, showing me her amazing body.

I crawl toward her and trace my fingers from her ankle to her thigh. When I reach the apex of her legs, I tap her thighs. "Spread your legs for me, babe." She does, revealing a wet spot on her panties. "Are you wet for me?" I ask as I run my finger over the trim of her panties, and her hips lift and chase the movement of my hand. Each time I get near her center, her breathing picks up. I push the panties to the side and run my knuckles through her wet folds. *Soaked. For me. Damn, I'm a lucky man.*

On the third pass, she whimpers, "Don't tease, Rocco." I'm not trying to, really. I'm just trying to get myself under control before I embarrass myself. After all, three years without sex can make one a little quick on the trigger.

Pulling back, I anchor my fingers in the sides of her panties and tug them down her smooth-as-silk legs, anticipating what's next. Not caring where they land, I toss the moist undergarments over my shoulder and then elbow her legs farther apart. I move closer, feeling the heat pouring off her. Jasmine raises her hips when I blow on her heated flesh, seeking more contact. My first taste of her is heavenly.

"You taste amazing." She's both sweet and spicy. It's nothing like I've ever tasted before. And already I know I can't get enough. She's addictive and something I'll never tire of. Licking slowly from back to front, I groan into her folds. When I reach her clit, I flick it several times before I suck it into my mouth. Jasmine whimpers as her hips flex. Running her fingers through my hair, she tugs on it, letting me know she's enjoying what I'm doing to her. Deciding she needs more, I slip a finger into her and curl it.

"Ohhh," she moans, making me feel invincible. Sex has never been like this for me, and we haven't even gone all the way yet. Will I survive it?

Panting, she says, "Rocco, please." *She wants more?* I slide another finger in and fuck her with them. Pushing her knees back toward her chest, I plunge deeper, feeling her muscles tighten around me. *I can't wait to feel her squeeze around my cock.* I can tell she's getting close, so I pump my fingers even faster and increase the suction to her clit. It doesn't take long to feel her come apart below me. Her body shakes and she lets out a long moan. The vibration registers deep in my bones. Once she's completely spent, I pull my fingers out and lick them clean, sighing my satisfaction. Jasmine's sated eyes capture me through her still-bent legs. Pushing them down, I lean over her and press my lips to hers, giving her a taste of herself.

"Mmm," she hums in the back of her throat. Even though we've been best friends for years, talking about our sex lives was always off-limits. I don't know what she's done, what she wants, or what she likes. However, I plan to rectify that soon. I don't need all the nitty-gritty details, but I want to know what her likes and dislikes are. I never want my woman left wanting. I always need her satisfied.

Chapter 23

Jasmine

From the moment Rocco kissed me on the rowboat after we confessed our shared feelings, my body hasn't stopped buzzing. It's like I'm hooked up to a power transformer. Everything is heightened, and I'm not sure how to handle it. Finally getting my feelings off my chest feels amazing. And hearing that Rocco feels the same is incredible. I'm not just happy, I'm ecstatic. Basking in the fact that my feelings for Rocco are reciprocated, I try my best to ignore my unease that something will happen to put a damper on our happiness. But as I lie back on my bed, sated while Rocco hovers above me, licking his lips, I'm enjoying this moment.

Singularly focused, Rocco bumps my pussy with his still-covered cock. "Are you ready for more, Jaz?"

I don't have to give it any thought. "Yes," I pant. Not wasting any time, he sits back and slides his boxers down his incredibly muscular legs. Jutting out in front of him, Rocco's cock reaches for me. Gently, I lean forward and wrap my hand around it. It's hard yet silky, and the groan he emits through his gritted teeth is enough to push me over the edge.

Lowering my voice, I playfully ask, "What's the matter, big boy?"

I smirk when a goofy grin tips up his kiss-abused lips. "That's right. I am a big boy," he answers while stroking his cock from root to tip. A drop of pre-cum appears from the slit, and I run my thumb over it. Bringing it to my lips, I suck off his essence. Rocco releases a growl, his eyes almost black with desire.

"You're playing with fire, Jaz. I desperately want your mouth on me, but I need to be inside you now."

"Take me," I answer.

He tips his head. "Are you sure? You know I haven't been with anyone in years and am tested regularly because of hockey, but I don't want you to feel pressured."

I smile. "I don't feel pressured. I've always used condoms and I have an IUD. At my last checkup before moving, I was tested. Please, let me feel you bare."

Rocco leans down, kisses my lips tenderly, then he thrusts in, bottoming out in seconds. Pleasure overwhelms me. My eyes roll into the back of my head and a moan falls from my open lips.

Pulling out and thrusting in again, Rocco pants,

"You feel like heaven." Our bodies work in tandem, chasing the same high. When I'm just starting to feel the effects of an orgasm, he surprises me when he stops and pulls out. Rooting around next to me, he confuses me when he pulls a pillow out. "Jaz, lift," he orders when he taps my hips. When the pillow is tucked under me where he wants it, he thrusts back in and everything makes sense. He changed the angle, and now he's getting so much deeper. It only takes a few thrusts before my toes curl. Goose bumps cover my body as he lowers his hot mouth to my breast and sucks in a pebbled nipple.

"Rocco," I whimper.

"I know, babe," he rasps back, thrusting even harder. A minute later, I'm seeing stars. My muscles clamp down on him, and he slips his hand between us, rubbing my sensitive clit, prolonging the orgasm. When I go limp, Rocco pulls out of me and rolls me over onto my side. He curls up behind me, resting my leg over his, and thrusts back in. He runs his hand up my side to my breast and massages it, pinching and rolling the nipple.

"Feels so good," I confess.

Rocco licks up my collarbone to my ear, sucking my lobe into his mouth. His warm breath sends a shiver down my spine. His hand drops to my hip and tugs me closer. His thrusts become more chaotic and his fingers finds my clit. Aggressively rubbing circles on it, he sets off another orgasm. And then he follows, holding me tight and growling into my ear. Feeling him come behind me is so empowering, but I want to watch him come undone. *I hope this isn't a onetime thing.* I feel Rocco relax behind me, then he moves off the bed. I hear him in my bathroom, opening cabinets and turning on water. *What is he doing?* A few moments later, the answer is obvious when he's at my side with a warm washcloth.

"Let's clean you up." Baffled, I roll onto my back and spread my legs. This sweet gesture isn't lost on me. It's completely unfamiliar but incredibly welcome.

"Thank you," I whisper. His grin and nod are all the reply I need.

When he climbs back into my bed, I snuggle close, resting my head on his chest and arm across his abs. "I always knew you were in shape, but your body is incredible."

He laughs and pulls me in even closer. "No, Jaz, *your* body is incredible." My cheeks flush. Lying here, wrapped around him, I realize something: I've never been happier. Sated and content, I drift off to sleep.

The next morning, I wake up, still cuddled up to Rocco, and memories of the night before flash through my mind. Half convinced it was a dream, I release a contented sigh.

"Morning, babe." Rocco's deep timbre, thick with sleep, rumbles next to me. Snuggling deeper into him, I answer with a happy hum. His warm muscular arms wrap around me and he places a gentle kiss on my head.

"What's the plan today? I mean, I'm okay with staying in bed all day. My mind is overflowing with ideas of what we could do," Rocco says without even a tinge of embarrassment in his voice. I'm not embarrassed either. I'm more relieved. But I have two major questions. What are we and how will it work?

"Have you ever been to Times Square?" I ask, knowing Rocco comes to New York multiple times a year but not knowing what the team does in their downtime.

He shakes his head. "I've been through it on a bus a time or two, but I've never explored it. Have you?"

"It's always intimidated me. But with a muscular hockey player by my side, I'll feel safe and protected." I throw in a flirtatious smile, hoping it will seal the deal. I've always wanted to see Times Square, but it always looks so crowded. I was afraid something bad would happen. I asked Melinda last week for the hidden gems and she delivered with a list that I couldn't wait to explore.

He pulls me in for a hug. "You know I'll always protect you, babe. Looks like we have a plan for the day. Want to start with a shower?" The waggle of his eyebrows makes me blush, thinking about all the fun we could have.

After he completely ravages me in the shower, we dress and head out to explore Times Square. The subway ride is entertaining, as always. Rocco and I spend the entire time snuggled together and talking about all the things Melinda recommended. Because it's lunchtime, we make our way to B & B, a rooftop bar that provides a fantastic view of the square.

"This is incredible," I gush while waiting for our food. We're high enough that the typical sounds of the city are muted but the sight is still impressive. The enormous billboards captivate us, advertising everything you could imagine. I heard somewhere that it costs five thousand dollars for a day of advertisement.

The server appears, dropping off our Long Island crab cake sliders and NY Buffalo wings. "These are incredible," Rocco praises, his lips lined with the signature orange buffalo sauce. I only ate one slider, leaving the other for Rocco because I want to save myself for a slice of Joey's New York-style pizza. I also heard there was a Shake Shack at Grand Central Station. A New York founded chain, their Shackburger and crinkle-cut fries are always amazing, so I have plenty of options for food later in the day.

After our lunch, we head down to the street. We stroll over to an Aural art piece Melinda mentioned that was on Broadway between Forty-fifth and sixth street. *Times Square*, an art installment by Max Neuhaus, was originally installed in the seventies. Then it was removed in the early nineties. In the early two thousands, the piece was reinstated. Being available twenty-four hours a day, most people walk over it, probably unaware of its existence. Because I'm aware of it, I point out to Rocco the musical hum it's responsible for. Because of the busy sounds of the bustling city, you have to focus on hearing it.

"Can we go see the naked cowboy we passed on the way here?" I ask.

Rocco rolls his eyes and mutters, "I look better naked."

"Yes, you do," I agree against his cheek before giving him a peck. *It's amazing being able to kiss him anytime I want.* Thankfully, the street performer wears briefs, even if they are white and leave little to the imagination.

After a quick song, Rocco pulls me away, growling, "What's next? Staring at that guy is making me feel creepy."

Patting his chest, I laugh. "This way. You're going to love what's next."

"It's not another half-dressed dude, is it? Because if that's what you want, I can give that to you anytime." He smiles widely, and I choke on air. Thoughts of him naked flood my mind, and my mouth waters. Licking my lips, he leans into me. "Looks like you have something on your mind, Jaz. Want to share?"

Shaking my head to clear it, I motion down the street. "This way."

After crossing a few streets and narrowly missing being hit by a cab even though we had the flashing man on our side, I lead him up to an elaborately decorated building. Painted maroon with a splash of gold, it draws you in with the giant silver hand coming out of the wall and the floor-to-ceiling glass overlook. Standing on the sidewalk, I can hardly believe my eyes. "This is magical."

"Where are we?" Rocco asks.

"Madame Tussauds Wax Museum," I reply excitedly.

Rocco has the same look of amazement on his face. "Have you ever been to one before?"

I shake my head. "No, but I've always wanted to go."

He leads me to get tickets, and before long, the most incredible wax statues surround us. Pretty soon I'm hobnobbing with New York celebrity Jimmy Fallon in a recreation of his *Tonight Show* set at 30 Rockefeller Plaza. We visit The White House and score some face time with POTUS.

"This way, Jaz," Rocco directs, leading me to the MARVEL Hall of Heroes. "Quick. Take my picture with the Hulk."

After I take a handful of posed pictures where it looks like Rocco is battling Hulk, I say, "Okay, but now you have to take my picture with Captain America. Or... maybe Thor. They're both so dreamy." Even though we're standing near each other, I swear I hear the crack of his molars as he grinds them together. His posture is tight, and the frown across his face is so adorable, I find it difficult to keep a straight face. *Such a guy.*

Laughing out, I say, "I'm kidding about wanting pictures with the Avengers. I want a picture with King Kong and Taylor Swift." It doesn't take long to find them and capture some quick memories.

Rocco's stomach growls, and it's almost as loud as the noise on the street. I pat his stomach, lingering on his drool-worthy abs, and ask, "Hungry?" He smiles widely, revealing his trademark dimples. *He is so handsome.* "Let's head over to Grand Central Station and we can get something at Shake Shack."

Rocco grabs my hand, leading the way. We saw the entrance for it on our way to Madame Tussauds. "Food first, then more exploring?" he asks.

Hearing his stomach growl again, I laugh and answer, "Yes."

Walking into Grand Central Station, my mind can't comprehend what I'm seeing. The architecture is incredible. Although I know it's over one hundred and ten years old, it remains contemporary and gorgeous. A true national historic landmark. The marble walls are breathtaking and then you look up and the constellation ceiling is mind-blowing. After our descent down the impressive staircase, my eyes are overwhelmed. They're being pulled in so many directions. I can't help but be mesmerized by the four-sided ball clock. It's brightly polished brass with what looks like an opal face. "It's stunning," I say as I gaze above at the iconic time piece.

Rocco pushes up next to me and asks, "Do you know about the Whispering Gallery?" I shake my head no. Melinda never mentioned that. "While you were looking at the clock, I overheard some people talking about it, and I asked them to tell me more." Dropping my gaze from the dazzling clock, I look at him, and he continues with what he's learned. "Apparently, by the hidden oyster bar, there's a section of the vaulted archway where one person can stand, whispering a message into the wall and the person on the opposite wall will hear it."

Surprised, I question. "Really? Can we try that after Shake Shack?"

"I'm in. Maybe I'll whisper dirty secrets of what I plan to do to you tonight when we get back to your place." His words are like a direct shot of lust to my libido, and my center throbs in delight. I rub my thighs together, and he smirks.

"Let's go eat," I say in a breathy voice.

Shake Shack is just how I expect it: Delicious. I'm not too hungry, but Rocco doesn't have any problem finishing my leftovers. Once we're done, we head to the Whispering Gallery to test out whether it really works. And Rocco is true to his word. If those walls were people, they'd be blushing as hard as I am. His dirty words delight and excite me, making me eager to skip the rest of our afternoon of exploration.

"Ready to go?" I finally whisper at him, my panties saturated with need for him.

Waiting for his response, I stare at the marble wall. Someone steps up behind me, and I shift to move out of the way until I catch a whiff of his incredibly sexy cologne. Rocco brushes my hair off my neck, leans in, and places lingering kisses from my shoulder to my ear before whispering, "All good things come to those who wait." Leaning back with a groan, he pulls me tight to him, and I feel his hard cock pressing up against me. I whimper. Dropping his voice, he asks, "Are you going to be my good girl?" Suddenly dying of thirst, I lick my lips and nod. He swats my butt and spins me around for an earth-shattering kiss. I'm lust drunk when he pulls away asking, "What's next?"

"Wh-what?" I stutter, waiting for my brain to function again. Finally, the fog clears and I boldly suggest, "How about my place?" Rocco just laughs.

"Remember what I said about those who wait?" I slowly nod, not sure where he's going with it.

He replies in a husky voice that sends a shiver down my spine. "Well, I'm going to make you wait. By the time we get back to your place, you're going to be wet, wanton, and willing to beg for me." My cheeks flame hot as I grow wetter and squirm in my discomfort. Looking at him through my lashes, his confident smile reminds me of the power he holds over me. I haven't ever been with anyone who talks dirty, let alone denies and commands me. I'm finding I like it. I like it a lot.

"Didn't you say there was a park nearby that has a fountain you wanted to make a wish in? And I believe you promised me pizza from Joey's for dinner."

Sexually frustrated with him, I grab his hand and drag him from Grand Central Station like they've ordered an emergency evacuation. We're speed walking and dodging people left and right as we head for the exit. Once we reach the sidewalk, I continue tugging him down Forty-second street for the three-minute walk to Bryant Park. We're vigilant. We bypass the New York Public Library and continue on. "This way," I say as I continue power walking like we're staring in a Jane Fonda workout video.

"Slow down, Jasmine. Can't we look around?" But I choose to ignore him, wanting to get home and to what he's promised. My skin is buzzing in anticipation of his touch. Annoyed, Rocco digs his feet in and plants his weight. "Jaz, isn't this where they have the famous ice-skating rink you see in all the movies?"

I stop, shaking my head, "No, that's Rockefeller Center. This is Bryant Park. It has some great stuff too, or so I've heard. This is my first time here."

"Wait. What?" he says as I keep marching forward. "What about the fountain you mentioned? Are we at least going to see that?"

I hang my head, embarrassed by my impatience. "Yeah, it's on the other side of the park. On Monday nights, they host movie nights where they show Paramount movies. I'm hoping to catch one or two this summer. Melinda says it's a fantastic time. You sit under the stars, the city skyline's your backdrop all while watching the big screen."

Being a huge movie buff, Rocco's mouth gapes open and his eyes go wide. "That sounds incredible. We should totally plan to do that during one of my visits this summer."

"Yeah, you'd love it. But how often are you planning to visit?" *Please, please, please say often.*

He squeezes my hand and then pulls me into a hug. I melt against him, burying my head in his chest. "I wish I could just stay permanently during the off-season, but I have weekly training in Chicago that I need to stay focused on. And I'd have to explain to everyone what I was doing. You know my friends and family; they'll get all up in our business. With this being so new, I want to keep you to myself."

His admission causes flutters in my stomach, and my heart races while I fawn at him. I'm sure I look like a love-struck fool, but I don't care. For too long, I have dreamed of this, and I'm going to savor every moment. Plus, I agree with him. I'm also not ready to share what we have yet.

"Let's go find that fountain," I suggest while still snuggled in. Rocco kisses my head and unwraps himself from me. His much larger hand cradles mine while we walk deeper into the park. When we find the fountain, we each make a wish, tossing in a coin. My wish, although secret, is for us and the longevity of our budding relationship. I look at Rocco after he's done, and he leans over and seals his lips to mine. Exiting the park, we go in search of Joey's pizza so we can grab dinner and finally head home.

After devouring the pizza, Rocco devours me. It seems he has an insatiable hunger for me. Who am I to complain? And I am more than happy to return the favor by sinking to my knees and begging for him. But when he orders me to do just that? I don't find it demeaning like I thought I would. It's fucking sexy, and I'm wet and craving him. All night long, we alternate between making one another come and sleeping. By noon on Sunday, we're both sated and completely spent. Rocco has a flight back to Chicago in the early evening, which gives us enough time to eat before he has to head to the airport. We're going to grab brunch and his suitcase from his hotel. The hotel he barely used during his visit. Next time, he'll just stay with me.

Hours later, when he's getting ready to catch a cab to the airport, I find myself withdrawing. I'm not ready for him to leave. I'll miss him terribly, but especially now that we're together.

His muscular arms wrap around me and he whispers against my head, "I'm going to miss you too. But I'll be back the weekend after next. Okay?" I nod my head against his chest, holding back my tears. He pulls back and dabs at my wet eyes. "Babe, you know you can come home, right?"

Sniffling, I answer, "I know, but I'm not sure that's the best decision."

He squeezes my arms. "Okay, but know I'm here to help you if and when you're ready. You just say the word."

Our last kiss before he gets into his cab and drives away lingers on my lips. I can still feel his warm embrace, and I wonder how long it'll last.

Chapter 24

Rocco

For two weeks, I focus on my workouts and training in the offseason. I find this is the only way to distract myself until I go back to New York City to see Jaz.

For days I've had the locker room to myself, but today Ace is joining me. He's still working on his leg rehabilitation, so his workout's limited compared to mine.

During the offseason, we try to work out together at least a few times a week. In previous years, as the perpetual single guys, we spent a lot of our weekends together. But since I've been visiting Jasmine every other weekend, our bro hangouts have been put on the back burner.

"Hey, Roc," he hollers as he enters the space. But then he freezes like a deer caught in headlights.

What is he doing? I pull off my headphones, stop my treadmill, and hesitantly answer, "Hey."

He grimaces. "What is wrong with you?"

I look down at my body, trace my hands over my face, and answer, "Nothing." Then I grin widely. "I've never been better."

Pointing his finger at me, he says, "That. That's what's wrong. Right there. You're doing it now."

I frown at him, not understanding what he's implying. "Ace," I growl in warning.

He laughs. "There's the Rocco I'm used to. All gruff and ruff. This is better. The smile that was plastered on your face when I came in was creepy as fuck." Then he smirks. I wipe my sweaty face and neck with my towel and then throw it at him. "Gross," he yells as he dodges left to avoid being hit.

"Sorry, I'm late. My siblings were all chatterboxes when I called home. I barely got to speak to my ma." He shakes his head while he steps up next to my treadmill. "Why are you so happy?"

I can barely control my grin as I increase the speed to a jog. "I'm still riding the high from my last weekend visiting Jasmine."

He smirks at me. "Dude, you've been back for over a week. Did something happen? Did you finally convince her to move home?"

I increase my speed and pant out, "I wish."

"Okay, if that's not it, what is it?"

"Let's just say we had some incredible *communication* all weekend long."

Ace runs his hands through his hair. "It feels like you're hinting at something, but I don't know what. Regardless, I'm happy you two are talking and getting along. We were all getting sick of the moody asshole you've been."

The last time I visited Jasmine before I left, we decided for the time being to keep our relationship just between us. I know everyone will be excited, and I'll hear a lot of "about time" comments, but we're still new and fragile. We aren't ready for the spotlight. Immersed in the puppy love stage, we're enjoying every subtle touch, tender kiss, and whispered secret.

I've done my research for this next trip to see Jaz, and I have an agenda. I looked at the top things to do while in New York, and museums topped the list. Sure, we could go to the traditional route visiting the American Museum of Natural History or the Guggenheim, but I want something unique and memorable. The Museum of Sex fits the bill, and I'm sure Jasmine hasn't been there yet. I'm not sure what to expect, but I'm convinced it'll lead to some great conversations. I also looked up some restaurants near it because I'm planning for a nighttime visit to the Empire State Building. I read the sunset is absolutely amazing to watch on a clear night from the eighty-sixth floor's outside observation deck.

On Friday afternoon, I fly into New York and make my way to the bank in lower Manhattan where Jaz works. Arriving just before five, I pace the concrete steps until I spot her exiting the building. When our eyes lock, it takes her a moment for recognition to register. When it does, an enormous smile appears on her gorgeous face. My heart thumps in my chest. Moving quickly, she almost runs into my awaiting arms. Sweeping her off her feet, her faint citrus scent invades my sinuses, and I breathe a relieved sigh. *Finally.*

"You're here," she squeals as she melts in my arms.

"I am. I've been waiting for so long to hold you," I murmur into her ear.

A click of heels next to us distracts me. Looking to my left, I see a woman staring at us. She clears her throat, and many thoughts invade my mind. *Do you mind, lady? I haven't seen my girlfriend in two weeks. Give us a moment.* The woman puts her hands on her hips.

"Uh, Jaz. I think this lady is trying to get our attention, but I don't recognize her." Slowly, I lower her back to the steps. *Already, I miss her body pressed to mine.*

"Oh my gosh. It's Melinda," Jasmine says as she pats my chest. *That name rings a bell.* And then I'm reminded that she's one of the few friends Jaz has made here. She also gave her some great recommendations for things to do and see here.

Smiling at her, I extend my hand. "It's so nice to meet you. I'm Rocco."

"Yes, you are," she says while flicking her eyes from me to Jasmine, who's still clinging to my side. When she lets her eyes roam over me, it feels like she's assessing me. But not sexually. Instead, it's more protective, and I find myself grateful that Jaz has made such a good friend. We exchange small talk until Melinda's phone alerts her to a message. "It's Henry. He was wondering if I'm headed home," she explains.

Jasmine leans closer. "That's her boyfriend." I nod, happy that we'll be alone again soon. Melinda excuses herself, and we walk to the subway for the ride back to Jaz's apartment. Sitting next to her on the train, I wrap my arm protectively around her, pulling her close.

She nuzzles into my side and asks, "What do you want to do this weekend while you're here?" She wiggles her eyebrows at me.

"What?" I ask, feigning innocence.

She cocks her head in challenge. "You mean you aren't going to suggest we stay in bed the entire time?" The thought of that makes me instantly hard and I smile widely. *That sounds pretty damn good.*

I shake my head no, earning a confused look from her. "I have an itinerary for us," I tell her.

She beams a megawatt smile at me. "Do tell."

Squeezing her closer, I admit, "I only planned activities for Saturday."

"Okay," she agrees.

"And I was hoping we'd repeat our prior Sunday," I say with a lust-filled grin. Jasmine blushes and I lean in for a kiss. As soon as our lips touch, my body buzzes like I've been electrified. I wrap my hand around her neck and pull her in closer. She gasps, parting her lips and allowing my tongue entrance. I find it incredibly easy to get lost in her. The train announces our stop and Jasmine pulls away. We're both dazed and panting. I restrain myself from throwing her over my shoulder and running up the subway stairs like I'm a love-struck fool. *Love struck?* Pushing that thought aside, we climb the stairs like the civilized adults we are, and stroll hand-in-hand to her apartment. Every step we take has me feeling more wanton. I need to get her alone.

When we're finally behind closed doors, I drop my bag and drag her to the bedroom. Gently, I push her onto the bed. Her hungry gaze follows my every movement, heating my body. *Too many clothes.* I pull my sweatshirt and t-shirt off in one tug, and I watch Jasmine's eyes go wide as they trace over my chest and abs. Licking her lips, I follow her gaze as it lowers to my cock. Slowly, to torture her, I lower my zipper, revealing my boxers. Stepping from them, I palm my heated, hard cock. Dropping my voice into a husky tone, I say, "Babe, you're wearing too many clothes."

She nods at me and quickly shoots up, tugging her

work clothes from her body at lightning speed. Thankfully, she wore a loose dress, so she's not getting tangled in it. Once she's down to a matching set of black bra and panties, she settles back and eyes me. It's my turn to lick my lips, and I crawl across the bed to her. I snag her ankle and pull her under me. Her responding squeal heats my blood and causes my cock to grow even harder. Growling, I palm it again, hoping to temper it. *I can't have it ruin things before we even get started.*

Hovering above her, I'm transfixed by the rapid rise and fall of her impressive breasts. I'm more of a legs man, but with Jasmine, no one part of her is better than another. "Do you know how beautiful you are?" Her cheeks pinken and she shakes her head no. But she is perfection. "You are perfection. From the deep emerald green of your eyes to your soft alabaster skin that covers every sensual curve you have. I love everything about you." Resting in a pushup position above her, I trace the lines of her cleavage with my tongue. Then I blow on her, inviting goose bumps to follow my path through her divine peaks. Pushing down the demi cups cradling her breasts, I run my tongue around her nipple before sucking it into my mouth.

"Rocco," she pants.

Resting my weight on one arm, I use my free hand to fondle and play with her other breast. She squirms below me as I tug, pull, and pinch her nipple. Her moans make me question if she'd ever consider wearing nipple clamps. *Conversation for another time.* Jasmine's hips flex up. *Is she wet?* Releasing her nipple from my mouth, I hear a pop, and her body shivers below me. I lean down and kiss her lips, mumbling against them, "Remove your bra," before I pull away. Scooting down the bed, I crawl between her exquisite legs. I run my palms up until I reach her hips. *How are they so damn soft?* I squeeze her hips before anchoring my fingers in her panties. Leaning forward, I place a kiss at each hip bone and then lower over her center. She lifts her hips to meet me and my mouth waters, eager for her taste on my tongue.

Looking up for permission, I recognize the desire in her eyes. It's the same that's pumping through my veins and propelling me forward. "Please," she whispers.

"Such good manners," I praise before tearing the silk and lace undergarment down her legs. My first lick is slow and torturous for both of us. I want to savor her flavor for a moment. "You taste so good," I say against her thigh before I give it a quick bite, remembering to lick away any sting I may have inflicted.

"Rocco," she moans impatiently while tugging my hair that's wrapped around her fingers. Lowering myself again, I place long languid licks from back to front. When I reach her clit, I circle it with my tongue before sucking on it. I take my finger and rim her entrance, sliding into her wet center with ease. I add another finger after a minute, stretching her out, making room for my cock. The sound of me thrusting my fingers inside her rivals that of the blood pumping through my veins, rushing south. My erection throbs painfully in my boxers, and I press it against the bed, moaning out.

Jasmine's eyes flash open and she stares at me between her legs. "Are you okay?" she asks. Nodding my head, I drop my focus back to her clit. After only a few sucks, she's tightening around my fingers and whimpering my name. Sitting back, I watch her unravel, and I decide I've seen nothing so beautiful. Once she's relaxed a little, I slide my damp fingers from her and bring them to my lips to clean them off. Shifting, I tug my boxers off and then move above her again.

"Jaz." Her eyes slowly open and she gives me a sated smile. "Hi, babe," I croon at her.

"Hi," she answers in a sleepy voice.

Smiling back, I ask, "Are you ready for me?" *Please say yes. I'm dying to be inside you.*

"Always, Rocco." She widens her legs for me. I palm my cock and run my thumb over the dripping wet tip. It throbs in my hand. Lining up with her entrance, I slowly thrust inside her. The immediate squeeze is heavenly, and I groan in pleasure. When I'm fully seated, I give her body a second to adjust before I begin to thrust. Jasmine reaches up and pulls my head to hers. She tugs my lower lip with her teeth. Opening for her, she licks into my mouth. A hum comes from her throat as our tongues wrestle. Wrapping her long legs around my waist, she pulls me deeper, making me bottom out. Her muscles tighten around my cock and a buzz travels up my spine. Grunting, I thrust even harder, seeking a mutual release. Moments later, pleasure overwhelms my brain and I tear my lips from hers.

"Fuck," I shout as I spill into her. Slipping my hand to her clit, I make quick, tight circles, encouraging her orgasm to continue as I keep pumping my hips.

"Rocco," she pants as she slides up and down my cum-covered cock, chasing another orgasm. I keep at it until I feel myself go limp. I collapse on top of her and then roll to the side, out of breath. Turning my head toward her, our eyes meet, and I can't stop myself from saying, "That was amazing." Jaz nods, a wide smile gracing her kiss-punished lips.

Her eyes flutter closed, and a minute later her breathing has evened out. Slipping from the bed, I head to the bathroom to clean up. Grabbing a washcloth, I get it wet so I can take care of Jaz too. She sleeps through it. I climb into bed and tuck her to my chest. I'm exhausted. We'll just take a little nap and have a later dinner. With Jasmine curled in my arms, I am completely content and at peace. Closing my eyes, it doesn't take long for me to fall asleep.

Chapter 25

Jasmine

Rocco is here! Those two weeks apart were harder than I thought they would be. Seeing him when I came out of work yesterday made my heart so happy. After we got back to my place, he rocked my world. *It was seriously the best sex I've ever had.* Sated and exhausted, I fell asleep, taking an early evening nap. When I woke up an hour later, I saw Rocco had napped too. We ordered Thai food, which we devoured naked in my bed before rounds two and three. We tried watching an Avengers movie after that, but we were exhausted and barely made it through the opening credits.

On Saturday morning, Rocco wakes me up at ten with a steaming cup of coffee and a streusel-covered blueberry muffin he grabbed from the bakery a few blocks over. I recently found it and told him about it during his last visit. "This is so good. Thank you," I rave. "Do you want a bite?"

"I got my own." He laughs as he sits on the couch and pulls another muffin from a white paper bakery bag. "And they're still warm," he adds before taking a large bite.

"What's on the agenda for the day?" I ask.

He leans back to settle in. "I thought we could do dinner on Fifth Avenue before watching the sunset from the Empire State Building."

"That sounds incredible, but what about the rest of the day?"

He raises his eyebrows and smirks. "I found an interesting-looking museum I thought we'd enjoy."

"Oh, yeah?" I ask, leery. "New York is known for having a variety of museums. Which one interested you?"

He takes a drink of his coffee, clears his voice, and answers me. "The Museum of Sex."

"Wh-what? Really?" I question with a stutter.

Rocco flashes me an adorable grin, highlighting those dimples I've loved since we were kids. "Sure, why not? It'll be fun."

Surprised and a little intrigued, I say, "Okay. I guess I'll get ready, then."

Once I'm dressed and ready, we hop on the train that goes to the Twenty-eighth Street station. Together, Rocco and I are learning to navigate the subway station. I won't admit it out loud, but it's finally starting to make some sense.

Heading to the museum, I see it's in the corner of an average sized building. The greenish-tan stone façade is beautiful, and the silver letters making up its name are contemporary and stylish. The giant X of the door handle matching the X of the sign. Then there's the window above, a subtle nod to the fun inside. A rainbow fringe sign proclaims the museum's new sensational exhibit, Super Funland. My body is buzzing with excitement, and I squeeze Rocco's hand. He laughs as he leads me into the whimsical museum. Both of us unsure what to expect.

"Jaz, come look at this," Rocco calls as he points out what looks to be Hugh Hefner's robe. The Artifact (XXX): Selections from Secret Collections section is filled with over 15,000 sex-themed objects that represent how sex has been perceived in our culture through art and science. They even have early versions of vibrators and how-to guides on oral sex and masturbation from the seventies. There's even a copy of *Playboy* magazine in Braille. Rocco points out movies like *Fifty Shades of Grey* and *Brokeback Mountain*, which were perceived as scandalous when they were released.

"Oh," I gasp when I enter the section of the museum that most resembles regular art museums. For some, the pictures covering the walls could be deemed pornographic. I, however, see the beauty in them. I'm fascinated the most by the women who are displayed with their breasts covered. They look like sexpots. They're empowered, glamorous, and sexy. As I move from one to another, Rocco stands next to me with his hand settled low on my back.

"Do you like those?" he whispers against my ear.

Nodding, I answer, "They intrigue me. I wish I were as confident as they are."

He nudges my hip, turning me to him. Then he pulls me closer, his erection rubbing against me. "You are every bit as sexy as them. In fact, I think you're sexier."

"Sure," I mutter under my breath as I try to turn away.

His hands anchor my hips, locking me into place. "Jasmine," he growls. I shudder. His face is the most serious I've ever seen it. Wanting to avoid the nagging feeling I'm in trouble, I look at my feet.

"Look at me," he chides. Feeling like a child who is about to be reprimanded, I look up at him through my lashes. "Higher," he commands, and I notice a weird reaction I'm having to him. I'm turned on. I don't know if it's the tone he's using, the sense of danger he's emitting, or the entire moment, but I can't deny it's making me horny. *Will he notice?* As soon as I look at him, he does, and he pulls me in for a hungry kiss. Lost in the moment, the rest of the world fades away. A loud gasp travels across the room, and I pull away. Refusing to let me go, Rocco places another soft kiss to my lips before we turn toward the noise.

Standing a foot away is a star-struck woman, staring at Rocco. "Are you Rocco Romano, the best winger in the league, number ten on the Chicago Steel?" Her questions all run into one, and it's adorable.

Rocco answers her. "Yes, I am."

A woman in her mid-seventies with light violet-colored hair, dressed in a purple velour track suit, steps closer. "Could I trouble you for an autograph?" Rocco smiles and takes the pen and paper she pulls from her fanny pack.

I love this woman's style. I hope when I'm her age, I'm as hip as she is. "Do you want me to take a picture for you?" I offer.

The woman smiles at me. "Aren't you sweet to offer. Do you know how to work this?" she asks as she pulls a new iPhone out of the fanny pack.

"I do," I answer as she cuddles up next to Rocco, who absolutely dwarfs her. Once I've taken a few pictures, she thanks us and then scoots back to join a sharply-dressed older gentleman. His sweater vest and fedora are on point, making him look dapper, as my grandfather would say.

Rocco pulls me to his side, wraps his arm around me, and kisses my head. "She reminds me of Nonna."

"You're right, she does. I love Nonna. And her

cooking. I could totally go for some of her lasagna or spaghetti and meatballs right now."

He nuzzles my nose. "You know, moving back to Chicago and being my favorite person gives you an all-access pass to Nonna and her incredible cooking." He points to the exit. "Let's go explore more of the museum."

Hand in hand, we enter Super Funland: The Journey into the Erotic Carnival. We purchase tickets to use on all the provocatively themed carnival games. We spend the next two hours laughing and having a ball. My favorite thing is the erotic mechanical bull. I don't last the eight seconds, but I have a blast trying to stay on. Rocco loves both the roll-a-ball horse racing game and the claw machine. We jump in the bouncy castle of boobs, and I get stuck in the corner behind some mammary tissue. Rocco rescues me once he's able to stop laughing. Winded and red faced, he pulls me free. We both take the mouth slide that delivers us between a giant set of black-and-white striped legs. Before we're done, we visit the siren to see if she'll give us a love potion.

"How does this work?" Rocco eyeballs the gold arcade game that's decorated with a bare-breasted mermaid.

Muffling my laugh, I point to the signs below. "It says insert your hand here and give her a whirl." I watch as Rocco squints at it. "That looks odd yet familiar." I snort, unable to hold back my laughter.

Crossing his arms in front of him, he demands, "Why are you laughing?"

Leaning over, I rest my hands on my knees, trying desperately to get myself under control. When I think I'm composed enough, I look up at him, then over to where his hand is supposed to go and I lose it all over again. A minute later, I stand up and ask, "You don't see what's so funny?"

He shakes his head. "Just tell me."

"What does that look like to you?" I ask, pointing to the lower half of the machine.

Annoyed, he shrugs his shoulders. With a smile on my face, I ask, "Are you sure that doesn't look familiar?"

"I said it does, but I don't know why," he explains before rolling his eyes.

"Guess we'll have to change that," I mutter to myself. He just continues to frown at me. "Rocco, it's a vagina. Don't you see it?"

He drops to his haunches and scratches his head as he examines it. "You're right." Then he laughs. "So... I reach deep inside her, give her a tickle, and see if she'll give me her love potion?" I nod and laugh.

"Let's see what you've got, big guy."

The siren doesn't sing, so Rocco doesn't earn her love potion. He pouts. I lean down and whisper in his ear, "You can redeem yourself tonight and see if you make me sing your praises." He nudges my chin and kisses me.

"You're on, babe." Rising to his full height of 6'2", he grabs my hand and leads me toward the exit.

Back on the sidewalk, we google the nearby restaurants he found and decide on a Mexican cantina that has great reviews. While waiting for our food, we stuff ourselves with chips and salsa, because what else are you supposed to do when hot, fresh tortilla chips are placed in front of you?

Following our early dinner, we walk the four minutes to the Empire State Building. Rocco had done his homework and discovered that you could access the outside observation deck on the eighty-sixth floor. Before sunset, we tour the building, enjoying the history lessons on the second and eightieth floors. Next we head up to the 102nd floor. "Oh my goodness, it's incredible," I proclaim as we step into the observatory and see the floor-to-ceiling windows that provide a 360 degree panoramic view of the city. It's completely overwhelming. After taking in that magnificent view, we're ready to see the sunset from the observation deck. I'm fearful of this, seeing that I've been afraid of heights since I was small.

My knees turn to Jell-O, and I cling to Rocco as he pushes through the doors leading us outside. "Please stay close to me," I beg him.

"I've got you, babe. I won't let anything happen to you," he assures, trying to comfort me. Finding a less packed area of the deck, we walk toward the edge to peer out at the city.

"That view is incredible," he says as he wraps his muscular arms around me. I nod my agreement, and he whispers reassuring words into my ear. Until now, I've never felt safer or more protected in my life. My heart hums its contentment as I rest my head against his chest. *This is love.* Although we haven't been together long, it's undeniable. I have loved him for as long as I can remember. I was just afraid to admit it. I'm not ready to tell him yet, but I suspect it won't be long. Not even ten minutes later, the first taste of sunset begins with its changing colors. Various shades of orange, pink, red, and purple streak across the sky, providing a beautiful backdrop to a city coming alive with its nightlife.

"Wow. That is absolutely stunning."

Rocco leans over and says, "So are you. Want to take a selfie so we can always remember this?" *Of course I do.*

When the sun has finally set and the sky darkens to black, we're treated to a brilliant show as all the buildings of New York City and its boroughs are bathed in lights.

"I can't believe it's only nine," I say as we head down to the lobby.

Exiting the building, Rocco smiles. "It feels so much later. Are you ready to go home, or do you feel like one more adventure?"

Lifting on my toes, I kiss his lips. "With you, I'm

always up for one more adventure. What do you have in mind?"

Rocco smirks and gets on his phone, typing away. When he's done, he pockets it, then answers me. "It's a surprise." Not even a minute later, a car pulls up to the curb near us. "That's us," he says as he ushers me to it.

After a quick ride to Central Park, we climb out of the Uber and see a horse-drawn carriage. "Those remind me of Cinderella," I say. "What are we doing here?"

Rocco leads me over to the white carriage. "Climb up, Jaz."

"We're taking a carriage ride? I've never done that before." I squeal with excitement as I climb up into the red crushed-velvet seat. The driver takes us on an hour-long ride, pointing out sights such as the Carousel, Sheep Meadow, and the Tavern on the Green. We even stop for a photo op.

When the ride ends, I'm more than ready to head home. Seated so closely next to him, sharing a blanket for the last hour, has left me feeling hot and needy. A few times during the ride, I wanted to crawl into his lap and enjoy another type of ride, but I restrained myself. We're in public, after all.

Knowing he's headed back to Chicago tomorrow, we both agree to be naked and wrapped around each other for the little time we have left. Rocco takes that seriously, wasting no time to strip off my pants as soon as we're past my front door. Anchored to the door, he uses his fingers to plunge me into ecstasy. Meanwhile, I'm trying to remove the rest of my clothes before I orgasm. My spine stiffens and my toes curl just as I'm tossing my bra across the room.

Standing on wobbly legs, I bite my lip and say, "You're too dressed." I reach for his leather belt, unbuckling it before I pull it free and drop it at my feet. I love the clunk sound it makes when it hits my wood floors. I drop to my knees as I reach for his zipper. Slowly, I pull it down, revealing a pair of black cotton boxers. Reaching into his pants, I curl my hands around back and squeeze his adorable ass. Shimmying his pants off his hips, they fall to the ground. Returning to the front, I palm his impressively hard cock, pressing a chaste kiss to the tip that is playing peek-a-boo at his waistband. Rocco lets out a deep, primal growl that makes me squeeze my legs together. My breaths speed up and my body hums in anticipation of what's going to happen next.

Chapter 26

Rocco

After the day we've had, the icing on the cake is staring down at Jaz while she pulls my hot, throbbing cock from my boxers and wraps her soft pink lips around it. She took out her messy bun, letting her natural curls fall around her face. She is exquisite, a dream come true. I moan as her tongue explores me as she sucks my cock deeper into her throat.

"Fuck," I say on a moan as I fist her soft brown hair. She hums around me, and my balls tighten. I'm not ready for this to be over, so I force myself to think about the most nonsexual things I can, like how big the rat was I saw in the subway.

Jaz places one hand on my thigh and squeezes it while the other makes its way to my balls. After a quick rub and tug, she migrates to my taint, and I tighten everything. Once she massages it, there's nothing I can do to stop the inevitable. A bolt of energy surges up my spine and I press my feet to the ground to make sure I remain upright as I spill into her mouth. My head falls back and my eyes roll into my head as my soul is sucked from me. I may have even blacked out for a moment because my vision is spotty when I open my eyes.

Immediately looking down, I see Jasmine wiping the corners of her mouth. "Naughty girl," I growl as I tug her to her feet. I kick off my shoes and strip off my shirt. Stepping out of my pants and boxers decorating my ankles, I tug Jaz to me. Leaning down, I pick her up and fireman carry her to the bedroom. I toss her on the bed, where she lands with a giggle. *I love how fucking adorable she is. I love everything about her. I love her.* That thought sobers me. It's undeniable, and I'm okay with it. I question if she feels the same way. For now, I'll keep it to myself, waiting for the right moment to tell her. When is that, you ask? I have no fucking idea. I just hope I recognize it when it's upon me.

Staring down at her, I find myself hard again. I stroke myself a handful of times before I lean over and grab her ankle. Dragging her closer to the end of the bed, I lower myself to my knees. Tossing her legs over my wide shoulders, I open her up to me. I run my hands down her thighs toward her glistening center. She squirms as I blow cool air on her heated skin. "Please," she begs as I lower my lips closer. A quick swipe through her folds has her arching her back and begging for more. *What the lady wants, the lady gets.*

"You taste incredible, Jasmine. You're my favorite meal," I say as she moans and gyrates. Wrapping my lips around her clit, I suck on it until she whimpers. Knowing she wants more, I give her just that, plunging two fingers inside her wet heat. In only a few thrusts, they are completely saturated and moving with ease. I curl them forward, getting her G-spot on my first try. Her hips flex, pulling her clit free from my teeth.

"Do that again," she demands once she's settled back down. I love that she's vocal in bed, asking for what she wants. She's ready for me this time, and her moans of appreciation fill the air as her climax peaks.

Sated, she throws her arms above her head. Her hair, which is a mess from all the writhing she was doing, hides her face from me. Climbing up on the bed, I carefully tuck it behind her ear. Leaning down, I kiss her, and she reaches up, pulling me closer. Without breaking the kiss, I shift my body above hers and lower myself so we're skin to skin. *This is a feeling I will never tire of.*

Her skin is warm and soft as she wraps her legs around my waist. I shift my hips, adjusting my cock, which is pulsating between us. Hungrily, she sucks her essence off my tongue as she grinds herself against me. I'm definitely ready for another round. There's nothing better than being buried inside her. Once she releases my tongue, I pull back and line up before I slowly push into her. When I bottom out, her legs tighten around me, and I groan. "That feels so good, babe." Thrusting in and out slowly, I almost pull all the way out before I push back in. We won't be winning any races for speed. This is not a fast fuck. I'm enjoying every moment, hoping this lasts forever. *Forever with Jasmine sounds amazing.* The buildup to this orgasm is slow and meaningful. Once I feel Jaz's inner muscles squeeze my cock, I increase the speed of my hips.

"Rocco, right there," she pants into my shoulder before she takes a bite. *Why is that so sexy?* I slip my hand between us and rub circles on her needy clit. Jaz moans and begs, panting with each sound that falls from her perfect lips. Our thrusts become crazed and reckless as we both chase the same thing. Her orgasm begins first, and I follow quickly behind. Continuing to thrust, she prolongs the experience. I pump my hips, hoping my cock remains firm until she's finished. When she finally settles beneath me, I breathe a sigh of relief. Looking down, I see her face is completely relaxed. Her eyes are closed and she's smiling through her slightly parted lips. I brush my lips against hers and she hums. Slipping from the bed, I wet a washcloth before I clean us both up. Once that's done, I climb back into bed and snuggle up behind Jaz, who's already fallen asleep. "I love you," I whisper against her head before I close my eyes.

Waking up without an alarm with the woman I love in my arms is a dream come true. It's Sunday, and later this evening I have a flight back to Chicago. I've already booked another trip for two weeks from now. In my spare time, when I'm not training, I have some research to do for our next weekend together. The warm body glued to my side shifts and I look down to see if Jaz is still asleep. She's not. "Good morning," I say while she rubs the sleep from her eyes.

"Good morning," she parrots back, adding a smile. *I love her smile. Yep, I have it bad.*

I lie back, putting my hands behind my head. She shifts closer and begins tracing her fingertips all around my chest. "What do you want to do this morning?" I ask.

Her eyes light up and she smiles at me. "Let's go over to Scramble."

Confused, I look at her. "What's Scramble?"

"It's a restaurant that I've heard has an amazing brunch."

My stomach growls at the idea of food. "We did burn a lot of calories last night," I say with a smirk. Jasmine just rolls her eyes at me. Throwing my legs over the side of the bed, I stand. I pull her toward me and then toss her over my shoulder. She squeaks, and I slap her butt. "Don't make me drop you," I caution as she laughs, wiggling in my arms.

Growling, I say, "This is serious, Jaz. You mentioned food. I'm a man on a mission." Hanging down my back, she mocks me with a drawn-out 'ooooh.' I squeeze her tighter to me as I head to her bathroom.

It's shower time. Since my stomach is threatening mutiny, I have to remain focused on cleaning.

Thirty minutes later, we step out the front door of her building. Scramble is only a few blocks over, and at ten thirty, it already has a good-sized line. Joining those waiting, we talk about ideas for my next visit. Central Park? Radio City? Or finding the world's best version of classic New York-style foods like pizza, bagels, and cheesecake.

"We're getting close," Jasmine says while bouncing excitedly on her toes. *She is fucking adorable.* Every time I think back, I question why it took so long to figure out my feelings for her.

"Jasmine?" a male behind me says. Turning around, I spot someone who looks vaguely familiar. He's an attractive guy with too big of a smile directed at my girlfriend. *How do they know each other?* Looking at Jasmine, I see she's smiling too, but it's more uncomfortable than happy. Feeling uneasy, I lower my hand, setting it on her back before I whisper in her ear, "Who's that?"

She looks up at me, her green eyes dull. "That's Anthony."

Her answer hits me like a hard check into the boards, and my mouth falls open. I didn't recognize him. In all the time they dated, I'd kept my distance out of respect for her. He wasn't my biggest fan. He didn't like how close we were. My mouth goes dry and I rasp, "Anthony, as in your college boyfriend, move to New

York with me, Anthony?" She nods, and it feels like I'm in freefall. *Shit.* Now she's in the same city as her first love, while I'm visiting from Chicago as often as I can during the offseason. *What's going to happen during the actual season when I can't visit as much?* My heart drops along with the hand I have on her back. Fear swirls in my gut.

Anthony speaks to the person he's with and then leaves his spot in line, approaching with a smug-as-shit smile. With hands clenched, I want desperately to punch it off his perfectly chiseled face. *Jealous much?* Yes. Yes, I fucking am. *She's mine.* He approaches her for a hug, and I resist the urge to rip his arms off. *Good luck eating breakfast without arms, motherfucker.* At the thought of that, I chuckle to myself, and Jasmine elbows me in the ribs like she knows what I'm thinking. She might. After they broke up, I didn't feel the need to hide my distaste for him. Obviously threatened by me, he always acted like he was perfect, but he proved he wasn't in the end. He wanted to take her away from her home, from everything she loves. In the end, it had been Jasmine who'd walked away, but he hadn't fought for her.

I'm not complaining. His indifference is my gain. I will do anything it takes to prove to Jasmine I want her. It doesn't matter the cost. I'll sacrifice it all for her. We've skirted around each other for too long to waste any more time. Who cares if they're in the same city? It doesn't matter. She's mine now.

Grinning wide, as if I won the Mega Millions jackpot, I place my hand on her lower back. *Staking my claim?* Dropping my voice, I extend my hand to him. "Hi, Anthony. I'm Rocco. I don't think we've officially met."

He drags his gaze away from Jasmine, frowns at me, and gives me a limp shake. *Pansy.* "No, I don't think we have. In all the years Jasmine and I dated, you were never around. The only time I ever saw you was when I was at the grocery store and you and some unnamed bimbo were on the cover of a gossip magazine after being photographed leaving a club or party."

My hands turn to fists and I shove them in my pockets. He's right. I wasn't around because I couldn't handle seeing Jaz with pencil dick, and every time I saw her, it caused a fight between them. I was trying to protect her.

Frustrated, I breathe out. "You're right. I wasn't around. I was biding my time, waiting for Jasmine to give me a chance." But I don't need to explain that to him. He's just here to measure dicks, hoping his midget will get a repeat. If we're measuring, his ruler wouldn't compare to my yardstick.

"Yeah, for the past six years, I've been busy playing professional hockey for the Steel. Jasmine always knew I was there and would be there in a heartbeat if she ever needed me." I pull her closer, placing a kiss on the side of her head. "Isn't that right, baby?" I ask while watching his eyes cloud with jealousy.

"What are you doing, Rocco?" she hisses in a whisper.

"Just having a little fun. He needs to know you're mine, and he needs to back off." She glares at me. I know she doesn't like how I've handled it, but I'm a protector at heart, and I won't allow him to get too close to what's mine.

Anthony looks from me to Jasmine. "Are you two together?"

I remain quiet, knowing he'll probably take the news better if it's from her. "We are," she says, then makes a noise in her throat like she's going to say more but stops herself.

He nods his head, defeat splayed across his face. "Oh. I figured one day you two would end up together. It's great to see you, Jasmine," he says, then he walks away, rejoining the friend he was with.

"That was weird, right?" she asks me when we're finally seated in a booth waiting for our breakfast.

I grab her hand from across the table and lace our fingers together. "It was, but only because he still wants you. And he doesn't like that we're together."

She nods. "Why has everyone else known we were going to end up together, while we were completely oblivious?"

I laugh before I kiss her knuckles. "I wish I knew. It would have saved a lot of trouble." For the rest of breakfast, we talk about what we should include on the agenda for my next visit. Central Park, Radio City, and a White Sox game are mentioned. It all sounds doable. I know I've been trying to convince Jasmine to come home to Chicago, but the more time I spend here with her, the more I see its charm. It's not home, but I've had a fantastic time exploring and discovering with her. It's been some of my favorite memories so far.

Chapter 27

Jasmine

With each visit Rocco makes, the more comfortable I grow living here. While that's fantastic if I want to stay, but I still don't, and I don't know how to tell him or anyone else that. It feels like admitting that I'm lonely and unhappy is admitting defeat. And I'm prepared to do that. My pride is getting the better of me, no matter how many conversations I have with Rocco and Nicole about it.

On one of his visits, we stuff the entire weekend with activities. We have plans to watch the Yankees versus the White Sox game at Yankee Stadium. Beforehand, we go on our second zoo visit. This time it's to the Bronx Zoo. I could honestly stay here all day. It's massive, and I know we won't see it all. But Rocco is set on making sure I see all my favorites: the sea lions, giraffes, gorillas, and tigers.

"The butterfly garden is that way. Ready?" Rocco asks while looking at the map.

"Rocco," I object. You can't miss the smirk on his face. Since we were kids, butterflies have scared me. Logically, I know they're harmless, but the way they flit around and land on people is disconcerting to me. I like to gaze from afar, but the thought of being trapped in a building with hundreds of them creeps me out.

With a chuckle, he points the opposite way. "Are you ready for your giraffe encounter?"

"What? We already saw the giraffes. What do you mean 'encounter'?" I ask in surprise.

He grabs my hand and tugs me back over to the zoo center and approaches an employee. "Hi. Is this where we meet for our giraffe meet-and-greet?"

The employee nods. "Welcome to the Bronx Zoo. I'm Marigold. You must be Rocco and Jasmine."

Rocco squeezes my hand. I'm sure he can feel the excitement coursing through my veins. I'm practically vibrating. "We are," I answer.

"Great. Let's go introduce you to our herd." We head back to the giraffe enclosure while she tells us about the group of giraffes they have at the zoo. The entire experience is only about a half hour, but Marigold crams it full of information, and the giraffes are even more incredible up close.

We grab a couple dollar slices of pizza for a quick lunch before we head over to Yankee Stadium to catch the pre-game warm-ups. Neither one of us are big baseball fans, but we agreed it would be fun to catch a game when the White Sox were in town. From what I've heard, these two teams have gone back and forth with wins and losses.

Three hours later, at the top of the 7th inning, the Yankees have a one-run lead. The weather has been agreeable too, not too hot or rainy. Being in an open stadium could ruin your experience, especially if you're a fair-weather fan.

Throughout the game, I enjoy all the traditional baseball snacks. Rocco heard about a special Wagyu beef burger, but by the time he gets over to that section, they've already sold out of the ninety-nine patties they prepare every game. So he settles for a regular burger, sweet potato fries, and a chocolate milkshake and seems quite happy with his choice.

When the game is over, the Yankees win by three runs. Yesterday, the White Sox beat them 2-1. Tomorrow, they have the last game between the two teams for the season. Riding home on the subway, we're surround by fans in Yankees gear. Talk about the game seems to be on just about everyone's lips, and it's loud. I'm thankful the game hadn't been between the Yankees and the Mets. Who knows what that would've been like.

When we get back to my apartment, we snuggle on the couch and plan out the next day. Rocco booked a later flight than usual, so we have a full day to explore. We decide to hit up Central Park again.

My exposure to it has been limited to the two times Rocco and I have been there, and the place is huge, so there's more for us to do. We book an early morning walking tour that not only shares the architecture and history of the park, it includes the shooting locales of many of the movies I remember from childhood.

The next morning, I yawn as I stretch to reach the to-go cup of coffee Rocco hands me before we head down into the subway. "Thank you," I mumble as another yawn threatens to escape.

"Hopefully, this and the fresh park air will wake you up," he says as he pulls me close. The warmth of his body reminds me of the comfortable bed he pulled me from not that long ago. I've discovered being naked and having him wrapped around me all night is the best way to sleep. It makes it almost impossible to leave our little love nest. *Love nest?* I guess that accurately describes it because I'm hopelessly in love with my best friend. I just haven't told him yet.

When we walk past the carousel, he tugs on my hand. "Want to go ride it?"

I smile and pull him toward the ticket booth.

After we've paid and waited for our turn, he stands beside me with his hand on my back as I sit on my brightly colored circus horse.

"Do you remember doing this at the state fair when we were kids?" I ask. We'd ridden it every year until he declared at eleven that he was too cool for it.

That broke my heart a little. But now, seeing him fully embrace it with me, the decades-old hurt heals over.

He looks up at me and smiles.

"I love you, Rocco," I confess, not expecting him to say anything in return but just needing to finally admit it out loud. He wraps his arms around me, burying his head in my side. When the ride ends, he helps me off the horse and leads me away from the carousel and over to a park bench.

"Let's sit," he says before lowering down and pulling me with him. I laugh as I almost land on his lap. Straightening myself, I turn to him and meet the most gorgeous brown eyes. Reaching up, Rocco cups my face and brings our lips together. Moving slowly, he passionately kisses me. When he's done, he pulls back, nibbling my lower lip, and lowers his forehead to mine. We're both breathing heavily, our warm breath mixing between us. He rasps my name out, and I pull back, suddenly feeling uneasy.

"I'm not good at this," he admits, which only confuses me more.

"Good at what?" I question, wringing my hands in my lap. My heart rate picks up, and I'm dying to know what he'll say.

"Feelings. I'm not good at identifying them," he murmurs, then hangs his head.

Wait. Did he think I told him I loved him because I was expecting him to say it back?

"Rocco, wait. Is this because I told you I love you?" He doesn't make eye contact but nods his head.

I rub his shoulder, trying to get him to look at me. He tries, but he can't seem to maintain eye contact. "I didn't tell you that because I expected you to say it back. I've just known I felt that way for a while, and I couldn't hold it in any longer." He nods again. "Please look at me," I beg, questioning if I made a mistake and whether it would ruin things between us.

When his gaze meets mine, his eyes are full of emotion.

"Did what I say scare you?" I ask.

He finally clears his throat and speaks. "It didn't scare me at all. Honestly, it made me really happy. It feels amazing to hear." He smiles, but it's forced.

"Okay," I hedge, hoping he'll say more.

"Truth is, I don't really know how to tell you what I feel. You're my best friend, but you are so much more than that. You're the woman of my dreams, and I am completely in love with you too."

Not expecting to hear that, I let out a gasp. This is what my heart has always wanted to hear, but instead of fully enjoying it, it's colored with a hint of sadness. In a few hours, Rocco's going back home to Chicago while I'm staying here. I lower my head, trying to hide my disappointment.

He leans over, runs his finger down my cheekbone, and tips up my chin. "Jaz, talk to me."

For the first time, I'm at a loss for words. I don't

know what to say. I put us in this predicament. It's my fault we're in two different states. "What do we do now?" I whisper.

Rocco pulls me onto his lap and wraps his muscular arms around me, holding me tight. "We don't have to make any big decisions right now. Can't we just enjoy being together?"

I nod my head against his chest, my thoughts and fears a chaotic mess vying for headspace. Opening my mouth, it all tumbles out in a shaky voice. "But what happens when the season starts and we don't see each other regularly? Will things change for you and you'll decide it's too much?"

Rocco squeezes me tighter and says, "Jaz, we've survived several seasons and remained close using phone calls, FaceTime, and visits. I understand your concerns. Will this be different? Yes, I bet it will. The stakes are higher. The feelings more intense. But aren't we more invested in making us work?" His words are the comfort my fragile heart needs. He places a soft, chaste kiss on my lips. He is the balm to my soul.

I moan softly, and he pulls away. "What is it, babe?"

"I just wish you didn't have to leave in a few hours. I really love when you visit. It makes everything better." Rocco gives me his megawatt smile, making my heart gallop in my chest.

"I wish I were staying too." He spins my body so I'm straddling him on the bench. I freeze, feeling uncomfortable. I know we aren't doing anything indecent, but there are families everywhere. "Rocco, what are you doing? There are people all around."

With our gazes locked on each other, he confesses, "Babe, I can't get enough of you. I'm not going anywhere."

"Rocco." I sigh. He knows exactly what I need to hear.

"I love you, Jasmine." Every time he says it, I feel giddy. Then he gives me a panty-dropping grin that has me shifting on his lap. "Whoa, babe. You have to stop that or this may become a show, and it won't be family friendly." I laugh as I lower my forehead to his.

"I love you too, Rocco. So much." He pulls me into a tight hug, and I'm not sure how long we hold on to each other.

A few hours later, at my apartment, we hug goodbye before he heads to the subway to ride back to JFK for his flight. It's been another unforgettable visit. One for the books.

Every place we visited, Rocco made special. Without him, I wouldn't have experienced so much of New York. But it hasn't made me desperate to stay like you might think. Instead, it just marked items off my dwindling New York City bucket list. I still want to go to another Broadway show, and Melinda and I have plans to do that in a week.

The last thing on my list is to experience Christmas in New York. I want to see all the beautifully decorated window fronts and, of course, the magnificent tree at Rockefeller Center. Most of all, I want to experience all of it with Rocco, especially skating on the iconic Rockefeller rink.

My thoughts about spending another few months here leave me feeling divided. Through our exploration, I've fallen in love with New York. But it isn't home. It has a unique charm all of its own, and the longer I'm here, the more familiar it becomes. Is that because I've been experiencing it with Rocco? With him by my side, I've developed a confidence that I'm not sure I'd be able to maintain if he wasn't with me. And in a few months, he'll be absent. When hockey season starts, he won't be able to visit often. Or maybe ever. Like he said earlier, I'll have to see how it goes and make my decision from that.

Chapter 28

Rocco

At Lucas and Samantha's annual Fourth of July party, Christian and Monica invited us all out to the Fields Farm for an event later this month. They've been rather secretive about the whole thing. All I know is that it's her family's cow farm, and they mentioned something about a barn dance. I don't know what that is, but there's no way I'll be caught dead in Wranglers, cowboy boots, or plaid. But the rest of my buddies are going, so I'm going too.

Ace is vibrating with excitement as we make the drive to the farm. He even traded his standard ball cap for the Stetson he wore when he first joined the team. I haven't seen it in years because we'd teased him about it. The ribbing was good natured, and he'd handled it like a pro. But he still stopped wearing it. If you spend more than five minutes with him, it's obvious he's all country. He doesn't need the hat to tell you. The drawl, manners, and saying y'all are so ingrained in who he is. Truth is, Ace is a stand-up guy in every way possible, and I'm lucky to say he's one of my best friends. He was raised on a farm, so going to the Fields Farm probably feels a bit like going home.

Days later, when we are at the farm, I hear the ladies gush. "Those are adorable," they say to Monica's brothers who have shown Sam and Lian, Shiloh's boys, the baby cows.

"Can we touch them?" Sam asks while Lian edges closer to the Great Dane-sized Holstein calf. Josiah, Monica's youngest brother, steps closer to help them do just that.

Ace moves closer to me. "Isn't this cool?"

"Sure man," I agree. "Remind you of home?"

He lifts his hat and wipes his brow before setting it back on his head. "Yeah, it does. We didn't have milk cows, but Ma always wanted a Longhorn, so for their fifth wedding anniversary, Dad got her one."

I laugh. "Wow. He was keeping the romance alive."

Ace grins. "They're still married and in love, so obviously it worked for them."

Looking across the farm, I see an area set up with chairs near Monica's parents' house. I elbow Ace. "What do you think that's for?"

He shrugs. "I've been to plenty of barn dances, and there is usually limited seating. But that, over there, reminds me of Sunday morning church."

"Maybe it's for something else," I say just as

Monica's other brothers, Mike and Will, show up to give us a tour of the farm.

An hour later, we're shown to the mysterious chair setup. Looking down, a paper has been placed on every chair. I peer closer and my eyes go wide with what I see. I elbow Ace again. "Holy shit. They're finally doing it."

He laughs. "I reckon it's time. They've been after each other for so long."

A half an hour later, we're directed over to a decorated barn to celebrate our friends finally saying "I do." Looking around the large space, I'm impressed with how beautiful it is. *Jasmine would love this.* Thoughts of the woman I love flood my brain. I wish she were here with me like she's been at so many Steel events as my plus one. Of course, back then, we were just friends.

Even now, months after getting together, we still haven't told anyone about the change in our relationship. At first it was because we wanted to keep it close, protected. But now, I'm scared to share it because what if she stays in New York and we don't work out? Losing her, now that she's mine, would absolutely devastate me. And I don't want to give my friends an up close and personal seat to my heartbreak. *But what if it doesn't end in heartbreak?* I'm lost in thought as everyone around me enjoys the reception honoring Christian and Monica. Maybe it's all the love and hope saturating the air, but my determination to bring Jaz home to Chicago has been reinvigorated.

Ace wanders over to me, sweaty and red faced. "Rocco, they're about to cut the cake." He smiles widely, like a kid on Christmas.

"Why do you look like you just skated drills?" I ask, taking in his happy, yet exhausted, appearance.

He slumps down into the chair next to me. "Because I just taught everyone how to do the Cha Cha Slide. Didn't you see?"

"I didn't. Sorry. I must have been lost in thought," I admit, while running my hand through my hair.

Ace grins at me. "Thoughts of what? Or who?" He waggles his eyebrows at me.

I sigh. "It's nothing. You said something about cake?" I ask, trying to distract him from any unwelcome interrogation.

"Could I have everyone's attention, please? It's time for me to make a toast before you hear from the bride and groom. Then we'll eat cake!" I hear Mike say over the speaker system. Clapping and cheers erupt from the kids in attendance. They'll need some sugar to keep them running for the next hour.

"This is amazing," Ace says as he shoves another bite of chocolate cake in his mouth. He isn't kidding. This is the best cake I've ever eaten. I'm not surprised when I hear that Kenzie at CakeStop made it. Samantha found her a few years ago and has been hiring her ever since for any Steel party she hosts. *Jaz loved her death by chocolate cupcakes Samantha had at the Fourth of July barbeque.*

<hr>

Although the weekend's festivities were filled with fun and laughter, it felt like something was missing. Like some*one* was missing. I'm desperate to get back to New York to see Jasmine next weekend. But instead of flying by like I hoped, the week drags by painfully slowly, like it's a sloth trying to make its way through quicksand.

Ten thousand and eighty minutes later, on the steps of her work building, I'm pulling her into my arms. Finally. Her delicious body melts against mine, and for the first time in weeks, it feels like I can breathe. Everything is right in my world again. When her lips find mine, our breaths intertwine and our pulses sync. *I never want to let her go.* Our hello is short-lived. I give her a quick kiss before I drag her to the subway, eager to get her back to her apartment.

Snuggled together on the couch, I can't remember ever being so happy. Pulling my lips from hers is an exercise in self-torture. But I need to tell her what my heart is screaming. Lowering my forehead to hers, I say, "I've missed you so much. I love you, babe." She sighs and nods her head against mine.

"I've missed you so much too." She lifts away and

looks into my eyes, her green eyes sparkling. "I love you. And I'm so glad you're here."

Wrapping my arms around her and tugging her to my chest, I declare, "There's no place I'd rather be."

Relaxed against each other, Jaz turns her head. "Do I smell chocolate?"

I laugh but say nothing.

She sniffs at the air, then pushes against my chest. "I'm not kidding. I smell chocolate."

Again, I laugh. She hits my chest. "Rocco, do you smell that? I know I've smelled it before. And we both know it isn't New York. Whatever I'm smelling is decadent."

"It's definitely not New York. I may have brought you a treat from home," I tease.

She licks her lips and practically trembles with excitement. "What did you bring me?"

Reaching down, I retrieve the pink box labeled CakeStop I hand carried on my flight, and hand it to her. Her eyes widen, and a dazzling smile stretches across her perfect pink lips.

"You brought me something from CakeStop? Is it Kenzie's famous death by chocolate cupcakes?"

"Guess you'll have to open it to see."

She carefully opens the box and peers inside. "I've never had these before. They look divine. What flavor are they?"

Smiling, I answer, "I know the death by chocolate is your favorite, but these are new to the menu, and I think you'll love them. They're called head over heels and they're chocolate with a raspberry mousse filling."

Jasmine takes one out of the box, eyeing it carefully. "I love the name." *I love it too.* Then she takes a bite. The moan that falls from her lips is purely sinful, hitting me straight in the cock. Pushing against my zipper, I want her to moan like that against me. She takes another bite, and her eyes roll back and she hums in her throat. I look at the box. That's strange. It doesn't come with a warning label. *May cause spontaneous orgasms.* Hearing her noises of pleasure has me rock hard and needy.

"Jaz," I pant. Her eyes blink open and they're full of happiness.

"Yeah?" she answers in a seductive tone that has my tip leaking.

"Babe, you're going to have to stop moaning before I throw you down on the nearest surface, smear that cupcake all over your naked body, and take my time slowly licking it off you." I readjust myself to make my point.

She forms an O with her mouth before she smiles. "Wanna bite?" she offers in a sultry whisper.

I nod, then lean forward, and she lifts the last bite to her lips and wipes the frosting all over them before she pops the last bit into her mouth. Releasing a growl from my throat, I pin her to the couch. Lifting both her arms above her head, I secure them with my much larger one. With her restrained, I take my other hand

and trail it down her neck, between her breasts, and to her waist. She squirms beneath me, but I'm not backing down. I drop my head to hover my mouth above hers, then slowly lick at her lips, capturing all the rich frosting she left behind. She tries to press her lips to mine, but I pull back until I'm just out of reach. She whimpers.

"What's the trouble, Jaz?" I ask, faking that she's not having any effect on me.

"Please, kiss me, Rocco," she whines. I answer by licking across her lips, and she whimpers again. Taking the hand that was on her waist, I move it to her lower lips and squeeze past her panties. They're already soaked with her juices. Sweeping my greedy fingers through her hot folds, her hips flex. Something primal builds within me, and I growl. "You taste delicious, Jasmine. I can't wait to get my lips on all of you."

A shiver rocks her body as goose bumps cover her. "Mmmm," she moans as her hips chase my fingers.

"Does that feel good, babe? Do you want more?" I taunt her.

She releases a breath from her puckered lips. "P-please, Rocco."

Her begging is just what I need to spur me forward. Quickly, I remove my fingers from her. Once they're out of her pants, I move them to my mouth for a brief taste. "Fuck. Jaz, you taste like heaven." Not at all satisfied, I rise from the couch, lift her up and throw her over my shoulder, and head to her bed.

I've been desperate for her before, but this, right now... I don't have the words to describe how badly I need her. It isn't about the orgasms we're chasing. It's more. It's *her.* I want to invade every part of her, just like she's done to me. I want us to be one forever. And the thought of that no longer scares me.

An hour later, after we've both succumbed to multiple orgasms, we lie facing each other, naked, sweaty, and sated, with our fingers intertwined between us. Like always, we end up talking about Chicago and our friends back home.

"It sounds like you miss Chicago," I say carefully, pushing a few stray hairs behind her ear. She lowers her head before she responds, and I question whether I'll like what she has to say.

"I do, Rocco. So much," she admits.

Hope flickers in my heart. "So why don't you just move home?" I ask, trying to sound the least confrontational I can.

She flops to her back, pushes out a deep breath, and groans. "I wish it were that easy."

"What's so hard about it?" I question. I'm not trying to push or bully her. I really just want to understand what's keeping her here when I know she wants to move home.

She lies silently next to me for a few minutes, and I wonder if she's fallen asleep. I look over and see her eyes are closed. Maybe this wasn't the right time to have this conversation. With my mind spinning, there's no way I'm going to fall asleep. Sitting up, I slip my hand from hers, and she startles.

"Rocco." Her saying my name is all it takes to stop me.

"I thought you were asleep," I explain.

She shakes her head. "No, I was just thinking. I know you deserve an answer to your question. I'm just really confused."

Even though she's still on her back, I pull her body to mine. "What has you so confused? Am I putting too much pressure on you?"

She laughs. "No. I know you want me to move home, and I want to do that too…"

"Why do I feel like you're about to add a 'but' to your answer?" I ask.

She turns toward me and says, "Because I am. It feels like if I don't give New York enough of a chance, I'm a failure. But it's hard to justify giving it a fair shot when all I want to do is move home."

"How long do you think it would take for you to feel you've given it a fair shot?" It's already been over seven months. I'm not sure what I'll do or say if she says years. Waiting for her answer is a practice in patience. And guess what? I'm not known for mine. I just want to know a timeline so I can mark it on my calendar and start counting down.

"I think I need to be here at least a year in order to be able to make a decision."

Looking for any loophole I can find, I ask, "Is it a

year from when you accepted the job, moved here, or began your job? Those are three separate dates."

Jaz smiles at me. "You want me home now, don't you?" Then the sassy little siren waggles her eyebrows at me.

I clench my fists and gruffly answer, "No, I wanted you home months ago. In fact, I never wanted you to leave to begin with."

"But if I'd never left, we might not be together now." Her words ring true, and I know she's right.

"Okay, but what do you say now?" I push, needing to know how much longer she plans to stay in this city.

"On the year anniversary of the day I accepted the job here, I'll make my decision. Okay?"

I nod, knowing I need to not push. "What day is that?"

She smiles at me. "It's December tenth." I want to groan out loud when I realize that's a little over four more months before I'll have an answer.

"Okay. If I can't convince you to move home right now, maybe I can convince you to at least come home for a visit," I say as I crawl over her, placing kisses along her naked hip. I spread her legs wide to accommodate my shoulders, then lock eyes with her before I even touch her. She wiggles in front of me, her pussy wet and glistening.

"What are you thinking?" she asks. Licking my lips, I lower to her center and drag my tongue through her soft folds. "R-Rocco," she pants, and I lick her again. Her hips raise with me. I move one hand over her pelvis to push it back down to the bed.

"Stay," I growl against her in between tongue lashes to her clit.

As she tries to follow my command, I feel her hips strain and her clit throb. She's so close. "Please," she whimpers. I slide one finger down toward her entrance and trace it, dipping the tip in occasionally. She makes an exasperated groan in her throat each time I deny her what she wants. After the third circle, I slide my finger into her, and she lets out a moan that makes my heart rate gallop. *I love that sound.* Pumping my finger into her makes her even wetter. I add another, and her muscles grip my fingers like an anaconda. I'm unable to move until she relaxes just enough for me to resume thrusting.

"Does that feel good?" I ask, already knowing the answer. Her garbled response tells me she's moments away from exploding. I add a third finger and lower my mouth back to her clit. I take deep sucks on it, flicking my tongue back and forth. Jasmine thrusts her hips forward and grinds against my face. Her juices cover my tongue, lips, cheeks. She's riding my fingers and my face simultaneously, and it's taking everything within me not to come all over her. My cock is so hard, I can feel my heartbeat pulsing against my thigh where it's pressed. When she finally comes a few moments later, I'm blown away by how breathtaking she is. Her blushed cheeks, her wild hair, her pleasure-filled eyes.

Her lips are slightly parted, and her pink tongue peeks out to wet them.

"So, about that visit. I was thinking you could come to Chicago for our first home series, and we could finally tell everyone we're together. How does that sound?"

"That sounds nice," she answers in a dreamy voice. I place a tender kiss on her lips before she falls asleep. Staring at her, I can't imagine my life without her. It's strange to think that the first time I fell in love, it would be with my best friend. I guess it was fate all along. Everyone always said we'd end up together. Guess we had to get out of our own way first.

Chapter 29

Jasmine

S tepping off the plane in Chicago, everything hits me. It's odd being back in the city where I was born and raised, and it just being a visit. The sights, sounds, and smells are so familiar and comforting. *Why did I ever leave?* Oh right, I needed space to figure some things out. And I've done that.

Less than a year ago, I was running from this city with a broken and tattered heart. I arrived in New York sad, confused, and unsettled. Over many months of self-discovery and exploration, I can admit that I'm the happiest I've ever been. And so much of that has to do with Rocco and his unwavering support and love. He's shown me what unconditional love is.

Last month, when Rocco returned to training with the team for their preseason, I was sad. It meant his visits would stop. Not that I need him near, but I want him near. So, we made a plan for me to come home for the first game of the season.

I didn't tell anyone I was coming back. It's going to be a surprise for everyone when I show up in the family box on Saturday. Stepping off the escalator to head toward baggage claim, something catches my eye. Standing there, dressed in a baggy sweatshirt and joggers, is a large man with a Steel cap pulled down low over his eyes. He's holding a sign with my name on it. It looks fairly benign until I get closer and see hand-drawn hearts all over it. From a distance, I wasn't sure what they were. Right away, I suspect who it is, but my suspicions aren't proven until his gorgeous smile appears. He's trying his hardest to be incognito, and it's adorable.

Speed walking across the baggage claim, I launch myself at him when I'm only a foot away. Rocco's muscular arms catch me easily and pull me to his warm chest. "Jaz," he whispers into my neck before he places a kiss there. The feeling of his lips on my skin is like a drug, and I crave more. Wiggling in his arms, I want to see him. Feel his lips on mine. Tell him I love him to his face.

"Thank you for coming to pick me up," I whisper against his chest where he's tucked me.

Placing a kiss on my head, he answers, "Well, I am the only one who knows you're in town. And tonight I have big plans. I get you all to myself."

His words make my heart flutter, and I cannot wait

to be alone with him. "What do you say we get my bag and get out of here?"

Rocco nods, then gives me a kiss before he turns me back toward the conveyor belt, which has already begun to turn. I take a step away, and he smacks my butt, causing me to jump. His deep, sexy laugh makes me smile. I look at him over my shoulder, and he gives me a sultry wink, letting me know there's more to come. *I can't wait.* My heart thumps in my chest as I make my way over to grab my bag. Five minutes later, we're in his Range Rover, making out like we haven't seen each other in years. When my chest tightens and I need air, I pull away from him, panting. "Can we go home?" I beg.

He smiles. "I love the sound of that."

"What?"

"You calling my place home," he says as he kisses my lips again. *I love it too.* Can you imagine? Me sharing a home with Rocco. That would be a dream come true.

Without another word, he pulls out of the parking garage and heads to his house right outside the city. He bought his house a year after he signed with the Steel, and has been slowly upgrading parts of it. It was a true fixer-upper, but with him being single and gone for a large majority of the year, it didn't need to be in perfect condition right away. In fact, he finished the remodel shortly after I moved to New York, so this is my first time to see it entirely finished.

Pushing through the garage and into the mudroom, I kick off my shoes and hang my jacket and purse like it's my home. Rocco follows with my suitcase and sets it to the side to follow me farther in.

"Rocco, this is stunning," I gush as I enter his mostly white kitchen. Splashes of gray give it a contemporary, homey feel. I run my fingertips over the large, white-speckled marble countertop. Bright stainless appliances keep it looking sharp and clean. Turning around, I excitedly smile at him. "Please show me more."

He returns the smile and beckons me forward. Hand in hand, we walk through the rest of the house, which is also done in shades of white and gray. He's furnished it all too, making it feel like a real home.

"This is incredible. I love it." He grins at the compliment, pulling me into his arms. Turning to his chest, I ask, "Can I see the upstairs too?"

"Go on." He nods toward the stairs. Without a second thought, I take off. At the top, he's created a state-of-the-art gym, filled with everything he'd ever need to keep himself in peak condition. *And he certainly is.* Ducking out into the wooden hallway, I continue on my exploration. Another two rooms sit empty, but they look to be the perfect size for bedrooms. "You should turn one of these into a man cave," I suggest, as he follows behind.

He chuckles. "I already have one of those in the basement."

My mouth falls open. "Really?"

Standing with his hands on his hips, he smirks at me before he answers. "Yes, one room is a movie theater, and the other is a game room."

Stepping closer, I run my hands up his chest and purr, "Can we watch a movie down there tonight?"

"As long as it isn't some chick-flick," he replies. Even though I don't really care, I pretend to pout, sticking out my lip and giving him my best puppy dog eyes.

He shakes his head, then licks his lips. "Jasmine." My name on his lips is like liquid crack to my body. It responds immediately, seeking the high only he can deliver, and he notices, flashing me a cocky smirk. *I'm in trouble.* As he steps closer, he says nothing, but his intense stare speaks volumes. My knees grow weak and my throat goes dry.

Swallowing the reaction I'm having, I force out my next words. "What's next on the tour?"

"My bedroom," he answers in a deep, throaty growl that sends shivers rushing down my spine.

Images of all the things we could do in there flash through my mind, making my heart race and my panties wet. "Want to see it?" he asks, and I nod excitedly. His hand finds mine and he drags me toward his lair. *Holy hell, is it hot in here?*

When he pushed open door, I see he has a king-sized bed in the middle of the room. All the furniture is black, and his bedding is snow white. Across the room, above his dresser, is a collection of artistic black and white photographs. Filled with curiosity, I step closer, and Rocco comes with me. When my eyes focus on them, I suddenly realize they're all familiar.

The first one in the grouping is of us as children. It was taken the summer I moved across the street from him. We aren't looking at the camera, but the moment that was captured by his nonna is one that I won't forget. Rocco was trying to teach me to ride a skateboard. He and his brothers rode them all over the neighborhood, and I'd always watched them with complete fascination. Toward the end of that first summer, after I'd begged him relentlessly for a week straight, I eventually promised him my monthly allowance as payment for teaching me to skate. Nonna snapped a picture as he was teaching me how to balance on one foot. He was also trying to get me to use the other to propel me forward. I was really struggling with it, and the picture shows my intense concentration.

Smiling, I remember how it felt to have all of Rocco's attention on me. Within days of meeting him, I knew that we'd be forever friends. It only took mere moments for me to recognize how special he was. "Of all the things we've shared, that is one of my favorites," I explain as I point to the picture.

Rocco laughs. "Mine too." He steps next to me, rests a hand on my back and confesses, "I wasn't sure you'd ever learn to skate."

Remembering back, I laugh. Rocco had been so patient with me. "Me either. And once I'd figured it out, it wasn't as fun as it seemed."

"I don't remember, did you ever do it again?"

"Nope."

Rocco wraps his arms around me, and we shift to the next photo. The photo stirs up so many emotions. We knew Rocco was going to be drafted into the NHL, but we didn't know what team he'd end up with. For weeks, it preoccupied me with worry that he would end up on the other side of the country. Because I stayed in Chicago for college, he invited me to go to Philadelphia with him and his parents to witness his invitation in person. Rocco's mom snapped a picture of us hugging just after the NHL commissioner announced that the Chicago Steel had selected him for the upcoming season. "That was such an exceptional moment," I whisper. Even today, I still remember the feeling of relief that washed over me as he hugged me tight to his muscular chest.

"It was," Rocco confirms. "I'm so glad Chicago signed me. They're the best organization to work for. I never want to go anywhere else."

"I'm really glad to hear that," I say as I snuggle into his side.

My eyes fall to the last picture in the collection. It's the most recent. When Rocco visited me in New York last month, we shared a moment I will never forget. Even though we aren't standing in front of a famous landmark, it doesn't mean it's any less special or meaningful. That day will forever be burned into my mind. We'd asked a passerby to take our picture. Standing in front of the rowboat we rented, and wearing faded orange life jackets, we hugged each other and smiled like fools. That day started out ordinary, but what happened in that boat changed everything for me. During our drifting in the middle of the still lake, Rocco admitted his feelings for me, and nothing has been the same between us since.

Remembering the emotion of that day and those that have followed, I smile, knowing it's just the beginning of the next chapter of our lives. I'm no fortune teller, but I'm confident our relationship will go the distance. Rocco has been, and will always be, such an important part of my life.

He moves behind me and wraps his arms around my waist, placing gentle kisses in to the curve of my neck. I tilt my head, giving him better access, and savor the heat of his lips as they trail across my skin. *It isn't enough. I want more.* Feeling needy, I turn in his arms and wrap my arms around his neck. Pressing my lips to his, our gentle kisses turn heated in minutes, and he grabs my hips, hoisting me in the air. Effortlessly, I wrap my legs around his waist. My center resting over his hard-as-steel cock. The heat exchanged between our bodies unlocks unbridled lust for this man. As our tongues duel, I grind my hips hard against him. He moans into my mouth and locks his hands on my hips, tugging me closer. The friction between us in unbelievable. "Ahhh," I groan into his mouth.

Rocco rips his mouth from mine, then stalks to his bed and tosses me into the middle of the mattress. "Undress, Jaz. I need you naked," he growls as he pulls his sweatshirt over his head. Seeing he's serious, I tug my tank top over my head and shimmy out of my cotton leggings. He licks his lips when he sees me in a matching bra and panty set.

"Is that new? Did you wear it for me?" he questions as he slowly lowers his joggers.

Nodding, I go up on my knees and crawl toward him. He drops his pants, leaving him in just his black boxer briefs. As confident as ever, Rocco puts his hands on his trim waist. Stopping in front of him, I reach out and trace my fingers along his Adonis belt. Goosebumps cover his skin, and I smile. *I did that.* My tongue darts out, and I lean forward, seeing his cock is playing hide 'n seek in his waistband. I place a delicate kiss on the head and he flinches. Wanting confirmation, my eyes flash up and see Rocco's brown eyes are a mess of lust and desire. Just thinking about that excites me. Instead of responding like a giddy teenager, I channel all the sex appeal I can muster. I lean forward again and trace the outline of his hard cock with my finger before I give it a firm squeeze. Licking and then blowing on the tip before I lie back on the bed and wait for him.

"Are you trying to kill me?" he asks as he pulls

down his boxers and fists his cock. *Why is that so damn hot?* I watch as he unravels before me. His body is shaking with need as he drags his thumb over his weeping slit. I lick my lips. "Jasmine," he growls, sending a shiver down my back. I want him now.

"Fuck me, Rocco," I demand. He shakes his head no but settles his hot, defined body over mine. My lady parts are screaming. "Do it now." But Rocco is taking his time, making me squirm beneath him. I need to feel him inside me. "Please," I whimper.

Crawling up my body, his skin rubs against mine, and everywhere we connect feels like a lightning strike. Frustrated and overheated, I blow out a breath just as he reaches my neck. He presses his lips against the soft skin and whispers, "You're beautiful. You were made for me. I love you." His words are gentle but filled with so much meaning.

"Rocco," I mewl, my heart feeling like it's pounding out of my chest. By the time he reaches my lips, they're dry from my constant panting. He rids me of my undergarments before he takes the entire night to cherish every hill and valley of my body.

Chapter 30

Rocco

When my alarm goes off at nine the next morning, reminding me I have an early skate before the game tonight, I drag my exhausted body from underneath Jasmine's. She moans as she snuggles deeper into the blankets. I kiss her lips softly before I head to the shower.

Two hours later, I'm walking back into my house to find Jaz curled up on my couch with a cup of coffee in one hand and her Kindle in the other. Sneaking up behind her, I'm able to read over her shoulder for a minute before she notices me. *Holy shit.* My eyes go wide as I read over a sizzling scene that involves cuffs, a blindfold, a feather, and whipped cream. *Sign me up for that.* I keep reading, taking mental notes along the way, until I hear a giggle. Knowing I'm caught, I slowly turn my head to her. Sitting quietly, wearing a sexy smirk, is my highly amused girlfriend.

"See something you like?" she teases.

Hell yes! I lick my lips before I answer. "I never knew you were into BDSM," I say. My heart rate speeds up, intrigued by the possibilities of the conversation.

She shrugs. "I've never tried it, but the way this is written... it's making me curious. At least the light stuff. I'm not ready for the whips, butt plugs, or Saint Andrew's cross."

My mind fills with idea upon idea of what we could try. I look at Jaz, who remains quiet. I let the idea go, assuming the conversation has been sidelined.

"Are you hungry?" I ask. Her emerald green eyes dance. "I called in an order to Mateo's before I left the arena, and it should be here soon."

"Really?" she excitedly asks as a beautiful smile stretches across her face. "I mean, it's not your nonna's cooking, but in a pinch, it'll do." Seeing that I'm one hundred percent Italian, eating at Mateo's is almost sacrilegious.

"I promise I'll take you home to see Nonna and my folks next time you're in town, and you can eat as many meatballs as you want." Her eyes twinkle as she laughs.

I'm careful not to overeat, as the first game of the season is tonight. Shortly after, we head up to my bedroom so I can take my pre-game nap. Snuggled up to Jasmine's side, I think about our future and what it could be. She lazily runs her hand through my hair while she reads, and it's easy to relax and drift off. I want this forever.

A few hours later, we head to the arena. Even though she's early, I show Jaz up to the family box. She's the first one there, but I'm confident the rest of our friends will arrive shortly. I wish I could stick around for their reaction, but I have to head to the locker room to get ready for the game.

Sitting on the bench and pulling on my gear, Coach comes wandering in. "Heard Jasmine is here." I nod before he walks away.

I'm beyond excited and unable to hide my smile. Soon, Ace is next to me. "She's here? Why didn't you tell us? Are we all going out after the game?"

Laughing at him, I hold up my hands. "Whoa, buddy. She's flying home tomorrow. It's just a quick trip. She's not even seeing her parents."

Ace frowns. Other than Nicole, he's been the biggest advocate for us getting together. I elbow him and whisper, "It's all part of my plan."

Shocked, he turns to me. "What plan?"

"I plan to make her mine and bring her home." His eyes go wide as my words sink in.

Lowering his voice, he asks, "Did you make her yours?" I just nod. "What?" he screeches. The entire locker room goes silent. I frown at him for drawing attention to us.

Josh, already dressed for the game, saunters up as I'm pulling my jersey over my head. "What are you guys talking about?" We both look at each other, refusing to answer. This isn't the first time we've been the center of the entire team's focus, but usually, it's over something one of us can easily explain. That's not the case today. Ace doesn't want to share my confession, and I'm not sure I'm ready to handle the teasing of all my teammates.

"Does this have anything to do with Jasmine being at tonight's game?" he asks, looking around the locker room. I grow nervous as everyone's eyes focus on me. *Maybe I can give them a half-truth and they'll let it go.* It's worth a shot.

Clearing my throat, I say, "Jasmine is in town for the first game of the season to cheer us all on." I let out a breath, hoping they'll drop it.

But I'm not that lucky. "Is that the only reason?" Josh needles. *What does he know?* Did Jaz already tell the ladies we're together, and Kenzie sent a message to Josh? Unsure, I know the truth will come out sooner than later. *Just bite the bullet.*

I lift my head, making eye contact with most of my teammates. "She's here visiting me because we're together." I've never seen so many opinionated athletes speechless. Then someone whoops and the locker room goes crazy like we just won the Cup.

Ace stands up and finger whistles, silencing everyone before he yells, "About damn time."

Finally, Coach steps up and we all settle down. "Okay, guys. Let's take that energy to the ice and win our first game of the season." As we head out to the tunnel, each member of my team gives me a "congratulations" and a fist bump. I take it all, wearing a dopey grin on my face.

We do as Coach asks and win the game 3-1. When I push out into the tunnel after I've showered, I walk into a gawking mass of my teammates and their significant others. They're all waiting to see Jaz and me together. Not wanting to leave anyone disappointed, I stroll up to her, drop my bag, and pull her into my arms. Then, just like in all the romcoms she's made me watch over the years, I kiss her like my life depends on it. Whistles, whoops, and hollers fill the surrounding air. Jaz and I both laugh as we separate. "The show's over," I declare before I drag her to the exit. If I only have a few more hours with her before she heads back to New York, I want them to be undisturbed, unhurried, and unleashed. I want this visit to be unforgettable and the last piece to convince her to move home.

Chapter 31

Jasmine

Since my trip home to Chicago two months ago, I've never felt more homesick. I've seen a new side of New York City in the almost eleven months I've been here. Through exploring sights, sounds, and tastes, I have experienced new cultures and people that I'd never been exposed to. The city is a melting pot of so many cultures, and if I'm honest, it's taken a piece of my heart. But all that aside, it still isn't where I need to be if I want to be happy.

I told Rocco I wouldn't feel like I gave New York a fair shot if I didn't spend at least a year here. As that deadline inches closer, I'm sure my decision seems obvious. But as I reflect on it all, I can't deny why I originally left Chicago. It was an experiment in self-exploration. And now I think I've done what I set out to do.

Two weeks ago, I spoke to my old boss about the possibility of returning to my previous branch in the new year. She told me a position had just opened and they were actively interviewing for it. I told her I would submit my application and would love to be considered for the job. Although she couldn't promise me anything, she confirmed that she'd be on the lookout for it.

This last week, I did a Zoom interview, and it went really well. Human resources even called to confirm my current references, which I consider a positive sign. Now I just wait. I booked a ticket home for Christmas so I could see Rocco and our families. Both families are over the moon that we're together. Finally. I'm hoping that for Christmas, I can surprise them all with the news I'm moving home.

It's ten at night on the Tuesday before I'm set to travel home, and I'm surrounded by the clothes I'm planning to pack in my carry-on. When I called my parents last week and told them about my quick trip home, they'd been sad I'm not planning to stay with them. If they think about it, they know I'll spend all my time with Rocco anyway. It just makes sense. But to keep them in the know, I confessed to them we were officially dating. My mom sighed and my dad grumbled, "It's about damn time."

Just as I fold another pair of leggings, my phone rings.

"Hello," I answer without looking.

"Hey, babe. How are you?" Rocco asks. His deep, smooth voice makes my brain mush.

Switching to FaceTime, I smile before I answer. "I'm better now that I'm talking to you."

"Are you packed yet? Did you remember my gift?"

I shake my head as I discreetly fold and pack the new pieces of lingerie I just purchased this afternoon. "What gift? I thought me coming home was your gift."

His hearty laugh fills the line. "It is, but I won't complain if you got me something."

"Rocco, you are worse than a toddler," I tease, earning me another laugh.

"I'm just teasing, Jaz. I was just calling to get your flight information and to tell you I love you." It doesn't matter how many times he's told me that over the past few months, it still surprises me. *I am so lucky*.

Flipping to my reservations, I read off the flight information, sending him a copy of the confirmation.

I hear the ding of his messages. His deep laughter fills the line before he asks, "How'd you know I didn't write it down?"

"Just a guess," I say. "Plus, I didn't see you do it."

"Thanks, babe. I am so ready to see you." I love when Rocco shows me his tender side. Most people wouldn't believe he had one, but I'm lucky enough to have full access to it.

"Me too. I love you. Two more sleeps," I remind him.

He grunts. "Two more sleeps and then I'm not letting you out of my bed for days."

Images of that flash through my mind, and I laugh. "Although that sounds amazing, we still have to visit our parents on Christmas or we'll be in trouble."

He raises his eyebrows, questioning me.

"With Nonna," I answer.

He winces. "Good call, babe. We'll get out of bed for a few hours to see Nonna and eat some of her food. But I don't care about upsetting anyone else."

It's my turn to raise my eyebrows and ask, "What about my father?" We haven't talked about marriage, but Rocco is traditional, and I know that if he ever asks me to marry him, he'll first ask my father.

Rocco slumps his shoulders, and I chuckle. "We'll have plenty of naked time when I get home. Remember, I'm staying with you."

"That's right. I'm enacting a new house rule for your visit. No visitors and no clothes." He grins, obviously proud of his suggestions.

"Deal," I answer as I grab another stack of clothes to fold. "I need to finish my packing and do a few things before I go to bed."

"Two more sleeps," he says again.

I smile. "Two more. Thanks for calling, babe. I love you."

"I love you too. Goodnight, Jaz."

n hour before I fly out, I get a call from my old supervisor.

Chapter 32

Rocco

Just days before Jasmine is set to return, I walk into Trey's office. Immediately, I notice something is different. The air is charged, making the hair on my arms stand on end. Peering around the suite, I look for anything out of the ordinary. Everything looks fine. I nod to Marcie, and her lips are pulled tight. Before I can even speak, Trey flies out of his office. He appears rattled and fidgety. Looking over at Marcie, she offers me a weak smile. *Is that supposed to be comforting?* The man looks unhinged.

"Hey, Rocco. Ready to go?" he calls at me. Nervous, I flash a panicked look at Marcie as he speed walks past me. He's acting like he's competing for an Olympic medal. *Is that a thing?* Marcie shrugs. I turn tail and jog to catch up.

I'm worried. *What is going on?* As we enter the

parking lot, I inform him, "I'm driving. No offense, but you look a bit off. Where are we headed?"

He forces a smile onto his panicked face, and says, "Okay, that's fine. We need to go to the mall."

On the drive to the mall, Trey fidgets continually. I'm barely in a parking spot when he hops out of the car.

"Slow down, Speedy Gonzales. Who's chasing you?" I holler after him. He slows down so I'm able to catch him, and I joke, "Is there a sale we're missing?"

Shaking his head, he answers, "No, I'm just feeling edgy."

I put my hand on his shoulder. "Are you okay?"

He stops and lets a big breath out before he spills his guts. "I'm going to ask Nicole to marry me on Saturday."

"Holy shit, Trey. That's huge," I practically shout.

He grins. "I know, but I love her and I want to make her mine."

"Congratulations, man. What do you need from me?"

Trey winces. "Do you know anything about rings?"

I laugh, earning a scowl from him. "Honestly, I'm not sure I'll be much help. Every woman's taste is unique. Picking a ring is a prayer followed by a crap shoot. Hopefully, you have luck on your side too, and choose something she loves."

"Thanks, I think," he mutters as he turns back toward the mall.

"No problem, man. Let's go find you a ring."

When we enter the nicest looking jewelry store, I push Trey forward.

An employee eyes us and heads over, smiling. *She seems nice.* "Good afternoon, gentlemen. Is there something I can help you with?"

Trey goes mute, so I answer for him. "My buddy is proposing to his girlfriend, and he needs to look at engagement rings."

The sales lady looks at Trey, asking, "Do you know what she likes?" He just shakes his head. While she's showing us a few rings, I see Trey wobble. *Is he going to faint? He looks pale.* I put my hand on his shoulder to let me him know I've got his back.

"Do you like any of these?" she asks.

"They're all beautiful, but she's going to be the one wearing it, and I want her to love it," Trey finally answers.

As I stand here in the jewelry store, I can't help but think about Jasmine. *What would she want? Would she say yes if I asked her? Am I ready?* I already know she's my forever, but we just haven't had that conversation. My mind busies itself thinking about the commitment of marriage and how it would change things between us. But as I watch Trey light up with excitement and anticipation, I can't help but think *I want that too.*

I need Jasmine home *now*. Even though I know she'll be back in days, the uncertainty of whether she's moving home for good weighs heavily in my gut. It's like I'm carrying around an extra fifteen pounds of anxiety, and it's affecting everything I do. Yesterday's practice was horrible. I was sluggish and my passes were atrocious. Too many of my teammates asked if I was okay. By about the fifth time, they pissed me off. I knew I was off, but not knowing Jasmine's decision was fucking with me. Being a selfish man, I wanted her home in Chicago, in my bed.

We haven't talked about living arrangements because our relationship is still new and we're living in different cities. But what if she moves home? She should live with me. Realistically, I understand she'll probably move back in with Nicole since she still lives in Jasmine's parents' rental. *But what about Trey?* While Jasmine and I had been fighting our way to our fairytale romance, Trey and Nicole had been falling in love. Earlier this month, I'd gone with Trey to get an engagement ring, so I'm not sure how long they'll be living apart. But am I jumping the gun? He still has to ask, and Nicole still has to say yes.

And if that happens, who knows when they'll tie the knot and whether they'll live together before then? Question upon question piles up in my brain, and I need relief. I thought calling her tonight might get me some. Nope. Two days can't pass fast enough.

And they don't. I swear, waiting for her plane to

land earns me several years and gray hairs, but it's so worth it when I see her riding the escalator. It's been too long since we touched. My hands shake like I'm a junkie looking for a fix. I suppose in a way I am. I crave everything about her.

"Jasmine," I whisper as she steps closer. I love everything about her. From her melodic cheerful laugh to the way her eyes sparkle when she smiles at me. Or there's the heat that exchanges between us when we're doing something as simple as holding hands. When her soft skin brushes against mine, I'm swept away by her feminine charm. Then there's the rich and fruity scent of her namesake body spray, that I catch a hint of every time my arms are wrapped around her. Not only does it feel right, it allows me to play with her soft, silky hair, which I've done since we were kids.

"Rocco," she answers, rising to her toes to kiss me. I suck her lower lip into my mouth, tasting peppermint and making her open to me. Quickly, I dart my tongue inside, turning our polite peck into a moment of passion. Jasmine melts against me, her hands going to my neck to twist her fingers through my hair. Wrapping my arms around her, I pull her closer and lift her off her feet. The beat of her heart matches mine. Only a few layers of clothing separate our chests. Something I will rectify as soon as we're home. The house rule of no clothing that I mentioned on the phone is still in play, and I will enforce it once we're behind closed doors. Thinking about Jasmine completely naked takes me from zero to sixty in one point six seconds. I respond faster than a Dodge Challenger SRT Demon 170, the fastest accelerating car in the world. Pulling back, I growl against her lips, "Ready to go home, babe?"

A throaty moan is her response. Setting her back on her feet, I make sure she's stable before collecting her suitcase. I almost convince her to get in the back seat of my Range Rover in the parking lot. I wanted to grab a quick snack before hitting the road. I thought it was a great idea. I could have a taste of her on my lips as we drive home. Unfortunately, she doesn't go for it. Now I just have a severe case of blue balls because she says she always feels gross after a plane ride. I may pout a little until she reminds me that the option to shower with her is available. I've never loaded a bag into my car so fast in my life. It's a good thing they don't clock your speed in the garage, because I whip around corners like I'm auditioning for the next race car movie.

"Whoa," she exclaims as we enter the highway going eighty. "Excited to get home?" she teases.

I nod and then groan. "It's been too long since I've seen you."

She laughs. "I agree. I'm glad I'm home for longer than my last visit."

"I wish you were home permanently," I grumble, avoiding eye contact. I know my requests to return home have been on constant repeat and I've annoyed her, as she's told me many, many times she'll tell me as soon as she decides. Out of the corner of my eye, I see she's fidgety and nervous. Her feet are tapping out a steady beat and her hands are twisted so tight they're blotchy, almost like they're straining for blood. Looking up at her gorgeous face, I notice her pink lips are pressed tightly together, like she's desperate to hold something in. *Why?* I flick on my turn signal and pull off the highway, needing to know what's going on.

"Jasmine, is everything okay? Is this because I mentioned you moving home again?"

"About that," she says, then pauses. I hold my breath. *Please, please, please say you're moving home.* "Do you want the good or bad news first?" Her words put me on edge. I can't imagine what she's going to say next.

"Bad," I blurt out, feeling my heart pound in my chest.

Reaching for my hand, she cradles it in hers tenderly. *Shit. This isn't looking good.* Silently, I prepare for the worst. She's going to tell me she's staying in New York. "Bad first."

Before she can say anything else, I rush out, "Whatever you decide, it'll be okay. We'll figure it out together."

She nods her acceptance.

"We won't be skating at Rockefeller Center for New Year's Eve this year." Her green eyes peer at me, waiting for a reaction. I release my breath.

Confused, I answer, "Okay, what will we be doing? Where will we be?"

"We'll be in New York like we planned. But I thought you'd rather help me pack than skate." An enormous smile spreads across her beautiful face, and I'm frozen, trying to process her words.

Anticipation builds and I stutter, "Wh-what are you trying to s-say?"

"Weeks ago, I applied for my old job. And I just accepted their rehire offer about an hour before my flight. Before boarding, I called and gave my two-week notice to my current supervisor and then spent the entire flight making a list of all that I need to do before moving back to Chicago."

My mouth falls open. "You're serious?"

She nods and I unbuckle myself before moving across the center console and tackling her in the best kiss ever. Feeling her squirm in the seat next to me, I consider taking things further. I'm about to unbuckle her seat belt when a police siren squawk behind us. I quickly pull my lips from her and drop back in my seat, taking a moment to adjust myself before an officer is standing next to my window.

Rolling down the window, I turn off the car.

"Good evening, officer," I say.

"Good evening. Can I ask why you're pulled over on the side of the road? Are you having car trouble?"

I shake my head. "No, sir, we aren't. I just picked my girlfriend up from the airport, and while I was driving, she told me some incredible news that shocked me. I thought it would be safer for me to pull over than continue driving."

The officer leans forward and looks at Jasmine. "Is that accurate, miss?"

She smiles, her kiss-swollen lips red and moist. "It is, sir."

"Okay, well, if you're fine, I would suggest you head on. Sitting on the side of the highway isn't safe either."

Smiling at him, I say, "Thank you, sir. Happy Holidays."

"Same to you, Mr. Romano." He smiles and walks back to his patrol car.

Jasmine teases, "Oh, Mr. Romano."

I lean over and nip her bottom lip. "Let's go home and celebrate."

Chapter 33

Jasmine

Rocco has a game in New York against the Chargers on New Year's Day. And while in town, he has permission from the coach to help me pack. Since I've only been here for a year, and my apartment came furnished, I don't have too much. We box up everything that won't fit into two suitcases and make a trip to the packaging store to ship the rest. Before today, I've never seen anyone so excited for someone to pay hundreds in shipping, but the perma-smile on Rocco's face sets me straight. Since New Year's Day falls in the middle of the week, my last day of work is Friday.

I fly back to Chicago that night after work, and Nicole picks me up because Rocco has a game against the Stars in Las Vegas. Since we haven't discussed living arrangements, I'm moving back in with Nicole. However, when Rocco's in town, I imagine I'll be at his house a lot, and what happens next is anyone's guess. I've figured out he's my forever, so I expect we'll live together at some point.

In the days before I return to work, my anxiety starts rearing its head. I'm not nervous about the work itself, as it's the same thing I'd been doing in New York, but thoughts about how my former coworkers would see me, consume me. But by the end of my first day, I discover I'd been worried for no reason. Most of my previous coworkers are still there, so it's like a mini reunion.

Instead of feeling like a failure, I'm living my best life. I have a job I love, in the city I love, with the one I love.

My parents are thrilled I'm finally home too. After I return, they both confide their feelings to me separately. I learn they weren't too happy when I moved to New York. But because they didn't want to squash my dreams, they remained quiet. Since being home, we've had family dinner together every week. Thankfully, we eat out, because my mom still doesn't excel in the kitchen like Rocco's mother or Nonna.

Speaking of Nonna. The first stop Rocco and I made together after he returned from Vegas was to visit her. When he told her we were finally together, the smile stretching across her wrinkled face was enough to make my eyes leak. Of course, that didn't last long when she swatted Rocco in the stomach, admonishing him for waiting so long. It was tough to hide my laughter, especially when she broke out in Italian and started waving her hands. I had no idea what she was saying. I suspected Rocco didn't either, but we both understood she was plenty upset. When she'd finally spoken her piece, she shuffled over to me and offered me something to eat, and there was no way I was passing up that opportunity.

I've been back in Chicago a few months, and I was right about our living situation. When he's in town, Rocco wants me in his bed. Standing in his kitchen, I hear the sounds of the garage door opening and then closing again. Reaching over, I add the carrots I was cutting to the salad I'm making to go with dinner.

"Babe," he calls out.

"Kitchen," I answer. And before long, he plants his large hands on my hips and trails soft kisses up my neck. I tip my head to the side, giving him full access, and he takes it, moving to my ear. When he sucks my lobe into his mouth, my body goes into overdrive. Shivers run down my back as his warm breath contends with his cool, wet touch. Closing my eyes to savor the moment, I breathe out, "I missed you today."

His deep laugh makes me smile. He leans forward, and I look over at him. He waggles his eyebrows. "Babe, you saw me this morning. Remember, I woke you up?" Setting down the knife I was using, I turn in his arms and make a pouty face. Then he smirks and asks, "Wasn't that enough?" Trying to keep a straight face, I just shake my head no. He licks his lips. "No? How much time until dinner?"

"I'm just finishing the salad. The rotisserie chicken's still warm from when I picked it up on my way home. So we can eat whenever."

He licks his lips. "You don't say?" I just nod, hoping we're thinking the same thing. Rocco steps away without a word, leaving me confused. He grabs the salad bowl and places it in the fridge. Then he turns to me and gives me a wicked smile, his eyes dancing suggestively. "Come with me, Jasmine." Hand in hand, we walk up the stairs and to the bedroom. With each step, my pulse pumps harder and my breath becomes labored. I'm feeling lightheaded as he leads me to the bed.

An hour later, we emerge from the room, freshly showered, fucked, and famished. Dinner has never tasted so good. Halfway through the meal, our phones ding in tandem. The message is from Trey and Nicole. Selecting the attachment, we see what appears to be a party invitation. Decorated in animal print, it promises to be a wild night. One that we won't forget. It's being held next month to celebrate their engagement, and we're instructed to dress in our favorite animal onesie. Setting down my phone, I do a happy dance because I'm thrilled for Nicole. A year ago, our lives were so different. I had just moved to New York, heartbroken, and she was working for a sleazeball. Now we're both madly in love with the men of our dreams.

"What are you doing?" he asks with a grin on his face.

I stop moving, put my hands on my hips, and answer, "I'm doing a happy dance."

Rocco palms his face and groans. "Really? Why?"

"What's wrong, grumpy? The party sounds like fun."

"Oh yeah? Which animal are we going as?"

I laugh, because it's completely obvious to me. "Raccoons."

Rocco pouts. "A raccoon? Why?"

"Because they're smart and mischievous." I smile at him.

"Aren't they also called trash pandas?"

Shrugging my shoulders, I say, "Okay, big guy. What animal do you want to go as?"

He smugly answers, "A horse."

I think for a minute, then ask, "Is it because you like to be ridden?"

He snorts. "Nope. But that's good."

"Then why?" I ask.

"Because, like me in the human world, they have the biggest dick in the animal kingdom." A massive grin spreads across his face, making me laugh. "True, they do have large penises, but they aren't the mammal with the largest on the planet."

His mouth falls open. "What?"

I roll my eyes. "Blue whales have the largest penis at eight feet long, and a horse's is smaller than that."

As he processes that size, I see his eyes go wide and he mouths *"holy shit."*

"Are you suggesting we go as blue whales now? Because I see one other problem with it."

He tugs his hands through his hair. "What now?"

"I don't have a penis, so how can we explain our animal if it doesn't apply to both of us?"

A few minutes go by and he finally grumbles, "Fine, we can go as stupid raccoons."

"Okay, great. I'll order our onesies from Amazon tonight."

The night of the party we dress in our black, white, and gray onesies. I'm glad I just opted to wear booty shorts and a sports bra under mine. Otherwise, I'd be a massive sweat ball. "I can't wait to see what everyone else is wearing," I say as I put my hair up in a high ponytail.

"I bet no one will be as sexy as you, my little trash panda." Rocco laughs, and I just roll my eyes. The party is a blast, and I never would have guessed the animals everyone else selected. Trey and Nicole are penguins. She explained penguins and love to me after her and Trey's magical Halloween, and even I can admit, it seems sweet. Lucas and Samantha come as sharks, and that makes total sense. The funniest couple is Mika and Shiloh, they come dressed as giraffes. Because of their size difference, they look like a parent-child team. Christian and Monica were the most obvious. They dress as cows since her family owns a dairy farm. Coach Tristan, Josh, and Ace show up without dates and are dressed as a zookeeper, elephant, and duck, respectively. Tristan's outfit makes sense, but Josh and Ace just confuse me. The entire night is a great kickoff for their wedding. Some of our best friends are marrying one another other, and it couldn't be better.

Chapter 34

Jasmine

The months are flying by, and I can hardly believe it is already May. I've been staying busy with work and hanging out with the Steel ladies. We get together mostly when the guys are on the road.

It's now playoff time again. Although coming close, the guys haven't won the Cup in three years, and the last month has been filled with so many testosterone-rich activities trying to keep them focused on winning that trophy.

At first, I think it's baffling when weeks before playoffs begin, they all revamp their diets to pack themselves full of extra protein. Then they all start meeting for specialized team activities like steam room Saturdays and meditation Mondays. Rocco explains they each have a purpose, and I suppose they probably do. The entire team adopts an odd superstition, and they religiously adhere to it. The day before a game, they paint their toes Steel colors. Their dominant side is navy blue and the other is gold. It took weeks to dial it in, and I hate to admit it, but Rocco's toenails are prettier than mine.

After beating all the teams they're paired against in the brackets, they find themselves in the championship against the Las Vegas Stars. The first two games of the series are in Vegas. The first is an overtime win for the Stars. Both teams played well, but the Stars were victorious in the end. The second game comes down to the last minute. The whistle is blown on Mika for roughing with a minute forty-five left in the period. During the penalty kill, Deacon Smith, the Star's best center, has an amazing wrap-around goal. While trying to defend his net, Jersey pulls his groin when he gets twisted up with another Stars player who had been camped out in his crease looking to rebound the puck if Smith couldn't put it away. Jersey collapses to the ice as the last seconds of the game run down.

"I hope he's okay," I say to the group of Steel ladies gathered in Samantha's living room. She offered to host us for the first two games of the series. Gathered around the television, we all watch as the trainers run onto the ice. They're busy assessing Jersey and what looks like his groin while the rest of the Steel exchange fist bumps with the Stars players.

"Jersey's tough," Samantha says confidently. "But

it's a good thing they're coming home tomorrow, then the team doctors can evaluate him."

"Mom, where's the groin?" Samuel asks. For almost eight years old, Shiloh says he is gifted. They had him tested, and he scores well above many children his age. *Maybe he'll be a doctor?*

Shiloh moves closer and lowers her voice while she points to the juncture between the upper thigh and lower abdomen. "It's this area here." He nods his understanding and then goes back to the couch and picks up a book.

I notice Liam had been watching his mom and brother's conversation. "Momma, did he hurt his pee pee?" he asks, at toddler volume.

"Oh, geez," Shiloh says on a groan. The rest of the Steel kids are babies, so she has nothing to worry about with answering him. "I don't think so, Liam. I'm sure once he ices and stretches, he'll feel much better."

Later that night, while I'm lying in bed, playing on my phone, I get a message.

ROCCO

Hey there, beautiful.

Instead of texting back, I hit FaceTime, and in moments a gorgeous man with chocolate-brown eyes fills my screen. "Hi, handsome. I miss you," I purr.

"I miss you too. I am so ready to be home," he grumbles.

I laugh. "Are you sick of rooming with Ace?" I hear a noise off camera and I wonder if Ace is in the room.

I watch Rocco's eyes shift over and then he frowns. "He's not you."

Off camera, I hear, "Oh come on, Roc. I'll spoon with you. Do you want to be the little or big spoon? I'm good either way." I cover my mouth to hide my laugh and see Rocco's eyes darken. He's pretending to be annoyed, but I know he's not.

"Hey, Ace," I say loud enough so he can hear me. "He likes to be the big spoon, but watch your nipples. He gets sort of handsy." I smirk, and Rocco growls in warning.

"What?" I ask as I bat my eyelashes at him.

He shakes his head, then says, "Ace, you and I are not spooning tonight or ever."

Ace's laughter fills the silence.

"Rocco, why don't you put in your AirPods?"

As soon as I know they're in, I tell him just how much I miss him as I strip out of the silk sleep set I'm wearing. I'm sure things are getting hard to hide on his side of the line, but I want to give him pleasant dreams. When I'm all finished with my show, I switch off my B.O.B. Rocco's sexy smirk is on full display, and he says, "Babe, I can't wait to get home tomorrow. I love you. Now I have to go take a shower before I go to bed." I blow a kiss to him before we hang up.

The next two games of the series are here in Chicago and I'm on the edge of my seat the entire time.

I've heard that Jersey suffered a bad groin pull, but with his trainer's help, he's doing his best to continue playing. It looks like the defense has stepped up their game to give Jersey more space. The Steel finish the home games with two wins, making them even as they go into the next game, which is back in Vegas. It's anyone's guess where the bricks may fall.

Vegas has the loudest crowd in the NHL community, and you're keenly aware of that every time you play there. The Steel win the first game, but the Stars secure the second. Both games are impressive to watch. The skating is superb and the level of play is incredible. Ace scores a hat trick the second night, and I'm sure they're going to win the game, but when the Stars skated onto the ice for the third period, it's like a whole new team had replaced the tired players with a bunch of Energizer bunnies. And there's no way the Steel could keep up. They lose 5-4 in that game. Even with all of Ace's goals, it isn't enough. As the guys fist bump following the game, you can feel the tension rolling off the players. Who would be the winner? The next game would determine it.

Chapter 35

Rocco

This is it. The last game of this year's Stanley Cup finals. We're tied at three wins apiece going into it, but we have home ice advantage. We haven't won the Cup in a few years, and we're hungry for it. The pressure I've felt at every practice the last week has done its job. I'm skating harder and smarter than ever before. We've worked hard and are ready to do battle on the ice tonight. But that isn't the only pressure I feel mounting on my back like a ton of bricks. After Trey and Nicole's engagement party, I made a big decision. One that started with a visit to Jasmine's parents to get their blessing. And after the playoffs are over, I plan to make more of my dreams come true.

Sweat pours off me as I skate to the bench, winded from another shift in the most important game of my life. We are currently in the second period, leading 2 -1 thanks to a brilliant goal by Ace during a recent power play.

"You good, man?" Josh asks as he sits next to me on the bench. I give him a nod before tipping my head back for some refreshing water. Coach stands above us, barking out orders to the guys on the ice as the last minutes of this period wind down. Mika wins the puck in our corner and sends a beaut of a shot to Lucas, who's at the center line. Before I can blink, he already has it cradled on his stick and is breaking off for the goal. I rise to my feet just as Rick Thomas, one of the Stars' best defensemen, challenges him. With some stellar stick work and skating, Lucas shifts left, goes up on one skate, and fires a shot at the goalie's exposed top right corner. It sails in with ease, lighting the lamp, and our bench goes wild. Lucas skates past the bench for fist bumps and congratulations. His smile is infectious. With another baby on the way, I'm guessing that he'll retire after this year, so I know that goal means the world to him. He returns to the center line for the next puck drop with fifteen seconds left before the final intermission. When the clock runs out, we skate off the ice and head down the chute. The locker room is in utter chaos as we all hoot and holler about Lucas's goal. That is until Coach walks in and whistles.

An eerie quiet permeates the humid, sweat-soaked room. When Coach speaks, we listen. "Let me start by saying *that* was a phenomenal goal. Absolute perfection and just what I like to see! Mika, you started it off strong with your beauty of a pass, and Lucas, you finished it with top-notch stick work and smart skating." Coach takes a moment to scan our smiling faces. Then he continues his speech. "But we still have one period. We haven't won the Cup yet. It'll take more focus and effort to maintain the lead. The Stars want the Cup just as badly as we do, and they're going to show up to the next period ready for a fight. So, let's give it to them. You all know you're capable of winning this game. You worked hard to get here. Now, let's finish it." The entire team cheers.

Coach wasn't kidding when he said the Stars were going to show up ready for a fight. Although I'm not sure if he meant it literally. Not long into the twenty-minute period, our team has already logged two penalties. Coach switches lines during the penalty kills, having Josh and Mika in on defense rather than some of our less experienced guys. They are both exhausted when they get back to the bench after their longer than usual shift.

The period whizzes past, and during the final five minutes, the Stars' Deacon Smith gets a breakaway and lines up with Jersey. We're in the middle of a shift change and are vulnerable. As soon as he can, Mika is off of the bench and racing for Deacon. Deacon fakes to Jersey's right and shoots left. The puck flies right over his lowered shoulder, cutting our lead to one point. Jersey is slow to get up. The training staff file onto the ice to check on him. I skate closer, trying to see if he re-injured his groin. From the way he's wincing, I'd guess so. He brushes them off, telling them he's fine and that he'll have it checked out following the game.

Before returning to center ice for the puck drop, I skate past Jersey and ask, "You good, man?"

His jaw is tight, like he's grinding his teeth, and he growls, "I'm fine, Rocco." I give him a head nod and skate away, hoping he really is.

The clock counts down, and we're able to maintain our lead. When the final second fades, it leaves us the winners of the Stanley Cup again. Pumping my fist in the air, excitement buzzes through my body. This moment feels incredible. Scanning the crowd, I see they've gone wild. It feels amazing to be at home for this momentous occasion. As I skate around the ice, feeling the breeze in my sweat-soaked hair, I celebrate with my teammates.

A young man stops me and hands over a championship t-shirt. To my left, some of my teammates are wrestling to fit the shirt over their bulky hockey gear. Laughing, I join them. The entire team is all smiles. We shake hands with the Stars before the presentation of the Cup to our captain. This is the third time Josh has lifted it above his head. This year has to be even more special than the previous one because now he has Kenzie and Issac cheering him on. I can relate because this year I finally have Jasmine by my side as officially mine.

I knew after the first time we won the Cup, when

she and I first kissed, that she meant more to me than just a friend. I was just stubborn and delayed the inevitable. I cannot wait to celebrate with her. I feel on top of the world. Excitement for what's coming bubbles up within me, and I'm ready to get showered and pull the love of my life into my arms.

A week after winning the Cup, when I finally feel like I somewhat have my life back, I take Jasmine out for a secret date. When she asked me what she should wear, I told her to dress casually.

"You look gorgeous," I say as she walks into the living room. Wearing a white cotton sundress and white Chucks, she is the epitome of summer sexy. My gaze traces up her tanned legs, and I wish it were my tongue. *Does she taste as good as she looks?* Stepping closer, I pull her into me and a whiff of her delicate jasmine perfume tickles my nose as I nuzzle into her neck. I place a tender kiss there, then pull away before I take things further. We have somewhere to be. After I help her into my Range Rover, I walk to the driver's side, carefully looking in the back to make sure I have everything for my surprise.

"What are we doing? Where are we headed?" Jasmine asks excitedly.

I reach over and tuck a stray hair behind her ear. "It's a surprise. But first you have to do something."

Confusion covers her face. "What?"

I open the center console and pull out an eye mask I'd hidden there.

"Is that an eye mask?" she asks breathlessly. Her cheeks are flushed, her eyes wide, and her breathing is labored. *Is she turned on?*

I smile and nod. "And you have to wear it until we get to our destination. Are you feeling adventurous?" *Please say yes.*

Jasmine licks her lips, and if we weren't on a schedule, I would definitely pull her in for a kiss. "Yes," she answers in a sultry voice. The timbre of it sounding like a siren's song, registering in my cock, calling him home.

I force myself to stick to my plan, and slide the mask over her eyes. When we're halfway to the location of the surprise, Jaz shifts in her seat. "Are we almost there?"

I laugh. "Soon, but when we get there, you're going to have to wait in the car for a few minutes while I get the surprise set up."

"Do I have to wear the eye mask?" she questions.

"You do. I'll let you know when you can take it off." The reason she's wearing the mask is that she'd know immediately where I'm taking her.

Ten minutes later, we arrive at the planned destination. I park, turn off the engine, and remind her she needs to stay blindfolded and in the car until I come back to get her.

Stepping out, I hustle over to meet Christine, the photographer I hired to capture everything. "Hey,

Christine. It's good to see you. Let me show you where I was thinking you could hide."

"Sounds great," she answers as she follows me to the back of the property.

Pointing toward a fallen tree, I ask, "Do you think you could get everything from behind there?"

She walks over to the log. "Is that where you'll be?" She points at a dilapidated structure sitting twenty feet away.

"Yep, that's it. Is it all I said it would be?" I joke, knowing how run-down and ragged the structure looks. It's all broken and misshapen wood, half-bent nails, and uneven lines. "It may not be pretty, but it has great sentimental value."

Christine nods, then says, "I don't mean to rush you, but if you want the best light, it's go time."

"Okay."

As I walk back to the car, I hear Christine say, "Good luck." *Luck. Do I need luck?* I'm suddenly nervous. I wipe my sweaty palms on my pants. *Game on.* Shaking myself free from my worries, I push out a deep breath before I open her door.

"Jasmine, you're going to have to leave the blindfold on until I get you to the right spot. I won't let anything happen to you. Do you trust me?"

She smiles wide, parting her pink lips and showing her perfectly straight white teeth. "Of course I trust you."

"This way," I tell her as I walk with her hand in mine. "We're going down a little hill, but there isn't anything in your way. I won't let you fall." Her hand squeezes tight as we make the slow descent. When we're at the bottom, I lead her over to the perfect spot. I remove her blindfold, and as she blinks, I lower down to one knee.

As she looks around, recognition of where we are sets in, and she gasps. "Rocco," she whispers and then she looks down at me.

"Jasmine, you have always and will always be my forever friend. From the time we were young, you were my confidant and partner in crime. Now you are so much more. I'm sorry for all the years I kept us apart by refusing to accept what was in front of me. You are my soulmate and my forever. I love you more with each new day. Will you marry me?"

Tears leak from Jasmine's eyes, and I worry something's gone wrong. Or that she doesn't want to marry me. *That can't be it.* I squeeze her hand I'm holding, desperate for her answer. "Jaz," I whisper. Her eyes connect with mine.

"What?"

"Are you going to answer my question?" I mumble, feeling embarrassed.

Her eyes go wide with panic and she whispers, "I didn't?"

Flashing her a pained look, I shake my head. She lowers down to me and looks me right in the eyes. "Yes,

Rocco, I will marry you." Then she leans in, brushing her lips lightly against mine.

When her words finally register, I throw my arms around her and pull her body to mine. "Eep," she squeaks against my lips before I claim her mouth. There we are, making out like horny teens while on our knees in the grass in front of our childhood tree fort. Whooping and hollering come from a few yards away. We pull away from each other, and our friends and family stand on my parents' deck, celebrating our good news.

Jasmine laughs. "Is this for real?"

"It is now," I say as I slide the three-carat solitaire on her ring finger.

"It's gorgeous, Rocco," she gushes as she stares down at her hand.

As we make our way back to the house, Christine rises from her hiding spot. "Did you get it all?" I ask.

She smiles. "I sure did. I'll get the proofs over to you this weekend. Congratulations to you both."

Disappearing around the corner of the house, Jasmine asks, "Did you have a photographer capture the proposal?"

I kiss her nose. "I did. I'm sure she even captured your deer-in-the-headlights look." Then I smirk at her.

"Sorry. I heard myself answer you, but that must have only been in my head."

"I'm just glad you said yes," I tell her as I lead her up the stairs toward everyone who's gathered. It's time to celebrate. It may have taken me a long time to figure out I have feelings for Jaz, but once I did, I was hers, completely.

As soon as we reach the deck, we're bombarded with wedding questions. Where? When? At least we know the who.

Nonna approaches us, and as I lean down to her, she squeezes my cheeks in her frail hands. "Congratulazioni, polpetta," she says, smiling widely.

"Polpetta?" Jasmine asks. "She's called you that since we were kids, but what does it mean?"

I smirk. "It means meatball."

Jasmine nods her head. "That makes sense. You could always put them away."

I snort. "And I know how to make them too."

She holds her hands up in defense. I notice the sparkle dancing in her eyes and the grin on her pinched lips. *What's she holding back?*

"Gratze, Nonna," I say, kissing her cheek.

Ma steps up next to us. She's smiling and her eyes are filled with unshed tears. "Congratulations, you two. I've been praying for this since you were kids." She wraps Jasmine in a hug before shifting to me. "You know Nonna and I will make all the food for your special day, right?" I nod. There's no point in arguing. I know they'll start making meatballs and marinara sauce for the freezer tomorrow.

Out of the corner of my eye, I see Jasmine's mouth

drop open in disbelief. "That's too much. We couldn't possibly ask you to do that."

Nonna frowns. I whisper to Jasmine, "It would be an insult if you refuse them."

Turning her to me, I can feel the apprehension emanating off her. I soften my approach, giving her a smile. She forces one in return protesting, "But, Rocco, that'll be so much work, and I want them to enjoy our wedding."

I pull her into my chest and place a kiss on her forehead. "I know, babe, and they will. This is just how they're showing their love for us."

"Okay. If you're sure it won't be too much," she says before turning back to my ma and nonna. "Nonna, Maria, we would love it if you catered our wedding."

Nonna grabs our joined hands and brings them to her chest. Her smile seems to be just what Jasmine needs, and I feel her body relax next to mine.

"Gratze, Nonna," I say again

"Ti amo, nipote," she answers back.

"Anch'io ti amo."

Epilogue

Rocco & Jasmine

Rocco

Ever since I asked Jasmine to marry me, life has been on fast forward. Regarding the wedding, we didn't want to wait, so we throw together something small for this August. All our friends and family are in Chicago, and it's the offseason, so it seems like a win-win. Now for the planning.

Jasmine

Two and a half months isn't long to plan a wedding, and even though we're keeping it small, there's still so much to do. I officially moved into Rocco's house after he proposed, and to tell you the truth, it isn't much different from how things were.

A few weeks after we get engaged, Trey and Nicole tie the knot in a small, intimate ceremony. They have a much larger reception planned for after they return from their honeymoon to Kauai. Rocco and I are their attendants, and the team and their significant others are all here. They reserved a rooftop bar for an evening party. In a corner of the space, they have a trellis and chairs set up for Trey and Nicole to exchange their vows. After that's done, we're ushered over to another section for drinks and appetizers while the restaurant crew sets up tables and chairs for dinner. Kenzie made the cake, and it's divine.

Rocco and I haven't decided on our final cake flavors, but the red velvet Nic and Trey selected adds another flavor to the five we're already hotly debating. It doesn't matter what we choose. We know anything Kenzie makes will be delicious.

"This is incredible," Nicole gushes as we drive up to my parents' ten thousand square foot colonial-style home. "I love the ivy growing up the red brick walls and archways. It's so romantic. Did they add it for the wedding?"

She's right. It's incredibly romantic and gorgeous. Parking, I shake my head. "No. When they bought it a few years ago, my mom brought in an expert gardener to help her with the landscaping. She wants to turn it into a bed and breakfast." My parent's house is the perfect place for the wedding and reception. Not only is the house large, but we can bring in a white tent for the dinner and dancing.

We push through the front door and freeze. "Where's all the furniture?" she asks.

"Movers came a few days ago to move it out to make room for the ceremony," I explain as I run my hand across the back of the rustic white Chiavari chair the florist is busy wrapping ivy on. All the chairs are facing a beautifully decorated arch where Rocco and I will exchange our vows. "Isn't it lovely?" I ask Nicole.

She smiles. "It is. Can we see the tent now?"

We walk outside to where the tent has been erected.

"This is gorgeous. It feels very whimsical to me," I say as we check out the tent.

Walking up to a finished table, I can't help but fall in love with how it's decorated. It's covered in white linens and white roses. Silver candelabras sit in the middle of every table, creating an even more romantic vibe.

"The place setting is beautiful," Nicole comments as I admire the bone-white china plates and sterling silver cutlery at each seat. Decorators scurry around us, busy tying satin ribbons to every chair and placing a silver name card at each seat.

"Look at that," Nicole squeals as we approach the cake table. A four-tiered lemon pound cake with the thinnest layer of frosting just barely covering the delicacy beneath, renders me speechless. Pops of yellow from the sugar-coated lemon slices cover the lemon-flavored buttercream layers of the heavenly confection. I just know it will taste as good as it looks.

"What are you girls doing out here?" my mom asks as she steps up alongside us.

I blush. "I wanted to see it all before everyone else."

She smiles and touches the pearls she's matched to her cranberry sheath dress. "Okay, you've seen it. But now you both need to get upstairs and dressed before everyone arrives. We nod and weave our way through all the tables and chairs and back into the house that's bustling with people. I think I spotted two of Rocco's aunts who agreed to oversee the assembly of the food so that Nonna and Maria wouldn't miss anything.

Twenty minutes later, there's a rap at the bedroom door, and I spin around. My father enters, dressed in a black tuxedo. "Jasmine, I have never seen you look so lovely." I pat the waist of my mesh embroidered maxi dress. I selected a looser-fitting garment that is both dreamy and romantic. With my hair loosely pulled into a low bun, and light makeup, I've never felt more beautiful.

"Thanks, Dad," I say as he places a soft kiss to my cheek.

"You ready for this?" he asks with a smile.

Smiling back, I answer, "I am."

He leads me down the stairs to wait for my

entrance. When the music starts, he leads me toward my forever. The ceremony is beautiful. Standing at the end of the fabricated aisle is the man I have loved for so long. He's dressed in a perfectly tailored black tuxedo with a red tie that matches the red roses of my bouquet. He and Trey opted for vests instead of bow ties and cummerbund because they reminded them of high school prom. And I can admit it was the right call. Rocco has never been sexier than he is right now.

When our eyes connect, his hand flies to his chest and he gives me a shy smile. His reaction makes me weak, and all I want to do is run down the aisle and jump into his arms. I look over to my dad as he prepares to walk me toward my forever, and I see him wipe away a lone tear. I squeeze his arm and smile at him. His nod tells me everything I need to know. He's happy for me.

When I reach the love of my life, I look up at him through my lashes, and the way he's looking back at me makes my heart pound in my chest and steals my breath. "You're gorgeous," he says as he takes my hand from my dad's. I can't control the blush that spreads across my face.

"Thank you," I answer.

For the ceremony, we opted for short and sweet, and within fifteen minutes we're pronounced husband and wife. Pictures last quite a bit longer, as we pose with everyone. Even though our wedding party is small, we still want pictures with our family. The extra time allows for our guests to visit while they make their way to the backyard for the reception.

An hour later, the DJ announces our arrival. "It's my pleasure to be the first to introduce you to Mr. & Mrs. Rocco Romano."

Rocco squeezes my hand as we walk into the tent, where we're showered with hoots, hollers, and clapping. He turns me to him and kisses me tenderly while his teammates catcall. His hand finds my back and traces the low V of my dress, then pulls me closer and whispers "mine." A shiver travels down my spine, and he growls low against my ear. *Holy hell.*

We walk to the head table, where Nicole and Trey have already settled, and take a seat. It's already been a long day, packed full of emotion and so many hormones. I was hungry earlier, but now I'm desperate. Both for Rocco and Nonna's cooking. I'm absolutely famished.

Our DJ continues to MC the evening.

"Rocco and Jasmine want to thank everyone for being a part of their special day. We're going to start the evening off with dinner, which I'm told was prepared by Rocco's mom and grandma," the DJ announces.

"Nonna," our guests chant, causing Rocco and me to laugh.

The DJ clears his throat, then smiles. "My mistake. His mom and nonna prepared tonight's dinner. Following dinner, we will have the couple's first dance and the mother-son and father-daughter dances. Later on, our bride and groom will do the garter and flower toss and then we'll have the toasts and cake cutting. At the end of the evening, we'll send off the happy couple with a surprise."

Sitting back, I wait while servers deliver homemade spaghetti and meatballs to everyone. "This is so good," I say to Rocco after my first bite. He nods as he takes a bite of his garlic bread. Thankfully, we make it through the delicious meal without a sauce mishap.

"Now it's time for the bride and groom to share their first dance," the DJ says after dinner has concluded.

Rocco takes my hand and leads me to the dance floor. Pulling me close, he anchors his hands on my hips, resting his thumbs on my hip bones. I love the possessive feel of it. The heat of his body against mine chases away the chill of the night, blanketing me in love. I thread my hands around his neck and pull him in close, placing my lips on his. "I love you," I whisper. He traces his tongue against the seam of my lips, and I fight the urge to moan. I open my mouth, and his hungry tongue dips inside, making contact with mine. Needing more, I pull him closer. Rocco takes the kiss deeper, licking into my mouth. A hum travels up my throat, and Rocco tightens his hands around my hips, pulling our bodies closer. I feel his erection pressing against my needy center, and I wish we were alone.

"Now it's time for the mother-son and father-daughter dance," the DJ announces, pulling us from the lust haze we're in.

Following those dances, we walk through the tent to greet our guests. Once we've spoken with everyone, we head back to the dance floor to boogie with our friends. We laugh as we dance to stereotypical wedding songs like the "Funky Chicken" and "Y.M.C.A." Over the next half an hour, we laugh and celebrate with our friends.

At one point, Ace leads me to the edge of the dance floor. Being the captain, Josh clears everyone else off the floor while Mika pulls a chair over for me. Lucas, Trey, and Rocco walk to the middle of the floor as the DJ announces, "Please give your attention to the dance floor, where the groom and groomsmen have a treat for you." A smorgasbord of songs blast from the speakers, and the Steel men break out in a variety of choreographed dances. I don't know who came up with the idea, or when they had time to put it together, but it is absolutely amazing. Pretty soon, I'm surrounded by the stunned wives of the other men on the floor with my husband. The shocked looks on the beautiful faces of the ladies that have become my nearest and dearest friends is something I will never forget. Whoever planned this gave me the best wedding gift. I only hope that someone recorded it, because I know I'll want to watch it a million more times. These guys are the absolute best, and we're lucky to be part of this amazing community.

The garter and flower toss follow, and even though Ace is one of the few single friends in attendance, he leaps into the air and catches the garter, shouting, "It's mine!"

I look to Rocco as we switch places so I can toss my bouquet and ask, "What was that all about?" Rocco just shakes his head and shrugs his shoulders. Scanning the crowd, I see Janica, his friend and roommate, and notice the blush covering her cheeks as she watches him. *That's interesting.* Curious, I tell myself it's something I'll look into after the honeymoon.

After Nicole and Trey toast us and we cut the cake, it isn't long before the evening ends. Our friends all gather in my parents' front yard, armed with lit sparklers to wish us off. We exchange quick hugs before hopping into Rocco's Range Rover for the drive to our house. Early tomorrow morning we're catching a flight to Italy to spend a week in the sun, exploring vineyards, landmarks, and the countryside. Rocco has promised me gelato and real Italian pizza. He also booked a cooking class where a private chef will teach us how to make an incredibly authentic Italian dish. It will be my first visit to the country where his grandparents were raised, but he's been there several times and is almost fluent in the language.

Lying in our bed that night, listening to the cadence of Rocco's breathing after he falls asleep, I can't help but reflect on the day. It was truly magical. Curled into the warmth of his body, I smile at how happy I am. How many people can say they married their best friend from childhood? Our path to each other was full of twists and turns, but in the end, it made the bond we have stronger. And I'm excited about the future in front of us.

———

Thank you for reading Delayed By You, the sixth book in the Chicago Steel series. If you'd like another peek into the Chicago Steel world, visit my website at https://907publishing. wixsite.com/my-site and sign up for my newsletter. While there, don't forget to snag the extended epilogues for the Chicago Steel books and any extras for the rest of the series. Keep reading to check out the World of Chicago Steel.

Acknowledgments

Thank you, thank you, thank you to those who've invested their time in me and my books. I am beyond grateful. With each book, I face new challenges. As I grow as an author, I hope and pray that each story gets better and better. I'm in love with the Steel men, and I'm so glad I'm not alone. Their stories flow through me as if they are real people, and I hope you feel the same as you turn the pages.

To Darren–Babe, no words can ever express how thankful I am that you support me in my dream to be an author. It isn't prosperous, but I appreciate that I can pursue this creative avenue without worrying about how it'll affect our family.

To my boys–Your support and encouragement have been just what I need when I'm feeling discouraged. Thank you for loving me, even if my career might embarrass you.

To Karen–I think I will call you Yoda from this point forward. Your guidance, encouragement, and teachings are invaluable and have helped me get to where I am today. I hope you know how much I appreciate you.

To Shauna–On this book, my thank you remains the same as it's been for every other book. Your help, guidance, and suggestions are unmatched, and I'm so thankful.

To Nicole–You are the best cheerleader ever. Your steadfast encouragement has helped me grow in leaps and bounds. I only hope that it's clear in each new book I release. Thank you for your unwavering support.

To my friends, family, and readers–Keep reading. I have so many more stories in my heart, and I cannot wait to share them with you.

Happy Reading!

World of Chicago Steel

Have you read Hooked By You, the first book of the Chicago Steel Series with Lucas and Samantha? If not, you can click on the link to start reading. The entire series is available with your Kindle Unlimited subscription. Here's a small taste of each to whet your palate.

Hooked By You–Chicago Steel Series Book One

Lucas

She's a goddess in heels. Absolute perfection. Well, almost. Samantha Fox is the heiress of Fox Sporting, my new management team. As one of the best wings in the NHL, I have never shied away from a challenge, and she is definitely a challenge. But if her company representing me doesn't stop me from wanting her, the fact she's engaged should, right? But the noticeably absent sparkle from her left ring finger makes me question. I vow to myself that I'll find out what that's all about. And if she's single, I plan to make her mine. Or at least, mine for the night. I just need one taste of the divine.

Samantha

Off-limits. That's what he is. Lucas Bouchard is the prestigious new client acquired by my family's company. From what I know, not only is he an amazing hockey player, he's a humble and generous philanthropist too. Also, he's a walking aphrodisiac. It doesn't matter that I've just broken off my engagement to a cheating, using loser. Every time our eyes lock, I find myself captivated. But he's not for me. No matter how many times I remind myself of this, though, it doesn't compute. Plain and simple, I want him. And keeping my distance might prove impossible.

Checked By You–Chicago Steel Series Book Two

Mika

She's the uber-sexy, single mother living next door. Everyone tells me to keep my distance. But there's something about her. Specifically, her eyes. They speak to me. Drawing me in like a siren. I want to know her, but she's more guarded than Buckingham Palace. However, after one afternoon in her presence, I find myself addicted and wanting more. Willing to do whatever I have to just to make it past her defenses.

Shiloh

My next-door neighbor is an insanely hot, single

professional hockey player. As if that isn't bad enough, he's a nice guy too. After spending an afternoon where he showed my son how to skate and took us out to ice cream, I want to let him in. My past cautions me to put on the brakes, but I find myself going full steam ahead, ignoring all the red flags waving at me.

Clipped By You–Chicago Steel Series Book Three

Monica

She's his. Or she has been since her freshman year of college. According to Monica Fields, no man will ever hold a candle to Christian Fox. Too bad he's completely unaware. Or is he?

Christian

Since meeting her, a sweet dairy farm girl has captivated Christian entirely. But he's a guy. And he's the one who isn't quite ready to be done sowing his wild oats. Will he ever be? In this game called love, sometimes chasing after a woman is just the wake-up call you need. But what if chasing her to her family's farm and following her through a field scattered with cow patties in limited-edition white Nike Air Force 1s is the only way to catch her? And, when you finally do catch her, will she want you? Forever?

Speared By You-Chicago Steel Series Book Four

Tristan

Since he was little, Tristan's dream has been to play in the NHL. Then he falls in love with his soul mate in high school. A few years after being drafted, an injury cuts his professional career short. Devastated, he questions what is next for him. Instead of seeking solace from the woman who's remained faithfully by his side, he pushes her away.

Stephanie

Since high school, Stephanie's known she is going to do two things: marry Tristan Murphy and get a degree in business. Her plan is to work for a non-profit that focuses on breast cancer. Several years later, though, she finds herself recently divorced and in a new city with a new job. And she's learned a couple of major life lessons. 1. Life can be tricky. 2. We don't always get what we want.

What happens when their paths cross again?

Slashed By You-Chicago Steel Series Book Five

Josh

As the captain of the Steel, Josh is always in control and confident as hell. In relationships, not so much, especially after being majorly burned. Then a gorgeous baker enters his life and changes everything. Her confections are pure magic, and now she's all he craves.

Kenzie

Kenzie's always dreamed of owning her own bakery. With a heart of gold, everything she does is filled with love. Busy running her shop, she doesn't have time for relationships. However, priorities shift when she catches the eye of a kind and sexy professional hockey player who has developed a major sweet tooth.

Delayed By You-Chicago Steel Series Book Six

She's always been his. He's always been hers. Best friends since they were kids, everyone always assumed they'd end up together. But Rocco and Jasmine forge their own life paths. Despite remaining close, she discovers she needs a break from the life she's been living in Chicago. When she moves to New York, things change for him. And he panics, thinking he's lost her forever.

Rocco

Since the day she moved in across the street when we were kids, Jasmine has held my attention with her sparkling green eyes and spunky spirit. She's independent and headstrong, and I've always admired that about her. Hiding behind my bachelor status, no one is the wiser about the secret feelings I harbor for her.

Jasmine

Rocco has always been by my side. Whether it's making me laugh, teaching me something new, or sharing confidences, he's been steadfast. When he morphs into a man seemingly overnight, I find it tough to temper my attraction to him. But he doesn't see me as anything more than a friend.

Happy Ho, Ho, Holidays-Chicago Steel Novella

Trey

As soon as I see her, I'm bewitched by the bohemian beauty. One look from her and I'm done. Too bad after spending most of the evening together, I forget to get her number or her last name. As the owner of the Chicago Steel, the city's professional hockey team, you'd think nothing is out of reach for me, but finding her has proved challenging. Months pass, and as my hope of ever finding her fades, she walks through my office door, hired to be my temporary PA.

Nicole

He can't be real. The summer heat must be getting to me, because everything about this man seems too good to be true. We spend most of the night together, talking and laughing. And guess what... he is the complete package. The one worthy of a trip home to meet the parents. If you ever visited home and hadn't written it off years ago. But as soon as he appears, he's gone without a way to contact him. Do I write it off as bad luck, or do I storm their headquarters demanding to be seen? But what if it's all one-sided and he isn't longing for me like I do him?

Also by Jessica Buss
Chicago Steel Series

Chicago Steel Series

Hooked By You (Lucas & Samantha)

Checked By You (Mika & Shiloh)

Clipped By You (Christian & Monica)

Speared By You (Tristan & Stephanie)

Slashed By You (Josh & Kenzie)

Delayed By You (Rocco & Jasmine)

Coming Soon

Tripped By You

Blocked By You

Chicago Steel Series Novella

Happy Ho, Ho, Holidays (Trey & Nicole)

Coming Soon

Owned By You

Stick By You

About the Author

Jessica Buss was born and raised in Anchorage, Alaska. She is married to her high school sweetheart and has two sons. Although she has both her bachelor's and master's degrees in Psychology, she stepped away from that field to be a stay-at-home mom. Now that her kids are growing up and she's getting more time to herself, she's giving this writing thing a chance.

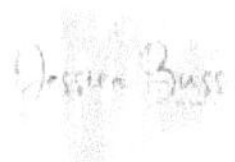

907publishing.wixsite.com/my-site

www.ingramcontent.com/pod-product-compliance
Lightning Source LLC
Chambersburg PA
CBHW071447140726

47997CB00005B/1618